BARBARIAN'S
TAMING

BARBARIAN'S TAMING

RUBY DIXON

BERKLEY ROMANCE
New York

BERKLEY ROMANCE
Published by Berkley
An imprint of Penguin Random House LLC
penguinrandomhouse.com

Library of Congress Cataloging-in-Publication Data

Names: Dixon, Ruby, 1976– author.
Title: Barbarian's taming / Ruby Dixon.
Description: First Berkley Romance Edition. | New York: Berkley
Romance, 2024. | Series: Ice Planet Barbarians
Identifiers: LCCN 2024001517 | ISBN 9780593639481 (trade paperback)
Subjects: LCGFT: Romance fiction. | Monster fiction. |
Science fiction. | Erotic fiction. | Novels.
Classification: LCC PS3604.I965 B3778 2024 |
DDC 813/.6—dc23/eng/20240117
LC record available at https://lccn.loc.gov/2024001517

Barbarian's Taming was originally self-published, in different form, in 2016.

First Berkley Romance Edition: May 2024

Printed in the United States of America
1st Printing

Book design by Kristin del Rosario

For all the bossy big sisters out there

BARBARIAN'S
TAMING

What Has Gone Before

Aliens are real, and they're aware of Earth. Fifteen human women have been abducted by aliens referred to as "Little Green Men." Some are kept in stasis tubes, and some are kept in a pen inside a spaceship, all waiting for sale on an extraterrestrial black market. While the captive humans staged a breakout, the aliens had ship trouble and dumped their living cargo on the nearest inhabitable planet. It is a wintry, desolate place, dubbed Not-Hoth by the survivors.

On Not-Hoth, the human women discover that they are not the only species to be abandoned. The sa-khui, a tribe of massive, horned blue aliens, live in the icy caves. They hunt and forage and live as barbarians, descendants of a long-ago people who have learned to adapt to the harsh world. The most crucial of adaptations? That of the *khui*, a symbiotic life-form that lives inside the host and ensures its well-being. Every creature of Not-Hoth has a khui, and those without will die within a week, sickened by the air itself. Rescued by the sa-khui, the surviving human women take on a khui symbiont, forever leaving behind any hopes of returning to Earth.

The khui has an unusual side effect on its host: if a compatible pairing is found, the khui will begin to vibrate a song in each host's chest. This is called resonance and is greatly prized by the sa-khui. Only with resonance are the sa-khui able to propagate their species. The sa-khui, whose numbers are dwindling due to a lack of females in their tribe, are overjoyed when several males begin to resonate to human females, thus ensuring the bonding of both peoples and the life of the newly integrated tribe. A male sa-khui is fiercely devoted to his mate.

The humans have now been on the ice planet for over a year and a half, and most have adapted to tribal life. New babies are being born of human and sa-khui pairings, and the tribe stirs with life once more. The last of the human castaways resonate, and the remaining men despair of ever having a mate. Josie, who ran from her resonance to Haeden, stumbles across the wreckage of the spaceship that Kira destroyed and discovers the unthinkable: two more human women are trapped in stasis there. Josie and Haeden return to tell the rest of the tribe, and a rescue party is sent out to retrieve the new women. Sisters Lila and Maddie cause issues amongst the tribe's hunters the moment the women arrive. Hassen steals Lila in an attempt to force resonance, only for Lila to run away from him. She's rescued by Rokan, who resonates to her, and they make their way back to the tribe.

Meanwhile, Hassen is exiled and Maddie remains angry that Lila was taken in the first place.

This is where our story picks up.

CHAPTER ONE
Maddie

It's weird when you don't fit in.

I thought that once I hit adulthood, I'd be all done with feeling like an outcast. That once I got past those awful high school years when I felt like a square peg in a round hole, it'd all just be a bad memory. That someday I could look back and laugh at how much it bothered me to be the weirdo on the outskirts.

Sitting here in a cave at a party for my sister, surrounded by aliens, I feel like I'm reliving my high school years all over again. It's pretty garbage, I have to admit. I wasn't popular then, being fat and opinionated. These aliens don't care if I'm fat or if I have a big mouth, and yet I'm still on the outskirts.

It's *weird*.

Someone dances past me, laughing. His tail smacks against my arm and then he spills a bit of his drink on the stone floor in front of me. Lovely. I absently swipe a bit of my tunic on the spilled alcohol because I don't want someone slipping on it in front of me while I sit and hold down a cushion in the corner of the room by myself.

It's not that people are unfriendly. Heck, it's not even that I'd have to sit alone if I didn't want to. It's that I'm really not sure where I stand with any of these people. I stare out at the celebrating tribe, not paying attention to the people who dance past with a skin of sah-sah, or the woman who pulls her top down to breastfeed not one but two blue babies. I ignore the exclamations over the fruit that they've managed to savor all damn night, and I sure as shit ignore when they start singing again.

Everyone's so damn happy. Everyone but me.

Me? I'm struggling.

In the space of the last month or so, my world has been upended. I went to sleep one night and woke up in the arms of blue space aliens on a frozen planet. Apparently I was kidnapped by bad aliens in my sleep. Apparently they took my sister, too. Apparently we were also stuck in sleep pods for over a year and a half and missed out on the bad guys being shot down.

It seems we slept through a lot.

Even if I thought it was all too strange to be believed at first, it didn't take long to realize this shit was legit. There are two suns, two moons, and endless frost and snow. The people here are blue, covered in a downy fuzz, and act like a blizzard is a nice spring rainstorm. Oh, and the parasites. I don't even want to think about the parasites, especially not the one living inside me now, helping me "adapt" to this alien world.

My sister is thriving, though.

It's strange. Lila's always been a shy introvert and even more of an outcast than me. She was born deaf, and though she got cochlear implants at age twelve and no longer needed me to speak up for her when lipreading was too tricky, I've always felt the need to protect her and care for her. But here? We've been separated and she's been killing it. Lila is usually the lonely, lost one and I'm the bold, outgoing one. I have to be because that's how you Get Shit Done.

Except Lila's doing fine on her own and now I'm just kind of . . . lost. I'm the single human that doesn't have a mate. I don't know the others. They're all pregnant or getting pregnant or juggling babies already and I'm sitting here, twiddling my thumbs with my VACANCY sign over my vagina.

Not that I want a baby, mind you. Or a mate. But it feels weird to be the only chick who's not hooked up in this place. Even my sister's lovey-dovey with an alien and mated.

She's happy here despite all the snow and ice and man-eating creatures and lack of toilets. She wants to stay (not that we have a choice).

And me?

I'm just kind of here.

Alone.

I rub at the wet spot on the stone floor while one of the humans—Georgie? Megan? I don't know which one—whips out a boob and starts breastfeeding her child mid–conversation with an alien lady. Lila's not attending the party any longer; she ran off to her cave with her alien guy to go make babies with him. Literally. She's literally going to make babies with him. It's something I'm still struggling to wrap my brain around. It seems that if my chest-cootie wakes up and starts purring, it picks a man I should make babies with.

I'm pretty glad mine is deciding to be mute.

Lila's thrilled to be "resonating," though. Of course she is—now she's one of the baby-crazy crowd of human women who've settled in with the aliens. Now she fits in even more, though she wasn't exactly having a tough time with that. She's mated to a popular guy. She showed up with fruit. She's taken to all the daily life tasks like they're a joy for her. Got a fire that you need made? Lila can do it. Skin a kill? Lila's right there. Make dinner? Arrows? Fucking slings or snowshoes or bear traps or whatever else these Grizzly Adams wannabes can come up with? Lila can do it. She can survive just fine because she's been learning how to be like them.

And they love her for it, too. The tribespeople have been learning sign language to speak to Lila and to make her feel welcome. I'm glad they've accepted her so readily, but it also makes me jealous . . . which makes me a terrible sister.

Everyone in the tribe adores her and they can barely tolerate me. I'm like a stinky fart that's lingering in the cave and everyone tries to ignore.

Not that I can blame them for treating me like a turd—I wasn't exactly Miss Pleasant to be around while my sister was gone. I was frantic with worry about her after she was stolen, and when they wouldn't let me go after her? I was kind of not nice about it.

Okay, I was a bit of an ass.

Well, more than just a bit.

But I was worried about seemingly fragile Lila on this hostile, cold planet. So I took it out on everyone else. I might have picked a few fights and dragged my feet, and okay, I threw a few things at people's heads. So what? Anyone else would have done the same if they were in my shoes, uncertain about the fate of their baby sister.

They don't understand what it's like to be so alone, even in a sea of people.

Everyone here's part of a family. There are happy women with babies, and men utterly devoted to their ladies. As I look over, the chief—Vektal—is tossing his baby daughter into the air and giving her exaggerated kisses just to make Talie laugh. And boy, does that baby laugh. It'd be adorable if it didn't make me feel so sour inside. He's got a wife and a baby. All of the humans here have someone.

I have Lila. Like I have in the past, I'm ready to shield her from the world's harms and interpret for her when someone doesn't know sign language.

Except my sister doesn't need me anymore.

Scared, timid little Lila has returned utterly confident in herself and in love with Rokan.

That leaves me . . . well, it leaves me sitting here by myself on a mat, mopping up someone else's spilled drink.

I sigh and stare out at the entrance of the cave, feeling alone and yet trapped at the same time. I don't fit in with these people, but I also don't have the option to find other people. There *are* no other people.

Sometimes I wonder what would happen if I just up and left. Would they hunt me down like they hunted for Lila? Or would they be all "good riddance" and not care because I've been a bitch?

I scowl into the shadows of the cave's entrance. It would be so easy to get up and just walk out while everyone's drunk and partying. But even as I stare, glowing blue eyes blink back at me, and a big, bulky form emerges from the shadows of the cave entrance, spear in one hand, a dead animal in the other. It's a hunter, returning from a late-night jaunt out into the snow.

And not just any hunter.

It's Hassen. The bastard that stole my sister. The one that decided he wanted a mate so much he'd just up and fucking steal her.

Him? He can kiss my fat ass.

Though the look he's giving me right now? That tells me he'd enjoy that far too much. That he'd do more than just kiss it if I bared it for his inspection.

And for some reason, I find myself prickling with arousal at the thought of Hassen folding his big body down to give my plump ass a kiss. Which is all kinds of wrong. He's exiled. He's a dick. He wanted my sister. None of these put him on the "Ice Planet's Most Desirable Bachelors" list.

As I glare at him, his mouth twists into a fang-bearing smile.

I jerk my gaze back around to the fire, scowling. Totally not gonna keep picturing him with his mouth on my ass. Biting one of my rounded cheeks. Dragging his fingers over my body and exploring the fact that I have no tail . . .

I give my cheek a hard slap to bring me back to reality.

Nearby, Farli gives me a startled look. "Are you all right?"

"Just distracted," I tell her. Farli's a good kid, and the closest thing I have to a buddy here, for all that she's, like, fifteen years old. Right now? She's my ride or die, because, well, I don't have anyone else. Even my sister, Lila, is off in a corner somewhere, making out with her new hubby. I can't even be mad about that—she's so happy and she is such a wonderful person that she deserves every bit of joy. I'm thrilled for her.

I'm a little jealous of her radiant happiness, sure, but still thrilled for her.

I'm just a selfish jerk of a sister who doesn't know what to do with herself when she's not needed anymore and suddenly finds herself with no friends. Funny how I always thought I didn't need friends. Funny how being stranded on an ice planet can totally change your perspective on things like that. In a small community like this, not playing by the rules gets you left behind.

Hassen knows all about that.

I peek over my shoulder back at the cave entrance again. Just in case Hassen is still there. But he's not, and I ignore the little stab of disappointment I feel.

The last thing I need is to get involved with the bad boy of the ice planet.

Hassen

It is a cold night for me.

The laughter coming from within the tribal cave spills out into the snow, and I can smell the burning meat cooking for the humans. Someone is singing, and I hear Warrek banging away at his drum. They are all good sounds, happy sounds. My people are light and carefree and full of joy.

That joy does not extend to me.

I stand alone in the snow on a nearby ridge, a fresh-killed quill-beast in hand. And I am torn, because I do not know if I should ignore the punishment the chief has given me and join the celebration, or if I should turn around and leave.

I am exiled. I am nothing to my people now. I did not think I would care, but . . . I do. Their scorn hurts me.

If I go inside, I will be met with uncomfortable looks, but they will not turn me away. Some will be filled with disgust at how I have behaved. Some will pity me in my punishment, because I risked everything and lost. It would have all been worth it had things turned out differently, but I am empty-handed and alone, and thus a male to be pitied.

I am not one to dwell upon what might have been, but tonight, I wonder. I wonder what it would be like to have the tribe celebrating my resonance. To hold my mate close and bring her to my cave, and together our chests would sing until our kit was created.

But I am happy for Rokan. He is a good friend and a good hunter. He truly cares for Li-lah, and together they will be very happy.

Li-lah . . . I have mixed feelings about. I am disappointed that she is not my resonance mate and yet I am incredibly relieved as well. I thought upon first seeing her that she was perfect—small, fragile, with dark hair and big eyes. I thought she would be the perfect female for me, and I listened to my heart and not my head, and stole her away. I kept her captive for hands upon hands of days in a hunter cave, and with every day that passed, I became more and more worried.

Li-lah cried. Many, many tears. She huddled in the back of the cave and stared at me, terrified. And me . . . I felt like a monster. I only wished to resonate with her, to cherish her and start a family with her. I want what the others in my tribe have with their human mates. I want to feel the warmth of another body against mine, to have someone to talk to. To see her belly full with my kit. I would never harm Li-lah, yet she flinched away from me every time I spoke to her. And then she would cry again. It soon grew to the point that I was looking for excuses to leave the cave so I did not have to endure her weeping and trembling.

And I was so terrible in Li-lah's eyes that she escaped. Left the safety of the cave and was taken by metlaks. Rokan had been in the area and helped me search for her, and when he returned, resonating to her?

I felt *relief*.

This cringing, terrified female was not mine. My gladness filled me with even more shame. Should I not be sad that Li-lah is someone else's? Should I not be jealous of Rokan? But . . . I am not. I am glad for him, even as I ache with loneliness. There are not many unmated females in the tribe. If I am to ever have a mate, I will have to wait for one of the other females to grow to adulthood, unless my khui chooses the last human, Mah-dee.

I snort to myself at the thought. Sometimes I wish it had been her I had stolen instead of cowardly Li-lah. Mah-dee does not cringe and weep. She throws things when she is upset, and bellows at all that stand near. She attacked me the last time she saw me. She is fierce.

Now *that* is a female.

I step into the mouth of the cave to deliver the fresh meat to those that sit near the fire. Normally there is a hunter standing on guard at the front of the cave. Tonight it is Bek, his arms crossed and his expression as morose as mine. He is not interested in the celebration, either. Nor is he interested in taking my kill to the others for me. He watches me with disinterest and then gazes back out to the night sky again. I feel a strange sort of kinship with Bek—he knows what it is like to have a human female and lose her. Though I think Bek still has feelings for his; I test mine and still feel nothing but relief that Li-lah belongs to Rokan. My loss is what she represented to me, but I think Bek truly loved his Claire in his way. Claire, however, has resonated to another and even now sits near the fire with her mate, content.

I feel eyes on me and scan the cave.

There, off to one side. It is the human Mah-dee. She is looking in my direction. I catch her gaze and give her a challenging look, daring her to continue staring at me. Does she think her distaste for me will make me scurry away like a diseased metlak?

To my surprise, a strange expression crosses her face and she quickly looks away again.

Curious. Her response reminds me of when Jo-see first resonated to Haeden. She chattered on and on about how much she hated him . . . and yet could not stop watching him when she thought no one paid attention. The hunters noticed, however. It is our job to be observant of our prey, to notice the behavior of others. Jo-see's lips said one thing, but her body language said another.

Could this be the case with Mah-dee? Is she attracted to me?

I feel a surge of pride and run a hand down my chest. My body is a fine one, and I am strong. I am a tireless hunter, and I am sure that if I were given the chance to test my skills, I could be equally tireless in the furs to please my female.

But it does not matter. I can take no mate because I am exiled. I have no cave to call my own. Until the brutal season arrives, my bed is the snow outside, and my task to bring in as much food as possible. Once I have worked hard enough, I will be forgiven for betraying the rules of the tribe.

Until then, I have nothing and no one.

My mood bleak, I toss the kill down in front of Hemalo. "Meat for you and your—" I stop, because Hemalo has broken the bond with his mate. They do not speak, and now he beds with the hunters. It is unthinkable to me—to have a resonance mate and choose to leave her. I do not understand him. "Meat," I say gruffly.

"My thanks," Hemalo replies, ever mild. "Will you join me by the fire for a bit? Rest yourself?"

I hesitate. I would like to join him by the fire. I would like to share a cup of sah-sah and laugh and eat. I would like to sit amongst my tribe and enjoy the evening, even if it is to celebrate the joining of another male to the female I stole. I would like to see if Mah-dee looks my way again.

But Vektal is sitting nearby, his daughter bouncing on his knee as his mate, Shorshie, shares a piece of fruit with other humans. He is watching me.

And his rules must be obeyed if I want to win my place back amongst my people. "I must not." I touch Hemalo's shoulder and then head off, back out into the snow and the dark.

Alone.

I have not yet earned the right to return. But I plan to.

CHAPTER TWO
Maddie

ONE WEEK LATER

"What do you mean, you guys are going out?" I stare at my sister like she's grown a second head, and then sign my question to her. Sometimes I forget that her cochlear implants are gone and she is now deaf again.

I mean, we are going out, Lila signs to me patiently. *A journey. The others want to see the fruit cave and harvest some of the fruit there, and grab a few plants to see if we can't grow some in this cave. Rokan and I are the only ones that know where it's at, so we're going to take a few of the others and show them.*

When do we leave? I ask. I'm not keen on trotting around in the snow again, but if it must be done, it must be done. Plus, staying around the cave all day with no one to talk to has been a bit boring. My cave buddy, Asha, doesn't do much more than eat and sleep, and my sister's been holed up in her cave making babies with her man. Stretching my legs with a walk sounds like a good idea.

Lila tilts her head at me, curious, and then begins to sign again, slow and deliberate. *It's going to be a very small group going.*

Okay? I'm not sure what that has to do with anything . . . and then I realize. *I'm not invited, am I?*

Lila looks pained. *It's not that. We're going to be traveling fast and it's going to be a hard push. And when we come back, we're going to be carrying a lot of weight in our packs.*

I see. And they don't want the fat chick slowing them down. The only thing that stops me from lashing out in a bitch-fit is the obvious pain on my sister's face. She's clearly torn between sticking up for me and being one of the cool kids.

That's fine, I sign to her and put a bright smile on my face, even though I'm not feeling it. *I rolled my ankle the other day anyhow, so I might as well stay close to the cave.*

The look on Lila's face is so full of relief that I feel like an asshole. *I'm so sorry,* she tells me. *I didn't realize you'd want to go.*

I don't. I just want to spend time with my sister, the only person on the planet that I'm a hundred percent comfortable around. But I'm going to have to get used to the idea that she has a man in her life and he's going to be taking up vast amounts of her time. *Should you be going?* I sign back, because I can't help being a bit petty and dickish. *What with being pregnant and all?*

Her face flames bright red and she hesitates a moment. *I don't think I'm pregnant yet, because we're still resonating . . . a lot.*

T M I, I sign in slow, sweeping motions and make a face. All the more reason not to go.

She giggles, and she sounds so happy that my heart squeezes painfully. I feel like I'm losing my sister all over again, and this time not because she's been kidnapped, but because she's in love.

There's no getting her back from this. The close bond we had prior to arriving here is gone forever, because Rokan will always be attached to her now. It's no longer Maddie and Lila against the world.

Now it's just me against the world, and it's the loneliest feeling ever.

I smile brightly at her to hide my pain and decide to change tactics. *So you guys are going fruit picking? Who all is going? And I'm serious—if you're pregnant or almost pregnant, Rokan can go without you, can't he?*

Her dark brows draw together and she gives a tiny shake of her head and begins to sign again. Someone else pauses, watching us gesticulate, and our conversation no longer feels private. I keep forgetting that the tribe is learning sign language through the computer at the elders' cave and nothing I say to my sister is secret. Lila signs, *Rokan has been nervous about something for a while. Says he's uneasy at the thought of leaving me behind.*

It's probably because my sister is deaf. He's smart to be extra watchful. I understand that. Lila can't hear danger, and there's a lot of danger on this barren, wintry planet. He's smart to keep her with him at all times. I can't fault the guy for that.

As for who is going . . . She pauses, thinking. *Tiffany and Salukh, and Claire and Ereven. Josie and Haeden were supposed to go, but Josie's feeling sick.*

It sounds like a couples retreat. No wonder I'm not invited. I'm fat, out of shape, and a total fifth wheel. *You'll have fun,* I tell her. *When do you leave?*

After lunch, she tells me, and her expression is eager.

Really? Today? I went and peeked out at the cave entrance this morning and snow was falling in big, fat flakes. *It's snowing.*

It's always snowing, Lila says with another happy giggle.

This is good weather, I promise, and the guys know the path to the canyon we are seeking.

Well, you guys have fun, I tell my sister and then pull her into an impulsive hug before she can worry. I squeeze her tight and stroke her braids. Really, it's good that she's going without me, I tell myself. I hate physical labor and sweating and hiking and things along those lines. I sure hate snow, whereas Lila loves the outdoors here. Go figure.

I still feel like I'm being left behind.

Lila squeezes me back and then pulls away. *I need to finish packing. We'll be back in a few days.* She smiles and then focuses on something behind me.

I turn and Rokan is there, watching his mate. Because of course he is. Those two are joined at the hip.

Go, I sign. *Have fun.*

She waves at me and trots over to join her mate. I watch his expression get all tender and hungry at the sight of her as he pulls her against him, and I have to look away. This must be how a mama bird feels when her baby birds leave the nest. Not that Lila's my daughter, but I've always looked out for Lila and protected her, even before our parents died and left us alone.

I see one of the women by the communal fire and head in that direction. It's Stacy, one of the new moms and the one who likes to cook. She's got her goofy-looking sheet of metal that passes for a frying pan and is holding it over the fire, making cakes. Not pancakes, sadly, but some shitty root thing that tastes like a potato mated with a dog turd. Everyone here loves them, but I guess I'm still only a month or two gone from my last French fry, and to me they are not the same. "Hey, Stace."

"Hi, Maddie," she says, and though she smiles, there's a wary note in her voice. Could be that I might have thrown one of those cakes at her head back when I first got to the main cave. Jeez, people sure do hold a grudge. "Hungry?"

I nod but don't sit down. "Thought I'd grab a cake or two to take back to my roomie." Pretty sure Asha hasn't crawled out of bed today. I'm not even sure she left it yesterday.

Stacy's expression softens. "Poor Asha. She's really struggling lately. Here, I'll make her a cake and put some of that peppery spice on it that everyone seems to like so much. You want some on yours, too?"

"Me? God no." I make a face. "I like having sinuses, thank you."

She chuckles and gets to work, patting some shredded root crap and then adding something that looks like lard from a tiny bowl and then seasoning from another. She forms a cake and then gently lays it in the skillet. As she bends over, I see her baby's on her back like a backpack, his fists waving in the air. Aw, cute.

"How is Asha as a roommate?" she asks. "Are you two getting along?"

"Oh, it's great. We both hate it here, so you know, that's a real bonding experience."

The guarded look returns to Stacy's face. "You hate it here?"

"Just a joke," I say quickly. Clearly Stacy takes my sarcasm for truth. Which it is . . . but just a wee bit exaggerated. I can't really hate it on the ice planet if my sister loves it here. "It's taking some getting used to, that's all."

But she still looks worried. "Should I say something to the healer about Asha? She's clearly depressed—"

"I'm sure she's fine." Great, now Stacy's going to be up Asha's ass, too. I'm sure my sour roomie will love that. "I'll talk with her, okay?"

Stacy flips the cakes with an expert toss, and then slides them onto a small plate that looks like it was made from the vertebra of something whale-sized. "I can—"

"Nope, it's good. I'm all good. I'll go talk with her right now. Thanks, Stacy." I snag the plate and rush off before she gets any ideas, even though I know I probably just pissed her off. I'm the one who has to live with Asha, though, and I'm pretty sure she wouldn't appreciate a pep talk.

I make my way through the busy cave purposefully, acting like I have somewhere important to be so no one else stops me. Everyone's always so chatty and there's not a lot of privacy. It's like sharing your living room with forty strangers, and everyone brings their crafts out into the main cave to work together or talk to one another. Two men have their skinning frames set up off to one side and are scraping while they talk in the alien language that everyone seems to know but me. Someone else has spread a blanket and is watching a baby crawl, and a few other people are gathered and look like they're doing sewing or weaving or something equally domestic and totally out of my repertoire. I know how to mix drinks and balance a cash register, not this other garbage. At some point I guess I'm going to have to learn, but the thought depresses me.

This isn't the life I signed up for. No one wants me here. I'm not useful. I'm not even pleasant to be around. I'm not making babies. Oh, and I'm fat, which means I eat more, and there's talk about food shortages in the winter months, which makes me anxious. At what point do they start giving me the stink eye because I'm chubby and like my food? Of course, Lila won't let them be mean to me, and then I'm even more depressed because I'm the one who should be protecting Lila, not the other way around.

The privacy screen is over our doorway, and I hesitate, holding the steaming cakes close. The whole "privacy screen" thing is supposed to work like a door, or rather, the sock on the doorknob that roomies hang to let the other roomie know not to come in. No one's supposed to acknowledge you even exist on the other side if the screen is up. Which I guess I get, but now I'm officially locked out of my own room and I don't hear anything but silence on the other side.

Asha locked me out so she could take a nap? Screw that.

I listen for a moment longer to make sure Asha's not having really quiet sex or something, because I would feel like an ass if that was the case. Except I'm also pretty sure Asha hasn't bathed or left her bed in days, so I doubt she's feeling sexy.

Fuck it. I push the screen aside and go in. "Yo, Asha. I got breakfast for you. Or I guess it's lunch at this point, but whatever."

The interior of our small cave is dark and depressing. I don't have much shit since I'm new, so my side of the room is nothing but a heap of furs that makes up my bed. Asha's got a few baskets lined up along the wall, but I've never seen her crack them open. Actually, I've never seen her do a hell of a lot. As a roommate, she sucks. Either I get to sit out in the open and have people "nice" me to death, or I can come and sit in a dark room with Wednesday Addams here.

Asha sits up as I enter, her hair messy, a scowl on her face. Her cheeks look suspiciously wet and she sniffs as she glares at me. She says something in alien that is probably along the lines of "Did you not see the screen?"

"Yeah, I ignored your screen," I say in English, dropping to my bed. "And I know you know English, and you know I don't know sa-khui, so don't even start with me." I pick up one of the crispy cakes and hold it out to her. "Hungry?"

"No," she says in a sullen voice. She holds a wad of clothing to her chest and lies back down. "I want to be left alone."

"I want to be home and eating a Happy Meal, but we don't always get what we want." Man, these cakes are so not great. I mean, I'm going to eat both of them, but I'm definitely going to be thinking of Happy Meals the entire time.

"Do you not have somewhere else to go?" Asha snaps at me.

"God, I wish." I shake my head and polish off the last of my cake before picking hers up. "This is where we come to be depressed, right? So I thought I'd join you in your wallowing."

She hugs the clothing—it looks like a man's tunic—to her chest and frowns at me. "What are you depressed about?"

My nose runs with every bite, but I devour her cake anyhow. "Oh, any number of things. But if you're talking about today, my sister's going on a field trip with her new hubby and I'm too fat and out of shape to go."

She snorts. "The walk will do you good."

"Thank you, Richard Simmons," I say dryly. "Besides, it's all couples going and I don't belong there." Loneliness washes over me like a wave, and I suddenly feel as tired and beaten down by the world as Asha looks. I crawl into my bed and lie on my belly, staring at nothing. "This place sucks," I say after a few minutes of silence. "I'm miserable."

And I am. I feel like weeping, because I'm alone and forgotten and I don't even have a soul-sucking job to distract me.

"So do something," Asha tells me, and she sounds irritated. "Do not just whine in my direction."

"That's rich—motivational support from you."

"You are angry because your sister does not need you. Anyone can see that." She shoves at her blankets, adjusting them, and then pulls them over her again, huddling underneath.

"It's amazing you can see anything, considering you never leave your bed," I snark back at her, but she's right. I'm flailing without my sister. Who am I if I'm not Lila's protector? All of who I was back on Earth has been stripped away, and while Lila was gone, I clung to her existence as an anchor. I told myself that when Lila got back, things would be better. We'd find our way together.

Except Lila got back and she no longer needed me.

"So what do you do when everything is terrible?" I ask Asha.

"I am going to lie in bed," she says in a terse voice. "You will have to think of something else, because I do not want company. Find another place to hide. This one is mine."

Dude. She's harsh. "I thought we were supposed to be roomies."

"No one asked me if I wanted a companion."

Well, she's got a point there. I roll onto my side and ignore her, trying out the whole "wallowing" thing. I have to admit, it's pretty damn boring. I'm used to doing things throughout the day, not hiding. This isn't going to work for me. I roll onto my back and stare at the ceiling, and then I look over at Asha again. "So you're basically telling me I need a hobby and that you already have the market cornered on 'moping' and I need to find something else."

"Something of that nature." Her voice is dull, tired. "Find something to amuse you."

"Like what?"

She sighs heavily, as if the very act of answering me is exhausting. "The rest of the tribe helps each other. There is cooking, and gathering, and tanning . . ." Her voice catches and she takes a deep breath before continuing. "And there are kits to watch over while the others are out hunting."

Oh. Hunting. I'm intrigued. I imagine myself with a bow and arrow, like Liz. She's a badass. I'd like to be a badass, too. "You know what? I think you might be right, Asha."

"Good. Now go away."

CHAPTER THREE
Hassen

From my vantage point up on a snowy cliff, I watch as Taushen wrestles to pull one of his nets out of the water in the valley below. He grabs a handful of the net, tugs, and then bobs and slips on the muddy banks. I stifle my laughter. How much sah-sah did Taushen drink last night? I saw him and Hemalo splitting one of the skins while sitting around a fire. At least he's alert enough to have remembered to toss the soapberries into the water before pulling his nets, or there would be fang-fish chewing on his boots right now. He picks himself up off the slushy ground and rubs his forehead. And tugs again.

And falls down again.

I bite the inside of my cheek to keep my laughter silent. Taushen is too young yet to know when to stop drinking sah-sah, though Hemalo should have known better. I wonder why they were drinking, then decide I do not care. I feel a stab of jealousy. I should have been drinking with them, enjoying myself. Now I am nothing. A bitter fool who must hunt endlessly for fires he is not welcome at.

I try not to let it eat at my gut, but I cannot help it. The tribe was all I had, and now I have nothing.

Now I am moping like Taushen, I imagine. I cannot do this. An exile must always work. While they whine and drink, I hunt and feed the tribe. I ran across Taushen's trail this morning, and decided to follow him after I saw the wildly weaving pattern of his footsteps in the snow. I have been watching over him to make certain he does nothing foolish or risky, but Taushen is smart. He stays close to the caves and checks traplines and nets instead of fishing while his head is aching and his reflexes slow.

I suspect Taushen is not the only one that drank too much last night and is moving slow this morning. I chuckle to myself as the young hunter tugs at his net again and then thumps down onto his bottom like a kit, staring out at the water. This is turning out to be quite entertaining.

I am so focused on Taushen that I almost miss the snow-cat that stalks nearby, slinking from the twisty leaves of a bush to a snowy overhang. I ready one of my bone knives, studying the creature. It is emaciated, fur matted, and the khui glow in its eyes is weak. Its movements are slow. Diseased, then, or riddled with worms and so far gone even its khui cannot keep it healthy. I watch it study me, then it slinks away. It is too weak to challenge for territory, and I relax my grip on my knife. A fresh snow-cat would make a decent meal for those back at the cave, but this one is not good to eat.

As I watch it retreat, a long, straight bone wobbles through the air and drops to the ground a short distance away.

I narrow my eyes, squinting at it. Am I seeing things? Is Leezh or Raahosh nearby? Was that one of their arrows? I have seen them hunt with the weapon, though, and trained with it myself. I know how to aim and hit my prey with one of the slim arrows, but that shot . . . it was not good. It would not kill the snow-cat even if the creature remained entirely still.

The snow-cat limps away, and in the distance I can hear a female letting out an angry string of strange human words. Curious, I get to my feet and crouch low, remaining in my hiding spot amongst the intisar bushes. Their spines pull at my clothes, but I nudge the leaves aside carefully, gazing out.

A figure swathed in many layers of furs moves through the snow. The form is small enough to be human, and curvy enough that I can guess which one it is. What is Mah-dee doing out here? Alone?

She wanders away, scooping up her arrow and then heading down into a nearby valley, presumably to chase the snow-cat she is hunting.

I glance back at Taushen. He is clearly not fit to be hunting this morning, and I worry I cannot leave him. At the same time, Mah-dee is alone and out in the wild. She will get hurt . . . or worse, if she corners the sickly snow-cat. I am torn.

I move back to the ridge and look over at Taushen again. To my relief, he has given up on his nets and is heading back in the direction of the tribal cave, a long, heavy fish slung over one shoulder. Good. That leaves me free to go and rescue Mah-dee from herself.

I turn back toward her and see she is already down in the valley, chasing after her prey. Her steps are slow and awkward in the snowshoes, and she uses the end of the bow as a pole to guide her. As I watch, she stumbles forward, planting face-first into the thick snow.

I sigh and head down the side of the hill after her, stifling my irritation. Humans are painfully unaware of just how dangerous it is for them to be out in the snows. Mah-dee is more unaware than most, but she is also newer than the others. If this were

Jo-see or Claire, I would have harsh words for them, but I suppose I must be forgiving when it comes to Mah-dee.

I hike down after her.

All thoughts of forgiveness and understanding disappear when she pauses in the snow again and draws her bow and I hear a metlak's warning cry, followed by the snow-cat's howl. Worry thuds in my chest. How can one small human find so much trouble so quickly? I speed up, drawing my knives.

Mah-dee is brave. She swings her bow toward the metlak's call, not backing away. Her form tenses, and in the distance, I see a metlak's dirty, yellow fur against the snow. It crouches low, then calls again.

Mah-dee fires at it, but her arrow flops to the ground close to her feet. She mutters something in human again.

The metlak charges.

I bellow a response, leaping forward. I cross the short distance between myself and Mah-dee in a matter of moments. As a hunter, my duty is to protect, and I surge in front of Mah-dee even as she fumbles for another arrow. Blades drawn, I snarl at the metlak, daring it to approach.

Its snarl turns into a screech of fear. It turns and scrambles away, as I suspected it would. They are cowardly but vicious, and tend to run if confronted or cornered. It did not run from Mah-dee, and I shudder to think what it would have done to her if she had stayed in place and continued to try to fire arrows. The thought makes my stomach clench, and anger bursts through my mind.

Stupid human.

I chase the metlak a bit longer, taking out my rage on it. The creature continues to hoot and screech its fear, and I do not stop until I am certain it will not circle back to Mah-dee. I slow my steps and then turn back, scanning for the snow-cat or other

dangers that Mah-dee might have stumbled into. I sense nothing, however, and relax enough to sheathe my blades.

Mah-dee is still standing where I left her, mouth open. The
bow is in her hands, half-raised, an arrow resting. "What was
all that?" she asks me. "And where'd you come from?"

"Did you not see my tracks?" I snarl at her. "Did you not see
the tracks of the metlak before you charged into this valley?"

She blinks at me. "Tracks? I . . . Oh. I didn't think about
that." She looks back behind her, at the churned-up snow left from
her snowshoes. "I guess that should have been obvious."

My irritation swells even greater. Even the youngest of kits is
taught to look closely at churned snow. "Who is with you?" I
will knock that hunter on the head for being such a fool as to let
Mah-dee run off by herself.

"No one is with me." She lifts her chin defiantly. "I'm alone."

"*What?* How?" There is no one protecting her?

Her brows go down and she gives me an incredulous look. "I
put one foot in front of the other and walked out?"

"And no one was there to stop you?"

"Last I checked, it was a tribe, not a prison. And I don't
know if you noticed, but people are a little busy lately. No one's
got time to hang out with a bored human." She says it in a casual
voice, but there is a tension on her round, funny-looking human
face.

An arrow slides out of the quiver she has on her shoulder—
her shoulder, of all places—and I absently pick it up. "Why is
everyone so busy?"

"There was a party the other day, which I know you know
about, because I saw you there." Her cheeks flush pink. "And then
Maylak had her baby, so a bunch of people set off to hunt one
of those really enormous creatures—"

"Sa-kohtsk," I say absently, moving forward and untying the quiver from her shoulder. "This goes at your hip, not over your arm."

"Oh. A sa-kohtsk, right. Anyhow, they need cooties for the baby. They gotta parasite him up. You know how it goes."

I do not understand *payr-uh-site* but I do know how a sa-kohtsk hunt works. The delicate khui is removed from the creature's heart and given to the newborn kit so he may live. Sa-khui children are born without a khui—the sa-kohtsk are native to this world and we are not. The khui burrows into the chest and wraps around the heart, lighting the eyes of the host. It keeps us strong and healthy . . . and gives us resonance. The humans are still not comfortable with the idea of such a thing living inside them, but those without a khui perish in a handful of days. "A khui is a good thing."

"So everyone keeps telling me." She shrugs. "And my sister and a few people are also going out to the fruit cave to go harvest and scope the area out. Cave's gonna be pretty empty for the next while."

"I see." I tie the quiver at her waist and then adjust where it hangs. Mah-dee stands there like a kit, oblivious to how close I am. My head is full of warring thoughts. I am angry that the tribe has gone on not one but two hunts and I was not included. Of course I was not. I am exiled. I am not welcome until I have been punished enough that Vektal is happy. The thought burns in my gut.

I am also still angry that Mah-dee is out here, alone. No one thought to protect the human? To see that she is kept busy? Give her something to do? "And so you came out here because . . ." I trail off, waiting for her to finish the thought.

Mah-dee's cheeks are bright red with emotion. She finally

slaps my hands away and scowls at me. "Like I said, because it's not a prison?"

"I do not know what this 'pree-sawn' is."

"Never mind." She sighs. "Probably wasting my breath trying to explain to you how I feel."

"But it is acceptable to waste my time and endanger yourself by trying to hunt?" I give her a curious look. "Is this a human thing I do not understand? Do you enjoy endangering yourself?"

She blows out an angry breath and her eyes narrow at me. Her hands go to her hips. "Fuck you."

I go very still. I have heard that human word before. They spout it from time to time, but I have dismissed it as babble. It was not one I learned when the elders' cave taught me their words, but one I overheard Jo-see say to Haeden recently, in between kissings. Lust blazes through me, surprising in its intensity. I study Mah-dee. Under the furs, I know her form is lush and thick, healthy and solid. She is not built like tiny Jo-see, but strong and plump with good health. Her hair is a strange pale color, but her round face is appealing for all its human strangeness. I am surprised . . . and honored that she has chosen me as a pleasure mate. "You wish me to fuck you? I accept."

Maddie

Mate with him?

"Wait, whaaaaaat?" I put my hands up as Hassen pulls me against him, and my palms slap against his hard chest. Oh, wow. He's . . . really warm. I didn't realize how chilly it was out here until I touched him, and now all I can think about is his scorching heating pad of a chest with the silky blue fuzz covering his body. My hands are on his pectorals and he's hard all over, which is fascinating and makes my girl parts sit up and pay attention.

"I will make it good for you," he says in a gruff voice. "Tell me how you like to be pleasured and I will do it."

His confusing words jerk me right back to reality. "Wait, no, I was telling you to fuck off, not that I want to fuck."

He tilts his head, and it's clear to me that he doesn't understand the distinction. Heck, with every moment he touches me, I'm starting to lose track of the distinction, too. He's all muscly and sexy and warm and, gosh, it really has been a while since I've had sex.

Actually, it's been a while since someone has touched me at all. I've been so isolated and alone out here, and Lila's occupied with her new man and I've felt . . . discarded.

I sure don't feel discarded right now, not with Hassen's glowing eyes burning into mine.

Slowly, regretfully, I give him another shove and push back, moving away from him. "I'm not having sex with you. That was a figure of speech."

He frowns. "Fig-yuur of speesh? I do not understand—"

"It means I was saying something you took the wrong way."

"What did you mean, then?"

"I meant you are being rude and annoying."

He huffs at that. "Then why did you demand that I fuck you?"

Okay, seriously. The arousal I felt at touching him is quickly disappearing behind irritation once more. "I. *Didn't.*" I grit out each word. "I was trying to tell you that I can do what I want. I don't need to ask anyone if I feel like hunting. You don't, right?"

Hassen gives me a puzzled look. "Why do you want to hunt?"

"Because I am bored. I am so damn *bored.*" I sling the bow back over my shoulder, irritated. "The other girls in the cave are all busy with raising babies or making babies. Everyone else is out hunting or gathering or whatever the hell it is you people do. Even my sister won't let me join her because I'm too damn fat and out of shape." I'm still stinging over that one. Since coming to the ice planet, I've been shedding inches like crazy because of all the physical activity. I thought I was actually looking pretty svelte, so to hear that I'm considered a burden hurts.

No, scratch that. It makes me angry. No one's giving me a fair shake on this planet, all because I was a little temperamental when I found out my sister was stolen.

Hassen reaches out and straightens the bow on my shoulder, pushing one side back that probably would have jabbed me in the eye if I'd turned to the left. "I understand."

That isn't what I expected to hear from the big, muscly jerk that stole my sister and just tried to make out with me. "You do?"

"I understand boredom." He gestures at the endless snowy hills around us, his face hard. "You think I do not get bored with no one to talk to? Hunting day in and day out with barely a word spoken to another? You think I do not long for company around the fire at night? I would gladly take Taushen's snoring over the silence of being alone."

"I . . . Oh." I suddenly don't know what to say. That sounds awful, and yet at the same time, I can't believe I'm having feelings of sympathy toward the douche that stole my sister. Because I know what it's like to be ignored. I know what it's like to feel like everyone in the world is against you. I know what it feels like to be on the outside and wanting desperately to be accepted.

I just didn't think I'd be feeling kinship toward *Hassen*. I've been told over and over again that Lila was never in danger with him, that he only stole her because he wanted to take care of her and mate with her, but I've been holding on to a lot of damn anger over that, regardless. He tried to force her hand, and that was not cool.

But now I'm also seeing another layer below "cocky jerk-bag." He still is, but he's also . . . lonely and desperate. He saw my sister as a chance and he took it. I should hate him for that. Instead, I keep thinking about how warm his fuzzy, velvety chest was.

I must be an idiot. "Well, if you're bored," I say lightly, "then teach me how to hunt. We can keep each other company." I twang the bowstring that's snugged between my breasts like a seatbelt. "I need to learn to be useful. Not just because I need to contribute to the food situation, but I need something to *do*."

I don't point out the thought niggling in the back of my mind: that I need to be able to take care of myself if I ever can't take it and want to leave the tribe. I keep telling myself that will never happen, and yet I keep thinking about it. Because I don't feel loved, or needed, or accepted, and I didn't realize how badly I needed those things until now.

Hassen regards me for such a long time that I can't tell what's going on in that head of his. Is he thinking about teaching me? Is he thinking dirty thoughts about me? Is he . . . focused on the fucking? I shiver at the thought, because that's another that won't leave my head.

Stupid head, always holding on to the wrong stuff.

I fiddle with the bowstring again and his gaze goes there. I freeze, because now that means he's looking right at my boobs. I hope he's not wondering why they're so much bigger than all the other girls' here. None of the aliens are fat, and that would be a hella awkward conversation to have.

"I am supposed to be exiled," he finally says, looking up at my eyes once more.

"That's cool," I say brightly. "I'll just teach myself. No biggie." I turn away.

He grabs my arm, and to my surprise, he growls—just like a bear. It's weird . . . and it makes my body thrill just a bit more than it should. "You did not let me finish, female."

"Pfft. Then go ahead and finish, *male*." I turn back to him and gesture grandly. "Continue."

Hassen crosses his arms over his chest. And okay, I really should not be paying attention to the fact that it makes his arms flex into the most incredible biceps, or that his pectorals are these amazing flat squares of muscle that are just begging to be petted again. "We cannot tell anyone that we are meeting. I do not wish for the chief to prolong my exile."

Oh. Is that his only concern? I smile, relieved. It feels like he just agreed to be my friend, and it's strange how happy that makes me. "Cool. So you're going to tutor me after all?"

He gives a quick nod and studies me again. "But not with this bow."

"Why not?"

"Your arms are not long enough to draw it properly. You are smaller than Leezh."

That's not something I hear often, and I preen a bit at that. I mean, clearly he's not talking about our figures, because Liz just had a baby and I'm still larger than her, but I like hearing it anyhow. "Then what?"

He grabs my hand and studies it, frowning to himself.

"W-what are you looking at?" God, I sound all breathless. But him grabbing my hand has kind of thrown me for a loop. His hands are so freaking big, and I feel all dainty and girly next to him.

"You have small fingers," he tells me, and it sounds like an admonition. "And small hands. Too small for my blades."

"Are there extras somewhere I can borrow?" Part of me wants to pull my hand back out of his grip, and the other part of me wants him to stroke his thumb down the length of my upturned palm. Or kiss it. Yeah, kissing would work.

Oh God, now I'm having weird sex fantasies about the guy that kidnapped my sister.

I snatch my hand out of his and he looks surprised, then seems to shrug it off. "The storage cave."

I think of the layout of the tribal cave. There's a room or two in the back of the "new" wing—the area with all the rough-cut rock—where a lot of extra furs and bones and things are kept. "I think I know where that is. I'll look."

"We will meet there in the morning," he corrects me. "I will pick out the appropriate weapons for your hand size and we will train on those."

I want to object to his chauvinistic "I will pick for the lil' lady" attitude, but I actually don't know if my hand size is going to affect things after all. Maybe I'm just being defensive. I look at the big knives strapped to his belt and try to imagine them in my hands. Okay, yeah, he might be onto something. "We can go back there now—"

"No. For now, I am going to take you home."

Arrogant jerk. "Why?"

"Because there are metlaks in this area and it is not safe for you." He puts a hand on my shoulder and slowly turns me back toward the direction I came. "So I am going to guide you home and then I am going to go and find Taushen and make sure that he made it back to the cave, too."

Taushen? Huh? "Okayyyy. What time are we meeting in the morning, then? Because I have to warn you, my schedule's pretty full," I say flippantly.

"*Sked-jee-ule?*" The way he says the word is funny, all drawn out and strange. "What is this?"

"It's a joke," I reply dryly. "Never mind."

I fart around in the tribal cave for the rest of the day. Really, there's nothing for me to do and everyone else seems so preoccupied that I feel awkward asking if anyone needs help. And really, there's not much I can do to help with a lot of stuff. I don't know anything about babies, or skinning, or fletching arrows, weaving, or any of that stuff, so I mostly end up sitting by the fire looking bored. Normally there are a few people gathered around shooting the shit, but today the cave feels incredibly empty. There are a few elders sitting around, and I can hear a baby crying in the distance. The fire keeps burning down to ashes and so I have to keep stoking it, which is . . . not something I'm good at. I end up shoving a lot of the big dried dung chips onto the fire and hoping for the best.

Which means that I've got a huge blaze going by the time someone drops by.

"Jeez, cold?" Stacy swings back through with her baby-backpack and gives me a curious look. "Do you need more furs? Because stoking the fire that high won't do more than just burn a lot of fuel—"

"It was an accident," I say, feeling defensive. "I didn't mean to make it so big. It just kept going out."

"Oh. Well, you have to stack the chips really close together to get it to burn for a long time. That's why some of them are bundled together." She bustles over to the fire and uses a couple of the poking sticks to shove all the fuel into a tight, tidy little pile. The flames die a bit and settle back to a less-than-blazing roar.

"Thanks," I say, and try to sound like I mean it. I hate that everyone's constantly correcting me on how to do even the most basic of things.

"Of course," she says, and the expression on her face tells me she is contemplating a strategic retreat from the fire. Damn, am I that unpleasant to be around?

I smile at Stacy, a little desperate for company. I pat one of the nearby stools, encouraging her to stay. "So what are you up to?"

The tension eases from her body and she relaxes. She doesn't sit in the stool next to me but pulls up one across the fire and produces her frying pan from her satchel. "Josie's been sick all afternoon, so I thought I'd make her some cakes. They're easier on the stomach than raw meat. Or cooked meat."

"Or that peppery dried meat stuff."

Stacy wrinkles her nose. "Yep. So I thought I'd make cakes." She pulls out her little pot of grease and rubs down the surface of the skillet, and I watch her. The skillet itself is pretty junky looking—a square with bent-up edges to form a lip, soldered onto a long metal handle with a bone grip. Where they got the solder, I have no idea. Stacy's the only one with a skillet, though, and that kind of makes her the unofficial cook of the group, just like Tiffany's the unofficial gardener. They both have skills they're putting to use.

I have nothing practical to offer, which is a real bummer. A bartender on an ice planet is about as useful as a runway model.

Stacy takes a chunk of the fleshy white root, dices it, adds a bit more grease and a few other ingredients I don't recognize before patting it into a cake, and then puts it on the skillet over the fire. "How's your roommate?"

"The same."

"She like the cake I made for her? Should I make her more?"

I shrug. "I can take her more if you make them, but I don't know if she'll eat them." I don't point out that she didn't eat the last one. Someone's here and actually talking to me, and I don't want to scare her off. "You seen Farli lately? She usually hangs out with me." The teenager is my best buddy in the cave, it seems.

"She went with the others for the sa-kohtsk hunt. Pashov went with them. Georgie, too."

"Are they going to be hunting?" I try to picture the chief's wife and teenage Farli attacking one of those things.

"Probably just going to help out and get away from the cave for a while before the brutal season hits."

Right. Because winter is coming, yada yada. I've been hearing a lot about it for weeks now, but I don't see how it can get much worse than it already is.

Stacy looks up and smiles at someone behind me. "Hey, Josie. How are you feeling?"

I look up as Josie drops onto the stool next to me. There's a pale cast to her face, and her hair is limp and sweaty. "Awful. Did I say I wanted morning sickness? Clearly I'm insane." Her hands go to her stomach. "Please tell me this doesn't last long."

"It doesn't last long," Stacy parrots.

"Liar."

"You didn't ask for the truth," Stacy retorts. "Here, I'm making you cakes. Maybe you can keep them down."

Josie puts a finger under her nose as if to block out the smell. "I guess. I wish Haeden was here." She blinks back huge tears.

"I hate that I've been sick all day and he's off hunting. I *need* him."

"Oh, honey," Stacy says, voice soft. "You're hormonal. He went with Maylak's hunting party. They're getting a khui for that cute baby of hers. You know he can't stay in the cave and stroke your hair all day."

"Can't he?" she says wistfully. She looks over at me as if noticing me for the first time. "Did you not go out with the others, Maddie?"

"Didn't feel like it," I lie. Obviously Josie has been in her cave enough that she doesn't know that I wasn't invited. I'm not going to disabuse her of that notion. "Thought I'd stick around and hang out here."

"It's boring without my Haeden," Josie says, sighing gustily. Stacy just rolls her eyes.

"Having a hard time staying busy?" I ask. God, I know how that feels.

"Not in the ways I want to be busy," Josie says with a pout.

"Overshare," Stacy says, flipping a cake and then sliding it onto one of her plates.

"Oh, come on. I'm pregnant. You weren't horny when you were pregnant, Stace?"

Stacy holds the plate out to Josie. "I'm sure I was, but I'm also pretty sure Maddie doesn't want to hear about your sex life."

Josie takes the plate from Stacy and looks over at me. "Sorry."

"Oh, it's all right. At least one of us is having sex." And for some reason, the moment the words come out of my mouth, I think of Hassen.

You wish me to fuck you? I accept.

I suddenly feel very restless. I think of the way his skin felt under my hands, the warmth of his body, how big and strong he was. How good he felt to touch. I shouldn't be noticing these things about Hassen of all people. And yet. And yet.

I'm attracted to him, and I haven't been attracted to anyone else on this planet. I couldn't get past the horns and the fangs and the tails—dear lord, the tails. But with Hassen, I'm not thinking about that. I'm mostly thinking about pectorals. And how velvety soft his skin was.

You wish me to fuck you? I accept.

Is it . . . wrong to want to tap the ass of a man that kidnapped my sister?

Probably.

Am I thinking about it anyhow?

Oh, yeah.

"I didn't think I'd be this bad when I was pregnant," Josie is saying. "Like, I thought once the baby was in, I wouldn't want Haeden to touch me until it came back out again. But oh, man." She sighs dramatically and wraps her arms around her torso. "Being pregnant just means I need sex all the damn time."

"We know," Stacy says dryly, putting a new cake on the fire. "You're noisy."

"Don't care." Josie's voice is cheerful. "It's just that sometimes you gotta scratch an itch, you know? And lately, man, have I been *itching*."

Stacy just laughs, but I say nothing. What Josie is saying is hitting me right in the feels. I've been restless and lonely ever since I got here to the ice planet. Is that what I need, too? Someone to scratch my itch? Josie looks so damn content and she's been barfing all afternoon.

You wish me to fuck you? I accept.

Maybe . . . maybe I should have taken him up on that. The

moment the idea crosses my mind, I don't hate it. I don't hate it at all. It can't be a "real" mating because we're not resonating. I can't get pregnant.

There's no one to judge me, either. The aliens are pretty open-minded about sex. Heck, I've seen couples making out in the public bathing pool, leaving little to the imagination, and no one nearby batted an eye. I've heard people having sex in their caves at night. It gets someone a little teasing and that's about it.

And to make it even more convenient?

Everyone's gone. They're out hunting or fruit gathering. The cave's practically empty and will be for probably another week.

This would be the perfect time to get my "itch" scratched.

Plus, there's a bonus in that Hassen is exiled. He's not supposed to be around. If things get awkward, it's not like I'm going to have to face him constantly. He's not going to be around the fire at breakfast. He's not going to be hanging out during the afternoon gatherings. He's exiled.

The more I think about it, the more I'm intrigued by the idea. I'm not opposed to a one-night stand. I'm sure not opposed to scratching the itch that's been plaguing me lately. I mean, if I get laid and I relax? That's a win. There are zero strings attached.

Of course, I need to find out how he truly feels about my sister before I decide to claim him for my selfish needs. If he's hung up on Lila, I'm not touching him.

But if he's not . . . I cross my legs tightly, squeezing my thighs together. Maybe it's wrong to focus my attentions on him. He's probably the wrong guy.

But he's so right in so many other ways that I can't help it. I toss around other ideas in my mind. Taushen didn't go with the others. Warrek didn't, either. Hemalo. A few of the elders. None of those even come close to making me think about wanting sex.

The moment I think of Hassen, though, it's all that's on my mind.

I could wait for the other parties to come back from hunting, but . . . I like the thought of the cave being so empty. It'll give me the freedom I wouldn't normally have.

It's right now or never. I glance at the entrance to the cave, but it's empty.

Okay, it's *tomorrow morning* or never.

CHAPTER FOUR
Hassen

I am at the tribal cave early the next morning, ready to start the day's hunt lessons with Mah-dee. I admit that I am looking forward to this more than I anticipated. While my days are filled with hunting as usual, it is the endless nights around a lonely fire that are starting to wear on me. It is not the same as being out on the trails, knowing that I have a warm fire and friendships to return home to. As an exile, I have nothing and no company to break up the endless days.

I thought it would not bother me, but it does.

Helping Mah-dee learn to hunt will not fix the ache of loneliness, but it is something to do while I check my traps, and she is fierce and interesting to speak with. I do not know if she will be easy to teach, but that is the least of my concerns. I am just eager to have company through the day.

I enter the cave, and it feels strange to have no meat at hand to feed the tribe. I feel like I should not be here, though there is no one to cast a judging stare. One of the humans sits near the main fire, but the rest of the cave is empty; it is too early for most to be awake. I set my spear down near the entrance and head toward the back storage cave.

To my surprise, Mah-dee is already there. Her back is to me, her yellow mane shining and cascading over her shoulders. She is not dressed to go outside, though, wearing only a light leather tunic and leggings. "You cannot wear that out," I say in greeting, moving past her to step into the storage chamber. "You are human. They do not stay warm."

"I know that," she says, a hint of irritation in her voice. "You think I haven't noticed that I'm human?"

"I would think you have." I look around the cave. There are baskets of furs, bones, horns, seeds, and anything else the tribe might need. I do not see more arrows, though, or slings. There are a few spears resting on one wall, but I can tell at a glance that they are too large for someone with small hands like Mah-dee. "What have you found?"

"I haven't been looking," she says, and sidles up to me. "I have a question for you instead."

I frown as I look over at her. A question? "What is it?"

The look on her face is wary, her hands clasped behind her back. "My sister is mated to your friend Rokan. How does that make you feel?"

I narrow my eyes at her and then move to pick up the smallest spear in the supplies. It is light and fragile, and yet I still suspect it will be too heavy for Mah-dee. "Why does it matter?"

"Let's just say it matters to me, all right?"

"Because we cannot be friends if I hold feelings for your sister? Is this why you ask?" I am not a fool.

She shrugs.

I pick up the spear, testing its heft. Light, but balanced. I hold it out to her. "Try this."

Mah-dee takes it from me and then gives me another pointed stare. "Well?"

I sigh, because I know she will not give up on this. More, it is a topic I am not keen to discuss. Just thinking about it feels as if I have to peel back a layer of skin and expose myself. "I . . . it is complicated."

"I've got time to listen."

I grunt and watch as she grips the spear. Her hands are small along the much thicker shaft. Perhaps spears are a bad idea and I should make her more arrows. Yet she was not skilled with the bow. "I am glad for Li-lah and Rokan."

"You are?"

I nod. "Rokan is a good hunter. He deserves a mate. He is happy with her. Thus, I am glad for them."

"That's a total cop-out of an answer." She pokes at me with the spear, stepping closer. "How do you really feel? You kidnapped my sister because you wanted her to be your bride. Don't tell me you don't feel anything."

"Oh, I feel things." I feel a great many things.

"Well?" She jabs me again, the spearhead dragging against my arm and leaving a scratch.

I grab at it and glare at her. "You wish to know how I feel? I am angry."

Her eyes go wide. "Go on."

"I am angry that I am a strong, capable male and yet my khui is silent. I am ashamed that I broke the rules of my tribe and stole a female that hated me and did nothing but cry every time I looked at her. I am sad that I am no longer welcome. I am disappointed that I risked all and gained nothing. And yet . . . I am happy for Rokan. And I am . . ." I let the words trail off, because I remember that Mah-dee is Li-lah's sister.

"You are what?" she prompts. "Spit it out."

"I am . . . glad that Li-lah is not my female." The words taste like grit in my mouth, but even as I say them, they are curiously freeing. "She and I . . . we were not a good match. I thought perhaps I would get used to her, that we would grow into each other, but . . . we did not, and I am glad for it. And then I am even more angry that I broke the rules of the tribe for her." I flick the spearhead away from my skin. "Does that satisfy you?"

For some reason, Mah-dee smiles brilliantly. "Actually, yes."

I grunt. There is no understanding females sometimes. "Then I am glad my pain pleases you."

"It's not that I want you to be in pain," she says, and puts the spear aside. "It's just . . . well." She considers me. "It makes things easier on my end."

I frown in her direction and turn back to the spears, searching for an even lighter weapon. Perhaps the one I handed her does not feel right and she needs a different one. "Easier for what?"

Her hand goes to my arm. "For me to do something for myself."

Mah-dee is not making sense. I glance over at her. "Eh?"

She stretches and grabs my vest, tugging me forward. There's a naughty smile on her face and a gleam in her eyes that makes my cock respond. I stiffen, because her touch should not be arousing. I am here to teach her, no more. When I pull back, Mah-dee pouts, her full lower lip thrusting out in a way that fascinates me. "Why are you leaning away?"

"I am trying to understand what you are doing."

She gives a little shrug and stands up on her toes, trying to move closer. "Maybe I want to kiss you."

"Eh? Why?" I am not entirely certain I have heard her correctly.

She licks her lips and I am suddenly fascinated by the way they gleam, shiny and pink. "Because I thought we might fool around a little."

"Fool around?" I do not understand these words together.

Mah-dee sighs. "I guess I need to show you." Her hand slides down my front, caressing my chest, and I freeze in place. Her fingertips trailing down my chest ridges and then tickling over my navel feel . . . incredible. My cock aches, hardening immediately. I remain still as her hand skims down even farther.

Then she cups my cock in her hand and looks up at me.

"Wanna fool around?" Her voice is a husky whisper.

My mouth is dry. The blood pounds in my ears and I can think of nothing except the small hand caressing my shaft. "You . . . you said you did not wish to fuck."

"Changed my mind," she says in that sultry voice. "We can play around with each other just for fun, you know? Let off some steam. No one's here to notice." Her fingers move up and down over the hard ridge of my cock in my loincloth.

She wishes to become pleasure mates? I am shocked. I thought she hated me. Is this why she asked about her sister? I gaze down at her upturned face, wondering if she is playing a prank on me. But there's interest and arousal shining in her eyes, and her gaze flicks to my mouth. Her lips part.

"Why?" I ask again, but my voice is a low growl as I am unable to hide my interest. Not that I can hide it anyhow—her hand is all over my cock. She knows just how interested I am.

"I'm bored," Mah-dee says, her lips curling in a smile as she strokes me again. "And jittery. I thought this might take the edge off. Haven't you ever had sex just to, you know, scratch an itch?"

I shake my head slowly. "I have never mated with a female."

"Then a male?"

I frown. "With *no* one."

"Oh my. You're a virgin?" Her eyes widen and her smile gets bigger. "This is going to be fun, then. We'll have to test your stamina." Her hand slides lower, cups my balls, and she gives them a squeeze through the leather.

I groan, my eyes nearly rolling back in my head at the touch. "Have you . . . mated before, Mah-dee?"

"Yup. Does that bother you?" Her hand squeezes my balls again.

I shake my head. "Right now the only thing that would bother me is if you stopped."

She giggles, and the sound is light and flirty and makes my entire body surge with lust. I grab a handful of her yellow mane, careful not to pull, and wrap it around my hand. "So you wish to kiss?"

"Among other things."

I lean in toward her. She turns her face up toward mine and her hands go around my neck—and I growl low, because I want those small fingers back on my cock, stroking it. I study her mouth. I have seen the others put their lips on their mates and act as if they are devouring their females. I wonder if there is more to it than just placing a mouth atop another.

She smiles up at me and licks her lips. "Let me take the lead." And then she pulls on my neck until I move closer to her. I am so tall that I am hunched over her smaller form, but it does not matter once her lips brush over mine. They are soft and sweet to taste, and I am stunned by how good they feel against mine. Why had my people never kissed before the humans came? This seems . . . natural. Good. Right. Her lips move against mine, nipping gently at the hard line of my mouth, and I let her lead because she wants to.

Mah-dee chuckles and bites at my lower lip. "Relax, big guy."

I try to. Nothing in my body is "relaxed" at the thought of Mah-dee's touch. Everything is tense and aching and desperate for more caresses.

Then her tongue flicks against the seam of my mouth. "Open for me. Just watch the fangs."

I do, and then her smooth little tongue slicks against mine. I groan even as she gasps and pulls back, her fingers flying to her mouth. "What is it?" I ask, worried. "Did I do it wrong?"

"Your tongue. It's ridged!"

"Yes?" I think again about the feel of hers slicking into my mouth, and then cup her face in my hands. "Yours is not? Show me."

She sticks her tongue out at me, and it is pink and soft and smooth. Fascinating. I rub my thumb along her smooth lip as she tucks her tongue back into her mouth, amazed by the differences. I have seen the other human females around the cave, but I did not stop and think of how those differences would feel against mine. "I wish you to stick your tongue into my mouth again."

Mah-dee chuckles. "Since you asked so nicely . . . let me know if you have any other surprises, yes?"

I think for a moment and then lean in to put my mouth on hers. Before I do, I tell her, "My cock has ridges as well." Just in case she does not know.

Mah-dee gives a little moan, pulling back before our lips meet. "Really?" Her breathing has sped up.

I nod. "It is good?"

"Oh, I think it is," she breathes, and then presses her mouth to mine again.

I part my lips and wait for her tongue. Mah-dee does not disappoint me; I feel her tongue brush against my lips and then slide into my mouth a moment later. The feel of it is incredible, and it makes me hungry for more. Unsure if I am supposed to remain still and let her slide her tongue against me, I test rub my tongue along hers.

She gives a soft little noise of pleasure that makes my cock throb in response.

My own need is threatening to erupt. I slide my tongue along hers again, and she tilts the angle of her head. Then we are kissing more deeply, our tongues meshing and twining as our mouths devour one another. Over and over, we kiss.

It is the best thing that has ever happened to me.

I want to keep kissing her, but Mah-dee pulls her mouth from mine, and her hands tear at my vest. "Take this off," she tells me. "I want to see the goods."

I am still dazed by the feel of her mouth against mine. I want it back. I want her tongue sliding into my mouth again and rubbing against me with its smooth, slick feel. I want the taste of her on my lips again. I growl as she tugs my vest down my arms, trapping them in the leather.

"Don't be such a baby," she murmurs as she pulls at the clothing. "I'm going to put my mouth on you again." Her hands go to my bared chest a moment later and she sighs with intense pleasure. "God, are you this hard all over?"

"Harder here," I tell her, and take her hand and place it on my cock again. It is a bold move, but I am learning that Mah-dee is a bold female.

"Mmm, yes, you are," she breathes, and rubs my cock again. "I can't feel the ridges through your pants. Guess they're going to have to come off."

She truly wishes to mate? I love that this human female is so fearless and bold, unlike her crying sister. "I am bigger than you. You are not afraid, are you?"

"Pfft. Nope. The whole size thing's kinda doing it for me," she says, and I do not follow all her words. I do not need to. There is arousal in her eyes and hunger as she gazes at me. That tells me enough. She looks up at me, a sly expression on her face, and smiles. Her fingers go to the laces at the sides of my loin-cloth. "Let's get rid of this ugly-ass diaper, huh?"

"Di-per?"

"Doesn't matter what it's called, because it's coming off," she tells me, and then gives the leather a hard tug. The knots tighten, and I push her fingers aside so I can show her how to undo the laces, because I want to see her reaction to my body. So far she has been eager to touch me. Will she be as eager once she sees my cock and its pronounced ridges?

My leathers fall to the floor, and I stand before her in nothing but my boots.

Mah-dee sucks in a breath, gazing down at my erect, straining cock. She drops to her knees in front of me. "Wow. Yes, please, this is definitely going on my wish list."

"I do not understand what you mean," I murmur, my voice thick. Her kneeling before me is giving my mind all kinds of wild ideas.

"Shhh," she tells me. "Don't interrupt. I need a few moments alone with this big guy." Her hand curls around my cock, and I hiss at the sensation. Nothing has ever felt better than that small touch. Nothing. "Damn, my friend. You are packing some serious heat under that furry diaper of yours."

"Sa-khui are naturally warmer than humans," I tell her, utterly distracted by her touch.

"Wasn't what I meant, but yeah, I noticed." And she leans in and rubs her face against my cock.

I groan loudly again and then bite down on my knuckle, staring at the open doorway. Even though the storage cave is tucked away into the back of the tribal cave, I do not want someone coming to see what strange creature is moaning and grunting back here.

I do not want anything to interrupt Mah-dee's studying of my body.

"Mmm," she breathes, rubbing the length of my cock against her cheek, and then rubs my cockhead against her soft lips. "I don't guess you've ever had a girl touch you like this before, have you?"

"Never," I breathe. I clench a fist at my side, because her touch makes me want to spill. Already my sac is tight against my body, my cock throbbing with the need to release. Yet I do not want that; I want her to keep touching me forever because it feels so very good.

"Then let me be the first to blow your mind," she says, looking up at me. She's got a wicked little smile on her face as she slips her tongue out and licks the head of my cock.

I stagger backward, almost losing my balance. There is a primal sound rising in my throat that I must work to swallow, but Mah-dee only grins and licks the head of my cock again, her small, smooth tongue lapping up my pre-cum.

And I cannot stop watching. I am utterly entranced by her pink mouth working over the head of my cock, her fingers gripping my ridged length, the look of pleasure on her face as she tastes me.

Did I think that kissing made today the best day of my life? My imagination was not ready for this. Nothing can be better than this.

But then she moans as she drags my cockhead along her tongue, sucking me into her mouth. Her hand slides between her thighs, and I smell the musky scent of her arousal.

It seems my imagination is a poor thing after all.

She pulls her mouth off my length and I feel the loss of her tongue keenly. Instead, she strokes her hand up and down my length, pumping me. Her gaze moves over my body and then she looks up at me. "All right, I need to ask about the elephant in the room. What's this?" She gestures with her other hand at my spur. "I have to admit that's new to me. And I've been trying to be cool about it, but like . . . I need to know."

"It is my spur."

"Super. What's it do?"

Do? I shrug, covering her hand with mine so she will stroke me harder. "It is there. I do not know that it does anything."

"Huh. Human guys don't have those." She tilts her head, studying it. "That's not going to make sex impossible, is it?"

"The other humans have not complained to their mates," I tell her.

"Hmm. Fair enough. Can I touch it?"

"I would rather you continue to touch my cock, but you can touch it, yes. I am yours to touch wherever."

She looks up and wiggles her eyebrows at me. "Don't make me test that theory."

Her words make new lust surge through me. This female is fearless. I did not realize how appealing such a thing could be.

I remain still as her hand moves from my cock and caresses my spur. "It feels hard," she says, curiosity in her voice. "How strange."

Her fingertips tickle me, and my cock jerks in response to her featherlight touches. "It is, yes."

"I wonder what sort of evolutionary purpose it serves, you know? There's a reason for everything, and I can't figure out the reason for this one."

"Does it need a reason to exist?" I cannot concentrate on her words, not with her small fingers stroking my spur like my cock.

"I guess it will remain a mystery for a bit longer," she says, and then leans in to give it a lick. "Can I play with your tail?"

My tail? I shudder at the thought, because then I truly will spill my seed. The underside of it is beyond sensitive. "I . . . would explore you now."

Her eyes brighten. "Would you? I love it when a man volunteers." She gives a little shimmy and slides her tunic over her head, tossing it to the side. She wears the strange strap across her teats that I have seen a few of the other humans employ, and she removes it quickly before shucking her leggings and tossing the leathers aside.

I move closer to her, admiring her body. She is small—all the humans are—but her body seems to be sturdier than the others, her thighs thick and full, her belly rounded. Her scent is light and musky, but lovely, and her teats are large and plump, tipped with rosy nipples that draw my attention.

I brush a knuckle over her pale skin, and she feels smooth but different than sa-khui skin. For a moment, I am overwhelmed. It has been a long time since I have felt the warmth of another's skin against mine. I did not realize it until I touched her softness. Living as a hunter with no mate is a lonely life, but a hunter in exile? It crushes my spirit. I swallow hard to rid myself of the knot in my throat. "I like the way you feel."

"Do you?" There's a slightly nervous note in her voice. She gives a little wiggle and puts her hands on my arms, stroking them. "I'm not too weird to you?"

"Perhaps I like weird," I tell her, gruff. She has no protective ridges on her arms or her round belly. She is vulnerable and soft everywhere. And yet . . . I like it. I like touching her softness. I like her smooth, pink skin and the tiny tuft of fur between her thighs. And I like her big, bouncy teats. They draw my hands and I cup them, fascinated. The females of my tribe do not grow as bountiful here as the humans do.

Mah-dee sucks in a breath, her nails scratching at my arms. There's a glazed look in her heavy-lidded eyes as I touch her, and I am fascinated by her response. I want to do more. I caress her heavy teats, tracing their shape. My thumb skims over the tight, pink bud of one nipple, and she makes another choked sound. So I do it again, stroking the nub with the pad of my thumb, over and over as I watch her face.

Her lips part and she closes her eyes. Another soft, throaty sound escapes her, and then I smell the musky scent of her arousal in the air. She likes it when I touch her teats like this. Is it the same as my cock, then? Because when she rubbed her face against it, I nearly came undone.

I would like to do that to her.

So I drop to my knees and pull her body against me.

She makes a tiny exclamation, but her hands go to my shoulders. Mah-dee runs her fingers through my hair even as I bury my face between her teats and begin to lick her flesh. Her breathless moan of pleasure is encouraging, and I nuzzle at her soft, soft skin until I find one of those pink nipples and tongue it.

Her hands tighten in my hair and she gasps. "Ohmigod."

"Tell me if you do not like what I do," I say between nips to the skin. Even her nipples are soft. My own are hard and rough, but hers feel tender under my tongue, and I lick the underside of one, dragging my tongue over it.

She shivers and moans against me. "I don't know if that's humanly possible."

Her excitement—and the tight grip of her hands in my hair—encourages me to do more. I glide a hand down her side, caressing her hip and bottom. She is plump everywhere, and smooth, and touching her like this makes my cock strain, desperate to be buried inside her warmth.

This is what it is like to have a mate, I realize with wonder. Holding your female in your arms and pleasuring her. Knowing that she is yours for all time. I am filled with longing so intense that it takes my breath away. I imagine Mah-dee in my furs every night, and waking up with her softness curled up against me. I imagine her body rounded with my kit. I imagine her by my fire, giving me those sharp, teasing looks of hers even as she nurses our son in her arms.

My hands tighten on her skin.

I want that.

I want *all* of that.

I squeeze one rounded flank, and then slide my hand over her thigh. I want to touch that thatch of fur between her thighs, and the pink folds it hides underneath. I want to discover the third nipple I have heard the hunters talk about. The sa-khui women do not have one, and I can only imagine what it feels like.

If she is aroused by my tongue on her teats, how will she react if I put my mouth on her there? I groan at the thought, and press my face in the valley between her teats again, trying to keep control. We should not be here, in the storage room, naked and exploring each other. I am in exile. My duty is to hunt and remain scarce around the caves.

And yet . . . I cannot seem to stop touching Mah-dee.

I will pleasure her first. Then we will stop.

I push my hand between her thighs, cupping her mound. The fur here is not soft like the mane on her head, but tight with curls. It is wet, too, damp with her arousal, and my mouth waters in response. I want to taste her. I want to see what that wetness tastes like on my tongue. But her thighs are quivering against my hand. I do not want to push her too far. "Do you want me to stop?"

"Are you kidding me?" She sounds as breathless as I feel. "Just now, when you're getting to the promised land?"

"Land?"

"Never mind. Just keep going." Mah-dee wiggles against my hand, rubbing her cunt against my palm. "I'll just be quiet."

I snort. "You have not been quiet since I entered this cave. I doubt you shall start now." She feels like all wet folds under my hand, soft and fragrant and slick. I drag one fingertip along the seam of her cunt, tracing it. "Are you sensitive here?"

"Oh my God," she breathes. "You have no idea how much."

"I want to learn."

Mah-dee's hand knots in my hair, her grip tight. "Then keep going."

I do. I explore her with my fingers, paying attention to each gasp, each hitch of her breath, and I learn her body. I find the entrance to her core, where she is slickest and hottest, and cannot help but push a finger into the opening, imagining it is my cock. Her soft cries and the way she jerks against my hand tell me that she is imagining the same. I want to push deeper, to thrust into her and see her body quiver, but . . . I want it to be my cock, not my hand. So I search for her third nipple instead.

I find it tucked into the front of her folds, a tiny nub hidden in the slick softness. She moans loudly when my fingers skate over it. I want to bring my hand to my mouth and taste her, but I want to keep pleasuring her, too. The need to please her wins out over my own selfishness and I circle my fingertip around her nipple, watching her expression. Her face is tight, her brows wrinkled together as if she is concentrating hard, her lips parted.

She is so lovely to look at that my mouth waters again.

There is another way to taste her, then.

I look around. There is a pile of extra furs in one corner of the storage room, behind a few baskets. I grab Mah-dee by the thighs and heft her in my arms as I get to my feet. She makes a small noise of protest, but it is muffled—she does not want us to be found, either. I carry her to the furs and set her on her back, and before she can say anything, I push her thighs apart and my mouth is on her. I give her a long, thorough lick, making sure to flick my tongue over her nipple. She tastes as sweet and musky as she smells, and I am filled with Mah-dee's scent, her flavor.

It makes me hungry for more.

Mah-dee whimpers. I feel her legs tremble, and then she hooks one thigh over my shoulder. Her hands grip my horns. She is not pushing me away. She wants more.

I am eager to give her more. With a hungry growl in my throat, I lick her again. And again. I use my tongue to give her pleasure, trying to make her produce more of those little cries that make my body tighten in response.

"I'm so close," she tells me, pulling on my horns. "Use your fingers, too. Thrust into me with them."

Her demanding tone fills me with a fierce response. If she wants more, I will give her everything I can. I double up on my ferocity, tonguing and licking at her nipple. I slide my fingers along the slippery folds of her cunt, seeking out her opening, and when I find it, she cries out again. She wants me to use my fingers? I shall. I thrust into her with one, and it is nearly my undoing.

She is so wet inside, so warm, and so very tight. I can feel her cunt clench around my finger in response to my invasion, and I imagine how it would feel around my cock.

I am very, very close to losing control. Gasping, I rear back, abandoning my efforts to pleasure her. If I touch her now, I will spend before my cock even comes close to her cunt.

And I want to spend inside her.

I press a hand to my forehead, willing my body to obey. My cock throbs incessantly, the head coated with my own slickness. I dare not lick my lips, because then I will taste Mah-dee. My hands are still wet with her juices, and I want to taste them even as I know I must not.

She approached me and wished to mate. I must please her and show her that I am worthy of her attention. Spending all over the furs instead of inside her will not do.

Mah-dee makes a small noise of protest. "What? Why'd we stop? Is someone coming? Because I know it isn't me, if you know what I'm saying."

I do not know what she is saying, actually. And I do not care if someone is approaching. At this point, I am too far gone. "Give me a moment."

"I don't want to," she says in a teasing voice, and her toe nudges my thigh. "I was so close."

"Me, too," I grit. "That is my problem."

"Oooh." Mah-dee sits up on her elbows. I dare to glance over at her, and it is nearly my undoing. She is lovely to gaze upon, her inner thighs still open and wet and inviting. She bites her lip as she looks over at me and tilts her head. "I don't think that's a problem at all, see. Because I want to come, too. So if you're waiting for permission, you have it."

"Permission?" If I were not in so much physical agony, I would find her words amusing. Does she think I am waiting for her go-ahead? I am trying to control myself so I can make it good for her. So she will ask me to mate with her again and again.

"Yeah. Permission. It's a fancy word that means have at it, big guy." And her toe slides over and brushes against my cock.

The control I have been struggling with disappears in an instant. I surge forward, covering her body with mine. She opens her thighs wide, welcoming me, and her arms go around my neck. My mouth lands on hers, and then we are kissing again, lips feverish as I press my cock against her entrance.

If she does not want me to be controlled, I will not be. If she does not want me to be patient, I will be an animal with her.

"Yes," she murmurs against my lips. Her hands twist in my hair painfully, and her body eagerly rises under mine. "Yes!"

I surge into her . . . and my eyes nearly roll back in my head. Her cunt grips me, hotter and wetter and tighter than anything I have ever felt. It is . . . indescribable. I feel as if my entire world has changed in the clasp of her body.

Underneath me, she gasps. "Spur," she breathes. "Ohmigod-spurohmigod." Her hand flutters between our bodies.

I can feel my spur, nestled in the slick valley of her cunt folds. "Is something wrong?"

"Fuckno. S'allgood," she mumbles. "Just gonna be over here, unraveling." Her eyes close, and the tight look returns to her face.

"Should I . . . get off you?"

"Do that and I'll kill you," she says, and her hands twist tight at my hair again. "Start moving again, because I need to feel more of that."

She likes the spur? Pleased, I stroke into her again. The breath hisses from my lungs at how snug she is, how tight a fit. Being in her cunt is so much better than my own fist. Mah-dee has ruined me for all else.

Mah-dee moans again, and I lean in to muffle her loud noises with my mouth. I kiss her deep, my tongue dragging against hers even as I thrust into her once more. She makes a sound of encouragement, and her nails dig into my scalp.

I can hold back no longer. I push into her, faster and faster, each thrust seemingly quicker than the last. My hips have never moved so quickly. I grip her hips to hold her in place, and pound into her even harder. It is as if all of the need and longing I have felt is channeling out of me and erupting into our bodies. I feel her cunt clench hard around my cock, and Mah-dee jerks underneath me. The noises she makes are wild as she pulls at my handfuls of hair, encouraging me to move faster, to push harder.

I do. And as I do, I feel her clench tighter, her cunt milking me like a fist. All the while, her moans grow louder.

Then, like a wave rising from the great salt lake, my sac tightens and then everything I have been holding back lets loose. I growl Mah-dee's name into her neck as I come, hammering into her soft body, losing myself in her. My hips work over and over as I spill into her body, holding her smaller form tight against me as wave after wave of pleasure washes over me. When it crests, I stiffen and collapse on top of her, balancing my weight on my arms so I do not crush her underneath me.

Time passes. I am conscious of nothing but my harsh, panting breaths, the slick feeling of our skin pressed together . . .

And the knowledge that this is my female, now and forever. Mah-dee gave herself to me today, and I am never going to let her go.

CHAPTER FIVE
Maddie

Oh yeah, I needed that.

My toes curl, and I utter a sigh of pure contentment. Itch? Scratched. Antsiness? Gone. Worry about the future? Can't worry about it when you've been boned into next week. Loneliness? Nah, I'm good.

Over me, the big barbarian wheezes as if I've killed him. I give a little wiggle, rather proud. I just rocked this guy's world, and it was pretty awesome. Of course, it was also awesome to be on the receiving end. That had to be the best sex I've ever had. It's like his equipment was made to pleasure a girl—ribbed penis? Yes, please. That wonderful, terrible spur that dragged alongside my clit with every thrust he made? Yes, please. That muscular body covered in velvet? Yes, yes, and yes, please.

I'm definitely glad I decided to fling caution to the wind and get me some of that.

I reach up and give Hassen's arm a little pat. He's sweaty, his velvety-feeling skin slick with perspiration. "You okay, big guy?"

"You . . ." he breathes. "That was . . . there are no words."

I chuckle, because I know exactly what he means. Of course, laughing means that my body shifts, and when my body shifts, I can feel his spur press against my clit, sending more ripples of pleasure through my body. "Yeah, that was pretty awesome."

He props up higher on his elbows and gazes down at me. From this close, his face looks craggy and hard and utterly alien, the ridges on his brow pronounced. I want to reach up and trace a finger over them, but that might be an invitation to round two, and I'm not sure I have the constitution for that. He strokes my cheek with one big finger. "I am honored that you have chosen me to be your pleasure mate."

It's like I can practically hear the record-scratch in the air. "Um, what?"

"I am glad that we are pleasure mates," he says again. "I will speak to my chief about acquiring a cave for the two of us, alone. It might be this one, but I do not mind." His mouth crooks in a half smile. "Much of these supplies will disappear in the brutal season." He leans in and nips my shoulder. "And this place will now hold special meaning for me."

Oh dear. He thinks we're mates? I try to wiggle out from under him, but it's impossible with his larger arms caging me and his cock still buried deep inside me. "No, no cave necessary. This was just a fling. An itch-scratching."

His hard brow descends, and he frowns at me even as he cups one of my breasts and begins to play with the nipple. "No, we are pleasure mates."

"If you mean we 'fucked,' then yes, yes we did. That's all it was."

"All it was?" Hassen looks at me, incredulous.

I push his hand away from my tit before he can get me all hot and bothered again, which, really, wouldn't take long. But this is an important conversation to have, and we need to set some boundaries before we fuck again. "Your people only mate when there's resonance, right? Pretty sure we didn't resonate just then."

"We did not. But my people take pleasure mates."

"Okay, and explain to me how that works. Everyone that fucks automatically mates?"

"Well, no—"

I fling my hands up. "Okay, see? So why do you assume we're mates? Why can't we just be fuck buddies?"

A possessive look crosses his face and he cups my breast again. "Because you are mine, Mah-dee. I am claiming you as my female."

"Whoa, whoa, back up. No one said anything about anyone claiming! We're just going to be friends."

He scowls. "Do you do this with all your friends?"

"Only the ones with magical spurs."

A look of alarm crosses his face. He sits up, and I want to weep with disappointment when his cock leaves my body. He grabs his loincloth from where it has fallen on the floor and starts to put it on again, an indignant look on his face. "You would pleasure-mate with any hunter in this cave? I am not special to you?"

Jeez, he sounds a little hurt. If I had known there'd be this much drama, I'd have rethought things. Most Earth guys are happy to hit it and quit it, but it seems that Hassen wants a freaking wedding ring. "If it makes you feel better, you're the only one I've pounced." And now that I've pounced him, I'm disappointed that there won't be future pouncings, because damn, that sex was amazing.

But it seems that it also comes with a side dish of possessiveness, and that's not what I want at the moment.

He scowls down at me. "But you will not be my pleasure mate."

"I don't think the timing's right," I say, trying to keep my voice light. I sit up on the furs, and my muscles are deliciously stiff. Gosh, I need a nice bath. Maybe tonight after we've gotten a day of hunting lessons in. "You understand, don't you?"

Hassen stares down at me, and then turns and stalks out of the cave.

Well, poo. Looks like our lesson has been canceled by Hassen's show of manly jealousy. I roll my eyes, hoist my well-fucked body off the furs, and dress again.

Maybe I'll just bathe and stick around the cave today after all. One thing's for sure, I refuse to feel guilty about his reaction.

The main cavern's empty of all but a few of the new moms, so I take a quick dip in the community hot tub in the center of the cave and wash my hair. I'm still not a hundred percent used to the whole "bathing in public" thing, but it's easier when the vast majority of the tribe isn't around to notice the size of my thighs.

Not that Hassen said anything about my thighs. He seemed to like them.

Okay, so maybe I'm moping a *little* over the fact that he turned out to be all possessive. Why couldn't we just be fuck buddies? Friends with all kinds of benefits? I don't need a mate right now. Hell, I'm still figuring myself out. I don't need to drag another person into my headspace, mostly because my headspace is way too much of a mess. I don't know how these other girls handle being mated lickety-split. I heard Georgie and Vektal were a couple the moment they met. I can't imagine.

Then again . . . I think of the spur and Hassen's big, ridged cock shuttling in and out, his big body looming over mine as we had sex, and I feel another quiver of arousal sliding through me.

Okay, maybe I understand it a little.

But seriously, why'd he have to get so . . . attached? All I wanted was to get all the stress out of my system and to feel the touch of another human being—er, alien. I didn't realize how lonely and isolated I was until I touched Hassen, and then I found myself craving him. I wanted more.

He apparently wants a *lot* more.

It's clear to me that I'm obsessing, so I get out of the bath, dress, and head to my cave before someone can stop me and start a conversation. I'm actually disappointed that we're not hunting today; I was really looking forward to that.

Maybe Hassen will get over his butthurt by tomorrow and we can pick up our lessons.

In the meantime, I guess I'm stuck with—ugh—Asha, Miss Cheerful herself. I guess I can change my clothes, since these smell a bit like sex and I don't know that I want to get caught smelling like arousal and leather.

I head back to the cave. Surprise, surprise, Asha's got the privacy screen up. I ignore it again and head in, moving to my furs. I have a change of clothing and I dig around in the small basket of my possessions, all the while trying to ignore my roommate. Asha is in her bed. Again.

She sits up when I start to undress, though, studying me. "What are you doing?"

"Changing."

"Why?"

"These leathers smell. Who are you, my mother?"

She's silent at that, and so I pull my new tunic over my head and glance over at her. There's a knowing smirk on her face.

"What?" I demand, and I can feel my face heating up. What is it she thinks she knows?

"If you take a pleasure mate, I suggest that you learn to be quieter." She fluffs her pillow—one that she's stolen from my bed, it seems. "You and Hassen woke me up."

Oh God. Guess we weren't all that quiet. It's even more embarrassing to think about, considering that the storage cave is a fair distance from my cave. Whoops. Guess that cat's somewhat out of the bag. "You heard?"

"I would have to be deaf not to." She smooths a hand along her blankets. Before I can ask if that's a dig at my sister, she continues, "I do not think anyone else heard, though. I did not see others around."

I relax a little at that. "So are you going to blackmail me with that bit of information?"

Her head tilts. "I do not understand."

"Use it against me. Make me do what you want so you don't say anything." I cross my arms over my chest. "I was kinda hoping to keep things quiet about the whole situation."

Asha gives a delicate snort. "Then you must learn to be quieter. As for manipulating you, I have no need. I do not care if you mate with all of the unattached hunters." She shrugs. "It is your business, not mine."

She's got my back? That's . . . nice. Unexpected, but nice. "Thank you."

Asha shrugs. "I was the same once. Before I resonated, I had my pick of the hunters. They all wanted me. It was enjoyable." Her expression grows sad again. "Then everything changed."

I say nothing, because I know she's thinking about the mate and baby she lost. And really, what can I say to her that she hasn't heard a million times before? *Chin up, kiddo? Everything's going to work out for the best*? Somehow I doubt Asha wants to hear that.

She twists her hands in her lap for a moment and then glances up at me. "I would choose more carefully if I were you."

"Choose?"

"If you are going to mate with the hunters, pick the ones that will be grateful for any attention. Taushen is young. He will follow where you lead. Harrec, too. Vaza is older, but he will be discreet if you wish it, I imagine, simply so he does not have to compete with the younger hunters." The look she gives me is calculating. "Hassen is a poor choice in a lover."

"I don't know if my girl parts agree with that." I squeeze my thighs together because, mercy. I'm still all noodly on the inside from the sex. Poor choice in lovers? Not in my book. "I thought he was pretty dang great. I mean, untrained, sure, but I can work with that." Actually, I kind of like that, because I can teach him to lick a fierce pussy for hours and I won't hear any bitching if I take too long to come. I dated a guy once who went on and on about how long it took me to get off compared to his previous lovers. It was a real pain in the ass, so he got the boot. Hassen's a blank slate in bed. I'm kinda turned on by that.

Not that we're going to have round two, of course. Not if he's going to be all Mr. Clingypants on me.

Asha rolls her eyes at me. "He is a poor choice in a lover because he is going to want to claim you. That one desperately wants a mate and a family. He is lonely. He will not take whatever scraps you toss him and be content. He will want more."

I chew on the inside of my cheek as I consider her words. She's not wrong. There's a ferocity to Hassen, an almost brutal eagerness. He held me down on the furs and plowed into me like the world was ending around his ears and he had to get his rocks off right then and there. And as he held my hips, there was a wild possessiveness in his eyes, and so much damn satisfaction. Like half of him getting off was entirely due to the fact that he was possessing me. And not just any chick. Me.

A little shiver moves through me. Okay, for all that it's not smart to toy with a guy that wants to be mates after one romp in the furs, he was hot as hell to play with. "Hassen doesn't know me very well," I tell Asha. "If he wants more, he's going to have to let me call the shots, not him."

She just shrugs her shoulders as if to say "whatever" and lies back down in bed, amused.

Hassen avoids me for the rest of the day. Which, okay, isn't exactly hard, given that I'm hanging around the cave and he's out in the wild, being an exile and doing exile stuff. He doesn't come around, and I'm pretty sure he's avoiding me.

His absence does mean that I spend most of the day hanging around Stacy, Josie, and a few of the other women. They're all nursing and baby-crazy (except for Josie, who's just pregnant and baby-crazy), so I feel like an outsider, even though I know they're doing their best to include me. I don't belong with the Baby Bunch, and after a few hours of talk about milk production and the best way to keep a baby's tail clean, I'm starting to wonder if I should go hide in the cave with Asha.

I'm bummed that I didn't get to go on hunting lessons with Hassen. Did I fuck everything up by having sex with him?

The next day, I decide to get one of the spears from the storage cave and go out and find him. If he won't bring the lessons to me, I'll go to him.

I sneak out—like the terrible person that I am—shortly after breakfast, when the firepit is empty and the girls are putting their babies down for midmorning naps. Hemalo and one of the elders are working in the main cave on a large leather hide, but they aren't looking in my direction, their backs to me. I grab the spear I hid near the door and race out, hauling my cloak and snowshoes along with me as I go. I'll dress properly for the elements once I'm out of sight of the cave itself.

Of course, once I'm out of sight of the cave, I'm greeted with nothing but endless snow. The area that the main tribal cave is in is relatively flat, and behind me there's nothing but steep cliff walls. Ahead of me, it's rolling hills of white dotted with some pink trees that flutter here and there. In the distance, I can see cliffs, and even farther away than that, the hint of mountains. The day is clear and cold, and the two weak suns are doing their best to give off some decent sunlight, but it's still not enough to warm the place up. I trudge over a nearby rise, slogging through the snow, and when I'm far enough away that I don't think anyone's going to race after me and drag me back to the cave, I stop to put on my snowshoes and wrap a cloak around my body.

And then I walk. The last time I went out to try and hunt, Hassen bitched at me about following footprints, so I'm going to do as I'm told. I find fresh tracks leading away from the home cave and figure they have to belong to one of the hunters. Using my spear as a ski pole, I trudge along, looking for Hassen.

Or another hunter.

Or animals, I guess, since I'm out hunting.

Of course, the farther I get away from the cave, the more open and vulnerable I feel. Last time I ventured out, it wasn't like this. Last time when I set out, I hadn't been attacked by a metlak and one of those ugly, skinny cat-things, though. I remember them and the fear and anger on Hassen's face when he realized I was out. That's when I figured I was in danger. Now I watch the snow, worrying that there are hidden dangers I'm not seeing behind every fluffy white hill.

I've been gone for maybe an hour when a large figure appears in the distance and starts stalking toward me, distinctive black hair fluttering over blue shoulders. Twin spears are crossed over his back. Yeah, I know that guy. It's Hassen, and he looks pissed.

Okay, he also looks pretty badass at the moment, and it's making me go sploosh in my nonexistent panties. Because seeing that arrogant swagger? That angry stalking thing he's doing? It makes me think of our intense little round in the storage room, and my body is screaming for round two.

I've never thought of myself as a particularly man-hungry sort of girl, but Hassen? He does it for me. Which is why I fooled around with him despite knowing it was a bad idea and knowing that he was the douche that stole my sister.

Plus, out of this entire happy tribe of do-gooders and mommies, he's an outcast. And boy, can I relate to that. He's the one that doesn't fit in, that doesn't belong when couples are gathered around the fire and being cozy. He's the one that never gets what he wants, and he sure isn't the hero.

That kind of makes him my people, though, because I know how all of that feels.

So it hurts that he's angry at me after what we shared. What we had yesterday was pretty awesome. I'm down for more awesome, but not if it comes with him trying to claim me. God, what would Lila say? She'd look at me like I'd lost my mind. And maybe I have. A quick throwaway fuck is one thing. Shacking up with a guy as a replacement for my sister is another.

And no matter what Hassen says to me, I know what it'll look like to everyone else.

It just reminds me that I'm making the right choice. That he might be good to sleep with on the down-low, but it can't mean anything—to him or to me.

As he approaches, I try to look cool. Like I've got things all handled and I know what I'm doing out here. "Oh, hey, Hassen. How's it going?"

"What do you do out here, Mah-dee?" He crosses his arms over his nearly bare chest, emphasizing the pectorals I didn't get enough time to lick yesterday.

I smile brightly. "I'm going hunting, of course."

"Again you are by yourself? What games do you play?" Hassen's frown is so dark, I swear people cringed three states over. "This world is dangerous."

"No games. I want to help out. I want to learn to take care of myself. There's no one at the cave except for pregnant ladies and elders. Everyone else is busy. And I had a teacher, but he got all butthurt and changed his mind about showing me how to hunt, remember?"

He steps even closer to me, and now we're practically touching. My breathing becomes quicker, because I'm thinking about yesterday. About his big body covering mine. About his cock pushing into me, and the way he kissed me, and—

"You changed things between us, Mah-dee." His voice is low, husky. Wounded.

Damn it. "Don't guilt me. You could have said no."

"How could I say no?" The look he gives me is devouring. It makes me prickle all over, and a familiar pulsing starts between my thighs. "I wanted it."

"You want a mate. I just want a bit of fun," I correct him. "It was never about commitment. It was about mutual need and pleasure. That's all."

"I do not want one night of you in my furs. I want you in them every night." He reaches out and caresses my cheek. His fingers are incredibly warm and feel delicious against the biting chill.

"I'm not saying it just has to be one night," I amend quickly. I know I wouldn't mind another round. "But I'm not committing. No girl in her right mind is going to sleep with a guy once and then move in with him." When he keeps touching my cheek, it takes everything I have not to lean into his caress. "Haven't you heard of casual sex?"

"No," he says bluntly.

Gah. "People don't sleep with other people just for fun in your tribe?"

"Sometimes they do. I am not one of them."

No, I guess he's not, considering he was a virgin until yesterday. Still, the whole "needs commitment" thing could have come up before I had my hands on his dick. He could have said something and then I would have found someone else to play with.

Except . . . I don't think I would have. Hassen's perfect for my needs because he's solitary. He's not heading back to the hunter cave to bro-down with the others to gossip. And he's an exile, so he knows what it's like to be lonely. And with this timing . . . it just made sense.

All right, the fact that he's the hottest guy on the ice planet doesn't hurt things, either. I mean, overall as a race, the sa-khui are good-looking. They're tall, muscular, well formed, and if you can get past the blue, the tail, and the horns? Oh, mama. In my eyes, Hassen puts the others to shame.

So, okay, maybe I wouldn't have found someone else to play with. I just wouldn't have played at all. I haven't been attracted to anyone else like I am to Hassen. "You're ruining what could be a good thing," I tell him, since he's sticking to his guns. "We could have fun together."

"Yes, we could." He caresses my cheek again, and his thumb skates over my lower lip.

I have a feeling we're not talking about the same thing. Damn it. And I wish that his touch didn't feel so incredible or make my nipples as hard as diamonds. "I'm not changing my mind. I'm not mating. Not you, not anyone."

Hassen's hand drops.

CHAPTER SIX
Hassen

Are all human females this stubborn?

I gaze down at my mate—because I do not accept otherwise—and she looks up at me with determination in her eyes, a defiant tilt to her small chin. It would be adorable if she were not so frustrating.

As it is, I am tempted to grab her and drag her into the snow and show her how good I can make her feel. Our mating yesterday is branded into my mind. I cannot forget it, and I relive each moment. Last night at my lonely fire, I took myself in hand and stroked off to the thought of her. Over and over again.

Two days ago, I would have questioned what was motivating me to continue. I was defeated. Alone.

Now I have purpose, and my purpose is Mah-dee.

She speaks of independence, of not wanting a mate, but when I touch her, she leans into my caress. She gazes up at me with hunger, and I know she thinks of what we did in the storage room. It is all I can think of.

So . . . I must convince her that I am the right mate for her.

That a pleasure-mating with me will be just as satisfying as resonance. That I want nothing but her for the rest of my days. That I would wake up every morning with Mah-dee's yellow head resting on my chest and cherish her because she is mine.

She has stormed into my heart like a bolt of lightning and left scorch marks wherever she has touched down.

I curse the day that I saw Li-lah, because she was tiny and frail and scared, and I thought she was what I wanted. I thought that she needed someone to take care of her and that I could be that male. I thought when I saw Mah-dee this morning that she was coming to me. To tell me she'd changed her mind.

Seeing her here, her expression stubborn? It has just convinced me that she is the mate for me. I do not need a mate that wilts and cries. I need a strong, capable female who will challenge me and push me to be better.

Mah-dee needs to let me love her.

But if she must be convinced, then I must convince her. I must coax her into realizing that I am the male she wants. If another so much as looks at her, I will tear his throat out like a crazed metlak. But I cannot think like that. I must find a way to return to the tribe, if only so I can provide a proper cave for Mah-dee. I must make it difficult for her to turn me down . . . starting now.

I look at the spear in her hands. "You wish to learn how to hunt, still?"

The look she gives me is wary. "Yes? You're not going to go all cray-cray on me, though, are you?"

"Cray . . . cray?"

She waves a hand in the air. "Nuts. Crazy. Whatever. I need to know if we're good."

"Are we?" I want to touch her soft cheek again, feel her skin against mine.

Mah-dee puts a hand to her chest. "I want to be friends. I really, really need friends here." Her voice catches in a way that makes my heart hurt. "And I was hoping we could be friends that also had sex. But if we can't, then I really just need a regular friend, okay? A hunting partner and a friend that will talk to me."

"I can be those things to you." I can be so much more, but I will settle for that for now. And I can convince her, with time, that I can be the best mate possible.

She is mine.

Her smile returns, and her features grow soft with relief. "All right, then. Let's just forget all about the sex and scratching itches and go back to being buds, okay?"

"*Buhds*," I agree, though I am not entirely certain what I am agreeing to. I think she means friends, and I will be hers.

"Then can you teach me to hunt?" She bounces a little, hugging her spear close in a way no hunter would. "I'm so damn bored. Please, Hassen. Help me get a useful skill so I'm not a big fat leech."

I cannot resist her, especially when she pleads with me. I nod. "It shall be as you wish." And if I am to woo her into being my mate, it works perfectly for me to be around her every day. "I must continue to hunt and bring in food, but you can accompany me when I am doing my rounds near the tribal cave. You cannot accompany me when I venture farther out."

"That's fine!" The delight and eagerness on her face make my cock ache with need.

"It will not be easy."

"I'm tired of sitting on my big ass anyhow."

Her ass is magnificent, but I do not tell her such, since we are *buhds*. For now. "I will not go easy on you."

"Fine."

"If you hinder my ability to hunt for the tribe, I must leave you behind."

"I won't!"

"And if I tell you to do something, you must do it."

"Not a problem." Mah-dee beams up at me. "Can we start today, or is this a bad time?"

"We can start today," I agree, glancing up at the sky. The weather is holding and there are no clouds on the horizon, which means no incoming snow. This is a good thing; Mah-dee is dressed lightly and I do not want her to be caught in a storm. "No one is expecting you in the cave?"

She snorts. "They'll probably be glad I'm gone. I think I make the other women uncomfortable."

I smile to myself. I have heard complaints about Mah-dee's throwing of things while her sister was with me. "If anyone asks, tell them you were with Asha. They will not like you spending time with me."

"Because you're the dick that kidnapped my sister?" Her words are harsh, but there is a teasing smile on her face.

"Because I am exiled," I say, refusing to take the bait. I take her spear and check to ensure that the head is tightly fitted and wrapped. One of the elders is forgetful and tends to put his broken weapons in with the good ones. "Part of my punishment is that I am to be alone."

"I won't say anything," Mah-dee tells me. "Are you sorry?"

"Sorry?"

"That you did it?"

My answer would have been very different two days ago. Two days ago, I would have said yes. But now there is Mah-dee, and all I can think of is that if I was not in exile, I would not be here with her. I would be hunting the sa-kohtsk for Maylak's new son. I do not regret my actions, because they placed my feet on this path and brought me Mah-dee. "No."

"No? Seriously?" Her jaw hangs open.

"I cannot change the past. But I also do not miss your sister." I reach out and tap her mouth, indicating she should close it. "I do not look back because I cannot change the past. You should not, either. That is one of the first things you must learn as a hunter—do not regret what you do not have. Make use of what you do."

Her brows furrow together. "I'm not entirely sure that all ties together, big guy."

"It does," I tell her confidently. "Now come. Today I will show you how to follow trails as I check my traps." I turn and start to walk away.

"When do I get to use my spear?" She huffs, trying to keep up with me. After a few steps, she reaches out and touches my arm. "Slow down a bit. It's hard to walk fast in snowshoes."

Her fingers feel like ice. I stop, and she nearly skids into me, losing her balance. I catch her before she can tumble to the snow. "Where are your gloves?"

Mah-dee shrugs. "The big furry mittens I have? Those suck. I can't hold anything tightly with those, and I thought I might need a good grip with some spear hunting."

I take her smaller hand in mine and press it between my palms to warm it. She does not pull away, which tells me she is colder than she would like to admit. "You do not wear gloves at all times, but much of a hunter's day is spent walking."

"Oh. I'll remember for next time." Her hand curls into a fist, and she shrugs her cloak down over her exposed hands, covering them from the elements. "I'm sure I'll be fine."

I grunt. "There is a hunter cave along the path we will take today. We will stop there and get you hand coverings."

"Sweet."

"Until then, however, you must keep up." And I turn and start walking again.

Maddie

He wasn't lying when he said he wouldn't take it easy on me.

I wheeze a few steps behind him as we hike through the endless snow-covered valleys and hills that seem to make up the entire fricking planet. I can't complain, because I said I wanted to hunt. I'm just out of shape and not used to trekking across so much snow. He's right, though; my fingers do feel like ice. I keep tucking them into my sleeves, but that only works for a little while.

I wish he'd hold my hand again, but I suppose it's my own fault that he won't. Instead, he stalks along, avoiding anything that looks like a path. Occasionally he'll squat down next to a set of footprints and then will indicate I should join him. When I do, he tells me about what creature passed through, how long ago, and anything else he can tell me. Some marks are crisp, which he says belong to snow-cats that lift their paws with every step. Others are more of a smear through the snow, which means a creature is dragging its belly. He points out each one and explains patiently, and when I've absorbed everything, he's off again, power walking to the next ridge.

And I have no choice but to follow.

Despite it being a little too athletic for me to handle, I'm enjoying the "hunting." The day is nice, and even though it's cold, there's a lot to see and I feel like I'm doing something useful. I didn't realize how much my uselessness was bothering me until now. I guess I'm worried that when winter comes, no one's going to want a fat, unmated human around eating all their food. If I can find my own, I can survive on my own. I won't be dependent on anyone.

We head toward a sheer gray cliff, and as we approach, Hassen points at something. "Do you see that?"

I push my sweaty hair off my brow before it crystallizes and freezes there, and scan the snow. "What am I looking for?"

"The cave. It is a hunter cave. The cliffs have small caves in them, and there are many hunter caves set up. You should always be on the lookout for one in case you need supplies or a place to rest."

"And do you know where all of them are?"

He nods. "I have visited them all many times. Hunters spend much of their time out in the wild."

"It's not all that wild out here, is it? We're still pretty close to the home cave, aren't we?" A few hours' walk, maybe, but to these guys, that's nothing.

Hassen glances at me. "It is an easy walk today, when the weather is good. On a stormy day? When the snow flies from the skies, even a short trip can be a dangerous one."

He has a point. "So are we going in?"

"We are. We will check if it needs to be resupplied, and get you gloves."

"All righty then. Lead the way." I could use a break and a chance to rest my feet, though I would never tell him that. Hassen hasn't been treating me like an incompetent fat chick and I'll be forever grateful. Thinking about my sister and the fact that she's out on a trip without me still stings.

When we arrive at the cave, I see there's a weather-beaten privacy screen pushed in front of the door. "Should we not go in? Is someone here?"

He pushes the screen aside, answering that question. "A screen does not matter in the wild. It is only in the tribal cave."

"When someone might walk in on you boning your man? Gotcha." I guess if you have a walk-in out in the wild, it can't really be unwelcome, because it's all about survival.

Hassen grunts acknowledgment of my words and pushes the screen aside, then waits. I assume he's waiting for me, so I move forward to go inside and he plants a hand over my chest, stopping me. Then he jerks his hand away as if scalded, realizing just what he was clutching. "Do not go in yet."

"No? Is someone in there after all?"

He shakes his head and squats near the entrance, so I do the same, hunching down next to him. "You must check for predators before entering a dark cave, Mah-dee. Use your senses."

Oh. Damn it. I hate that he's right, and I hate that it didn't even occur to me to check. Back on Earth, I wouldn't trip into a dark cave without checking my surroundings. It shouldn't be any different here. It just reminds me how pathetic my survival skills actually are. "So how do we check? I'm guessing that throwing a burning torch in probably isn't the most practical of responses."

His mouth crooks up on one side as he glances over at me. "Do you have a burning torch on you?"

"Nope, or else it'd probably already be in the cave."

He chuckles, and the sound makes my insides squeeze. I feel like it's rare that I hear him laugh, and when I do, it's . . . nice. Real nice. He should laugh more often. "Then we cannot send in a burning torch," he tells me. "What do you do, then?"

What do I do? Other than have many regrets over the fact that he doesn't want to fool around just for fun? I chew on my lip, trying to concentrate. "I . . . don't hear anything?"

He nods, gesturing at his eyes. "Use your senses before all else. Look for tracks in the snow." He gestures at the fresh powder at our feet, then gestures at his nose. "Look for smells. Metlaks have a foul scent to them. A creature that makes his home here that is not frightened by the sa-khui smell is usually a scavenger, and they will leave spoor in their home." He reaches out and brushes a finger over my cold ear. "And listening. Always listening for trouble."

I nod. In a nutshell, I need to be more observant. I have to think about my surroundings instead of just mindlessly stumbling around and hoping for the best. I think about all the days I spent back on Earth with my head bent over my cell phone. I imagine how horrified Hassen would be at that, and it makes me grin. "Got it."

I check everything, and when I don't find any problems, I turn to him again. He nods, and I venture into the cave, spear in hand. It's a small cave, little bigger than a closet, and just barely tall enough for Hassen to stand up in. Everything is quiet, and even though there's sunlight outside, there's not a lot in the cave itself. I can still make out neatly stored baskets tucked against a rocky shelf, and several bundles of furs alongside them. "Cute place."

"Every hunter looks out for another on the trails," he says, moving into the cave behind me. His body is so big—and yummy—that he's blotting out most of the sunlight. "We must check the supplies to ensure they are well stocked. It would not be fair of us to use what is here and not replace it, but sometimes there is a reason to rush home. And sometimes scavengers come in and upset what is left behind for others. So we must check everything first. If something must be restocked, we will add that to our list of duties. Understand?"

I do. There's a lot more to being a hunter than just wandering out with a spear and stabbing at things. It's about taking care of others—not just other hunters, but the tribe. For a moment, I'm overwhelmed at what a selfless task it is. Hassen and any of the other single hunters could survive on their own, but they choose to work tirelessly to bring home food for the tribe. In turn, the tribe cares for them when they are injured or sick, gives them a place to sleep, and people to socialize with. It's all very "circle of life," and I'm fascinated by how different it feels from my old life back on Earth. There, I felt like I had to work to pay bills. I dreamed about quitting on a regular basis. But there's no paycheck for these guys, and there's no quitting.

And for Hassen, especially, there's no reward. There's no one to come home to after a long day. I feel a twinge of guilt for his situation. He shouldn't have stolen my sister, but . . . I'm starting to understand why he did.

I gaze up at him, his features nearly hidden in shadow except for his glowing eyes. No wonder he wants to grab me and declare me as his mate. He's desperately lonely, and I'm positive that being exiled is only making things worse. Maybe I shouldn't have slept with him. Maybe that was selfish of me.

But . . . we both enjoyed it. And I can't change what's happened. All I can do is focus on right now. "Okay, so what should I do now? Build a fire?"

"Do you need a fire?" he asks. "Are you warm enough? Do you need to cook? Can you see?"

"I'm fine."

"Then we do not build a fire," he says. "Because if we build a fire, then we must go and replenish the fuel supplies for the next person who will stay here."

"Gotcha." Survival seems like a never-ending job. But in a way, I'm kinda motivated by that. You take, you give back. It just makes sense. "I guess I can see well enough . . . if you move out of the doorway."

He moves forward a bit, and our bodies brush against one another. Everything feels like it stops, and I'm acutely aware of his presence and just how alone we are. And I think about yesterday all over again because how can I not? But he moves past me with a flick of his tail and goes to sit on the far side of the cave, and I'm left feeling all achy and sad that we're not going to experience round two of storage cave seduction.

"We will check the supplies here," he says. "Come."

So I go to his side, and for the next while, he goes through the contents of each basket and each rolled-up fur, explaining what is stored here, what it is used for, and if anything is running low. Apparently we need more dung (a phrase I never thought I'd say in my life) and dried trail rations, which we'll bring by in the morning. As we unroll one of the bundles of furs, there's a gentle thud outside.

I jump to my feet at the same time Hassen does, and I move near the front of the cave, peeking out. There is another thud, and in the distance, I see a fur-covered form standing near a pair of the pink, bendy trees. He's muttering to himself and digging in the snow, a pair of carcasses at his feet.

A moment later, I feel Hassen's hand tighten on my shoulder. "Taushen."

"I see that," I whisper. He's probably about a hundred feet away, but I still feel completely conspicuous, given that we're standing in the entrance of the nearest hunter cave. If he comes by here, he'll see us. "Are we in trouble?"

"No," he tells me, and I feel his thumb move against the furs covering my body, like he wants to stroke my skin. "He will not come here. He is burying his kills in the cache nearby."

"Pretty sure if he sees us, that will be bad," I say to Hassen. He's in exile and not supposed to be hanging out. And me? I'm pretty sure if they find out I'm here with him, I'll be assigned a watchdog back at the cave that won't let me go anywhere without asking permission. Fuck that.

"Then be quiet," Hassen murmurs. His hand slides to my waist, and I shiver. I can feel the heat of his big body pressing against mine. We're a few feet inside the doorway, hiding in the shadows, and I have one hand gripping the hard bone edge of the privacy screen. I tell myself it's so I can quickly fling it up in case Taushen looks in this direction, but I'm probably lying. With Hassen's closeness, I have a feeling that if I let go of this thing, I'll just melt to the ground in a puddle of goo. Needy, *needy* goo.

"What should we do?" I whisper.

"We put the screen up and we wait for him to leave." His voice is soft and low, and I'm pretty sure I just felt him brush my hair off one shoulder. I'm pretty sure that's making me all hot and bothered, too.

I force my fingers to unclench off of the screen and put it up. It's not a perfect fit and I can still see out into the snow, where Taushen is digging, completely oblivious to the fact that Hassen and I are hiding a short distance away.

I hear Hassen take in a deep breath.

No wait, he's sniffing.

Is he sniffing my hair?

Oh God, why is that so freaking hot? His hand is still on my waist, and I'm acutely aware of its presence. He's not moving it, and I really, really wish he would. But he's not moving at all. He's just standing with his front pressed to my back, like a big, sexy shadow.

Then, as if he can hear my thoughts, his hand on my hip moves. I feel him pull up my fur coverings, and in the next moment, his warm fingers brush over my belly.

I suck in a breath when his hand immediately goes to the waistband of my leggings and he pushes into the front of them. And I whimper when he presses his head against mine and nips at my ear. "Silence, Mah-dee."

Right. Silence. "I'll be quiet."

"We do not want him to hear us," Hassen murmurs, and his tongue brushes against the shell of my ear, sending shivers through my body. His big hand cups my pussy and I have to stifle my groan. Silence. Right. Must be silent. "You would not want him to watch."

For some reason, those words make me look out across the snow, to where Taushen is. He's standing with his hands on his hips, his back to us, tail moving. Maybe he's taking a break from digging, or maybe he's about to turn around and come over here.

If he did, he'd find me with Hassen's hand down my pants.

And that hand, coupled with the fact that we might get caught? It makes me so incredibly wet.

I bite down on my lower lip when Hassen's big fingers glide through my slick folds. "Quiet," Hassen tells me again, though his voice is strained. "You will be quiet when I touch you?"

"T-totally s-silent," I manage, even though I feel like I'm

about to climb out of my own skin. I'm frozen in place, staring at Taushen, half-daring him to turn around, half-horrified that he might.

Hassen's other arm goes under my furs, and then he's pushing down my leather bra-band and cupping my breast. I bite back my moan and sag against him as his fingers stroke my pussy. God, this isn't fair . . . and I don't want it to be. I should be pissed that he's taking advantage of the situation, but all I can think is that this is exactly what I wanted, with a tease of voyeurism thrown in to boot.

I never thought I'd be so turned on at the sight of a guy digging a hole.

"So wet," Hassen breathes into my hair. "Is your cunt always this slick around me?"

Oh God, he said "cunt." Oh God, that's so freaking hot that I'm pretty sure I juice just at the sound of his deep voice. "I . . . Maybe."

"I should pull your pants off and lick you until you scream my name," he tells me. "But then you would not be quiet, would you?"

I shake my head. I would totally be noisy and love every moment of it. And then Taushen would see, and for some reason, that just turns me on even more. "You need to be q-quiet, too," I tell him, voice stuttering when one rough fingertip moves over my clit. "Oh, fuck, that felt good."

"Do you want me to make you come like this?" he asks, rubbing his finger against the hood of my clit as if he's been doing this sort of thing for ages. "Or do you want me inside you when you come?"

"Oh sweet Jesus, is that on the table? I want the dick." Do I *ever*.

He continues to pet my slippery pussy even as he pulls a layer of furs off me, tossing them to the ground. "Then you must be very quiet, Mah-dee."

Taushen's digging again. There's no chance of him coming over here . . . which is good, because I'm starting to breathe so loud I can hear it echoing in the cave around me, and I don't even care. I brace one hand on the cave wall as Hassen rips another layer of furs from my clothing, and then he's tugging my leggings down around my knees.

A second later, I feel something hard and hot press against my back. Hassen's cock. I moan, reaching backward because I want to touch him. He doesn't let me, though. He grabs my hand and holds it to the wall, then bends me forward. I brace my hands on the cave and spread my legs as wide as I can with the pool of my leggings at my feet.

Hassen's big body presses against mine once more, and then I feel his cock push at the entrance to my core. I whimper encouragement, arching my back and pushing my hips out. A moment later, he thrusts into me, so big and so good that it nearly blows my mind.

Or maybe the thing that's blowing my mind is the spur that's prodding at my ass. I've never been into that sort of thing before, but feeling it there makes me all squirmy and that much more turned on. Dear God, these alien men have such *naughty* equipment. God must definitely be a woman, because this is a gift from heaven if there ever was one.

"Quieter," Hassen rasps, his body against mine. He's so huge it feels like he's covering me from head to toe as he presses into me from behind. "He will hear."

I didn't even realize I was making noise. I'm too lost in sensation. I wriggle against Hassen, a silent demand for more, and his hand skims down my front, caressing my breast before returning to my clit and massaging it.

Oh God, he's trying to kill me, isn't he?

I groan his name even as he anchors a hand to my hip, thrusting again. It feels like I'm being pierced twice—once by his cock and once by his spur—and it's sensory overload. I'm panting as he pauses to rub my clit again and bites gently at my shoulder through my tunic.

Everything in me explodes. I come so quick and so hard that it's shocking, even to me. Ripples of pleasure turn into an avalanche, and every muscle in my body locks up in response. I can't move, can't breathe, can't speak—all I can do is stand here and silently vibrate with ecstasy.

He hisses my name and then he's pumping into me again, and his fingers rest on my clit as he begins to drill into me from behind. And did I think I was orgasming before? Clearly I didn't know the meaning of the word, because I'm coming all over again, and it feels harder and more intense than before. Wave after wave of pleasure pounds through me as Hassen fucks me with quick, rough strokes. I'm lost in the endless orgasm, unable to form coherent thoughts. I've never come so hard or so long, and it doesn't seem to be stopping.

But then Hassen's groaning against me, and he grinds his hips—and spur—into me with one last hard stroke, and my toes curl as the newest orgasm pulses through my body. He holds me close, catching his breath, and then pulls out of me.

And I practically stumble. It's a good thing I'm clinging to the rock, because I don't know that I have any strength left in me. It's all been (happily) dicked away. I drop to my knees and press my cheek to the cold floor of the cave, not caring how ridiculous I look. The world is spinning and I'm pretty sure it's going to take me days to come down off this endorphin high. Totally worth it.

"Mah-dee?" Hassen's hand touches my backside, which is raised up in the air. "Are you well?"

I think your dick broke me. "I'm fabulous," I say in a breathless voice. "Boneless but fabulous."

He rubs his hand on my ass. "This is going to get cold. I do not want it to freeze—I like watching it move when I take you."

With any other guy, I'd probably be insulted at him telling me my big ass is jiggling when we have sex. But the way Hassen says it—like a caress—tells me that he likes my ass. "I'll move in just a minute. I need to get my strength up."

He taps my butt cheek. "Rest, and then we will go out onto the trails again. Taushen is gone."

Wait, he expects me to hunt after that? Moreover, he expects me to be able to walk? I roll onto my back and stare up at him. "I think you are overestimating my recovery. I'm gonna need a few more minutes."

He chuckles. "I do not understand many of your words, but I will let you rest if you need to rest." He adjusts his pants, retying them, and looks quite pleased with himself.

"Yeah, so while I let my lower half recover, maybe we should talk about what we just did."

Ever graceful despite his enormous size, Hassen folds his legs under him and sits on the floor next to me. He reaches out and smooths some of my sweaty hair back off my face, and just that small caress makes everything tingle in response. "What do you wish to say?"

"I thought you didn't want to do the whole 'casual sex' thing." And I mentally brace myself for another round of chest-beating-man proclamations about how I'm now his woman.

But he only shrugs. "I have given thought about what you said."

"Oh?"

He nods. "If you wish to use me to scratch an itch, as you say, it is only fair that I use you to scratch mine."

Er, okay. So that isn't what I expected to hear. Instead of talking about how I should be his and we should set up a happy little cave together, we've moved on to "using" each other. Is it weird that I feel a little wounded by that? I shouldn't, because it's what I wanted . . . but damn. The guy sure moves on fast. "You're not going to ask me to marry you again?"

His face is blank. "As an exile, I can offer nothing to a mate. I realize that now. You were right to turn me down."

Oh. "That wasn't why—"

"It does not matter. If this is what you want, this is what we shall do. It means pleasure for both of us. I do not see a problem with this." He caresses my cheek.

I smile and can't help but feel like this is a lot easier than I expected. He's caving in to what I want just like that? "What made you change your mind?"

"Your nearness," he says bluntly. "I could smell your hair and feel your body against mine and I wanted you. So I took you."

I shiver. "Yes, yes you did."

Hassen

Mah-dee is smiling at me. She is pleased with my declaration that I wish nothing more than to mate with her.

It feels as if I am deceiving her, yet I will go along with it. The truth is, I have not changed my mind. In my head, Mah-dee is mine. She is my mate. But being close to her and not being able to touch her is torture. I will not choose that. I will choose another route.

Let her think I have given up on my quest to claim her as my own. I have slept on my anger, and I now have a plan. I will not blindly rush forward. I will enjoy these few days with Mah-dee while the weather is pleasant and she learns to hunt. And when the heavier snows come, I will endure the brutal season as an exile, and hunt harder than ever before. When it is over, I will talk with Vektal about rejoining the tribe as a hunter. Then and only then can I claim Mah-dee as a mate. By then, Li-lah will be carrying Rokan's kit and all will have forgotten that I stole the weak, crying sister when I should have stolen the fierce one.

Today was a risk. Not because Taushen might have seen us, but because Mah-dee might have decided that she did not want to be touched by me again. The fact that she craves my touch as much as I hunger for hers makes me weak with relief. Mah-dee initiated mating with me yesterday. I was not sure she would welcome me today.

The fact that she has means I can show her how much I need her. I plan on taking Mah-dee out on many "hunting" excursions.

And I will claim her every chance I get. I want her to need me as much as I need her.

CHAPTER SEVEN
Hassen

FIVE DAYS LATER

Mah-dee throws her spear with a limp grip. It wobbles in the air and skids into the snow a few paces away from where she is standing. The tree she was supposed to hit waves back and forth in the stiff wind, taunting her poor hunting ability.

I cross my arms and do my best to look displeased. "That was a terrible throw. You said you practiced."

"I did *try* to practice," she tells me in a grumpy voice as she trots forward to scoop up her spear. "It's hard to get up and go when you're exhausted all the time. I gave it a few tosses back at the cave but figured I'd do my practice out here with you."

"Exhausted? Am I exhausting you?" I reach for one of her large teats, caressing it through the many layers of furs she is wearing. "Shall I stop in my attentions?"

She squirms away, laughing, but the flush in her cheeks and the brightness in her gaze tell me that she likes my touch. "It's not the sex—though, okay, it's pretty amazing and hard-core on its own. It's all the hiking and the hunting. I don't know if you've noticed, but I'm out of shape."

I study her figure, frowning at her words. "I like your shape. What is wrong with it?"

Laughter peals from her again. "Just for that, you are totally getting laid again."

"Now?" I gesture at the open, rolling hills around us. "Here in the snow?"

"Not right now! There is zero privacy right now." Mah-dee sticks her tongue out at me again.

"You like no privacy," I remind her, and am pleased when a bright flush touches her pink cheeks. In the days since our first mating in the storage cave, we have mated as often as possible. A few times have been in the storage caves, in the middle of the day, and Mah-dee burns hottest when she thinks we might get caught.

When she burns hot, I do, too.

She brings her spear back toward me and then holds it out. "Do I need to work on my grip, you think?"

"If all your throws are like that one? Yes."

"Okay." She wraps her fingers around the long pole of the spear and looks up at me. "Like this?" Her grip moves up and down. "Or should I hold it tighter here? Maybe give it a little stroke when it's ready to throw?" And her hand moves in a way that has nothing to do with hunting.

I can feel my cock harden in response to the sight of her fingers moving up and down the pole. The little grin on her face tells me that she knows exactly what she does and how I will respond. "I would tell you to hold the shaft tighter in your grip, but I do not think we are talking about hunting."

She blinks rapidly. "Why, whatever do you mean?"

"Is something wrong with your eyes?"

Mah-dee snorts. "No. There is something wrong with my brain if I'm trying to use human techniques to flirt with you, though."

I grin at that, grabbing her by the waist and pulling her against me. "Do you flirt with me, then?"

"Duh. Do you see anyone else out here to flirt with?" She flings her spear aside into the snow and throws her arms around my waist.

"Is it because you want to make me need you? Or because you wish for me to bury my face between your legs and lick your cunt again?" I did so just before our lessons, but I will gladly do so again if she wishes it. The taste of Mah-dee on my tongue is better than anything.

She appears to consider it, and then sighs. "I think if we do that again, we're not going to get much hunting done."

"Mmm." I am not sure I mind that. My Mah-dee is enthusiastic about many aspects of hunting . . . except for the killing of animals. Yesterday, we found a lame dvisti kit alone on the steppes. It was easy prey and I suggested Mah-dee bring it down. She could not do it. She cried instead, and hid her eyes when I put my spear in the creature's throat. My mate has a soft heart, but she does not yet understand that sometimes a killing is a mercy.

I wish I could protect her from these things, but if she is to survive, she must be strong in both body and spirit.

"I suppose we had better go back to hunting, then." She snuggles close to me, pressing her cheek to my chest. "I do need to get better, and we've spent more time practicing other things."

I stroke her yellow mane. I want to tell her that she has no need of learning to hunt if I am her mate. That I can take care of her and provide for us if she will accept me . . . and if the chief will accept me back. Each night around my small fire seems to grow longer and lonelier.

But for now, we can hunt together and mate in the hunter caves. As long as I have Mah-dee at my side, I will take what I am offered and be thankful.

We kiss and I hand her back the spear she has dropped. "Let us go, then."

We hike, moving up one of the gentle slopes that surround the valley that is the tribal home. Mah-dee likes to come up here, because we can see from a very far distance. I let her lead, because it is important that she learn how to find game trails on her own. But when we get to the edge of the cliffs, Mah-dee points at moving specks in the distance. "Is that a herd of dvisti?"

"Too small," I tell her, walking along the cliffs a few steps to get a closer look. I count three hands of specks and see two long squares behind two of them. Sleds. Which means . . . "It is May-lak's party. They must have killed a sa-kohtsk." I eye the sleds, curious at the sight. Normally the sa-kohtsk meat has a strange, bitter taste to it and my people leave it for predators, taking only the khuis that twine in its heart. The fact that they are bringing sa-kohtsk meat home with them tells me that there are more concerns about the brutal season and whether there is enough food for so many mouths.

I should have gladness in my heart that my tribesmates are returning healthy and whole. I watch them walk, and no one is limping or moving slow. One jogs ahead, and then circles back, his movements almost playful. They are happy with how the hunt turned out, then. I should be glad.

But I am not. I am disappointed to see them, because that means it is that many faces returning to the caves. The freedom Mah-dee has had to come and go as she pleases will disappear with the return of the others. I will not be able to sneak into the storage caves with her and mate. She will not be able to slip out of the caves and see me. I bury my anger and frustration and turn back to her. "Come. Let us find a game trail."

"Everyone's coming back? Should we . . . should I go back to the cave?" Mah-dee looks up at me, curious.

Her words are like a knife in the gut. "Do you wish to go back? I can take you."

She chews on her pink lip. "Actually I'd rather spend the rest of the day with you, if that's all right. I can see them anytime."

Warmth fills my chest. I nod, because I do not trust my voice. That she would choose to stay with me this day is a gift. I hold a hand out to her.

Mah-dee moves forward and laces her small, cold fingers with mine. "So what does this mean for you and me?" she asks.

I hate that I must say the words. "Today will be our last hunting trip. It is as you have said. There is no 'you and me.'"

Maddie

There's a party that night, but it's a subdued one. Everyone's tired from their journey, so it's not the most energetic of re-unions, but everyone gathers by the fire and Maylak passes around her fat, wriggly baby boy, Makash, who now has brightly glowing eyes. They even pass him to me, and I don't point out that he's ginormous and looks strange to me after seeing so many pale blue half-human babies. Makash is deep blue and his horn buds are twice the size of the others'. Even his tiny chest has the hard plating already.

Maylak flutters around the group, touching everyone, and

looks anxious despite her happiness. I guess she's worried that someone might have gotten injured while she was gone, but the people left behind were a boring group. I doubt anyone left the cave other than me or Taushen, who stayed behind to hunt for fresh meat for the elders and preggos. Josie sits next to me by the fire, but I might as well be invisible for all the attention she's paying. Her mate is back and she's clinging to him like he's about to disappear again. I suppose it'd be cute to see them so lovey-dovey if I didn't feel so mixed up myself.

Hassen isn't here. The entire tribe has come out to hang together and eat and catch up. Heck, even Asha's sitting at the fire, a good distance away from her mate, and she's holding Maylak's baby with a blissful look on her face. No Hassen, though. He's not allowed.

I glance out at the cave entrance, but there's no one around, thick snowflakes blowing in and melting on the stones. Right after the others got home, a storm started. I suppose I should be worried about Lila, but she's with her mate and a bunch of other people. They're fine. Instead, I'm thinking about Hassen. He's all alone out there, and while he knows how to take care of himself, I can't help but worry. All it takes is a twisted ankle and . . . I shake those thoughts free from my head, because I can't go down that path. He can take care of himself.

I just hate that no one has his back right now.

It is as you have said. There is no "you and me."

He's right. I just didn't expect it to bother me so much to hear. I've loved the last week—it's been so much fun and I haven't felt bored or lonely. In fact, I've woken up every morning eager to face the world and see what new things I can learn or discover. Is this how Lila feels?

Someone drops into the empty seat next to me. It's Harrec,

one of the other young hunters that just returned with the group. I smile faintly at him in greeting and turn back to the fire, feigning interest in the story someone's telling, when all I really want to do is go to the cave mouth and see if Hassen's waiting outside, watching us. Wanting to be with us.

Man, that thought is a real bummer.

"Are you hungry, Mah-dee?" Harrec offers me a skewer with several overcooked chunks of meat on it. "I made this for you."

"Thanks?" I take it, even though I've already eaten. Seems rude, otherwise.

He grins at me, looking friendly. "Enjoy the good-tasting meat. When the snows come, it will be many soups."

"I like soup," I tell him, nibbling at one of the chunks.

"Do you have enough bowls? If you do not, I can make you some. I am not as good with carving as Aehako is, but I would be happy to help you."

Do I have enough bowls? That's the weirdest question I've ever been asked. For some reason, I look across the fire and see Asha. She smirks at me, her hard eyebrows going up. Oh, shit. Is this flirting? Is Harrec flirting with me? About *bowls*? "I'll have to take inventory when I mosey back to my crib, and I'll let you know the sitch." I deliberately pick a lot of human slang to baffle him. Maybe it's me being a bitch, but I smile widely as if I just said the most normal stuff in the world.

He gives me a firm nod, looking pleased even though I'm pretty sure he has no clue what I said.

A steaming cup of tea appears near my head and I rear back, surprised. It's one of the elders—Vaza, I think? He offers me the cup with a smile. "Drink, yes?"

"Oh, uh, thanks." I take the cup and now my hands are full of both food and drink. Everyone's suddenly so friendly.

To my surprise, Vaza steps over the stone I'm sitting on and pushes in between me and Josie, who looks surprised at the intrusion. "If you like the tea, I can bring you more. It is my special blend."

"I'm sure it's great." I give Josie an apologetic look as she moves to her mate's lap. Her mate looks pissed, though, his teeth bared protectively over his woman.

Vaza's oblivious, though. "There is a certain leaf that grows near the water that makes the best tea."

"You don't say," I murmur.

Harrec gestures at the food. "Is it good? Do you want more?"

"Great," I tell him, and take another obliging bite. Asha just smirks across the fire, clearly enjoying my pain.

Not for the first time this night, I'm pretty bummed that the others are back. I'd much rather be spending my time with Hassen.

※

The next morning, I get dressed in my double layers of furs to go out hunting, but I realize ten minutes later that it's not going to happen. I can't get away from the tribe. Specifically, the men of the tribe. The moment I leave my cave, Taushen's there, asking if I need more leather to make warm clothing for the brutal season. When I head to the fire to grab breakfast, Vaza's there with more of his tea. Then Harrec drops by to ask if I want to help him mend his nets. I manage to choke down a few quick mouthfuls of a not-potato cake before murmuring excuses and making my way toward the entrance of the cave. If no one's around, I might be able to slip out and go say hello to Hassen. I'm sure he's waiting nearby.

But at the entrance, Maylak is there, and Asha, who is holding

Maylak's little girl while Maylak nurses her newborn. They are both standing and talking to Rukh and Harlow, and the healer has a concerned expression on her face. They all seem to be having an intense conversation, though, so maybe I can sneak past them—

"Maddie! Oh good, another human. I need your help." Harlow waves me over and the small group turns their gazes to me.

Shit. I have no choice but to head over, pasting a smile on my face. "Hi. What's up?"

"I'm trying to explain to Maylak that it's very important that I go to the ship—the elders' cave. I want to visit one more time before the brutal season hits." She adjusts the baby in her arms and looks over at her mate, who has a large pack on his back. They look like they're ready to head out the door. "It's about the computer."

"Oh?" I'm not seeing where I factor in with this.

"Yeah, I noticed last time that things weren't adding up when I'd ask the computer questions, and the more I sit and think about it, the more I'm worried that there's something wrong with it." She looks at her mate, then back to me. "I worry the data's corrupted and I'm trying to explain that to them, and no one's grasping it."

"I'm no computer genius myself, but I ran into that problem before on my laptop. You think it has a virus? How did it get a virus if it's been crashed here?"

"I don't know if it's a virus, but . . . things don't make sense. It's a computer, so it's supposed to relay nothing but facts, but I keep finding discrepancies. Like . . . okay. You know how long the sa-khui have been here, right?"

"Um. Two hundred–something years, right?" I seem to recall someone telling me about that.

"Two hundred eighty-nine years." She jiggles her baby on her hip. "That's what it says every time you ask it. But when I talk to the tribe, it doesn't make sense. Maylak says the oldest in the tribe is Vadren."

The healer inclines her head. "He has seen one hundred and sixty-two brutal seasons."

"Wow, that's pretty crusty."

"It gets weirder. I was thinking about that, right? So I went to talk to Vadren, and he said his father lived to be a hundred and fifty seasons. And his father before him was about the same."

"Uh, I'm no mathematician, but that doesn't add up."

"Right! And he says that no one has ever had any technology for as long as he remembers. He learned to spear hunt, and his father learned to spear hunt from his father. If his dad was a kid around the time of the crash, wouldn't he remember something?"

I shrug. "I guess? Maybe they're off-the-grid types and decided to go back to nature when they landed here permanently?"

"I was wondering about that, but then I kept thinking about it, and it bothers me." There's distress on her freckled face. Her baby grabs a fistful of her orange hair and tugs, and Harlow absently pulls his hand free. "I know I've had a few instances where I'd get a schematic from the computer and parts would be missing or seem incorrect, and I thought it was me. But now I'm wondering if there's corruption in the system somewhere. And I'm worried because I don't know if it's safe to use for the language capabilities. What if it beams a laser into someone's brain and fries them when it's supposed to be teaching them sign language?"

Yikes. "Yeah, that doesn't sound good."

"So would you check it out? Or do you think it's just me looking for things to do?" She casts a worried look to her mate.

"No, I think if you want to go check it out, it can't hurt, right?" Plus, I'm selfish. Only half the tribe has the sign language so far, and I want my sister to be able to communicate with everyone. She's worked really hard to teach the computer her "hand-words," as the others say, and I don't want her to be hampered by an inability to communicate. Then again, I also don't want someone's brains turned to goo just because they're trying to learn how to talk to my sister.

"I am worried," Maylak says in her low, gentle voice. "I feel you should stay here, with the tribe."

At this, Rukh scowls. "I will watch my mate. I protect her."

"It is not that," Maylak continues. "It is . . . I just worry. I feel . . ." She sighs. "Perhaps it is just a healer worrying over nothing."

"We make this trip all the time. We'll be fine," Harlow assures her.

Maylak nods, but doesn't seem convinced. "Just be cautious."

Harlow casts a smile in my direction and then looks at Asha. "Did either of you want to go with us?"

"Oh, I'm, um, busy." I smile brightly and hope they don't ask too many questions about that. "Got a lot on my plate."

"Gathering all the unmated males close?" Asha says in a teasing voice.

I scowl at her. "Waiting for my sister to come back?"

She simply smiles, unbothered by my pissiness.

Maylak, Rukh, and Harlow start to talk again, and I edge backward, trying to extricate myself from the conversation. I glance out of the cave, hoping to see a familiar figure on the horizon, but it's empty.

"Looking for someone?" Asha's voice is amused as she comes

to stand at my side. In her arms, the little girl sucks her thumb and watches me with big, glowing eyes. Asha's smile returns. "One hunter in particular, perhaps?"

"Shut up." I scan the outdoors again. "You haven't seen him today, have you?"

"I have not. Perhaps he is bothered by all the males you are attracting, given that you do not wish to take him to your furs permanently."

I frown at her. "What do you mean?"

"Would you like some tea, Mah-dee?" she mocks. "Perhaps some leather for more clothes?"

Oh. That. "I'm not encouraging them! I don't know what's changed for them to suddenly start paying attention to me."

"It is because you smile now. Before, you scowled at everyone and threw things. Now you smile, and now they notice you." Her look becomes sly. "They do not realize the reason why you smile, I imagine."

I can feel my cheeks heating. Yeah, I know why I'm smiling now. It's because I'm getting laid. Actually, it's more than that. It's Hassen's company. It's that I've found someone that really understands me and my situation. I don't feel so abandoned. I feel like I have a partner in crime now. "Well, I want them to leave me alone. How do I get them to do that?"

"You resonate," she says in a dry voice.

"Well, aren't you just a big bundle of help?"

"No."

"Sarcasm."

She shrugs and cuddles the little girl in her arms close. "Then take a pleasure mate."

Argh. These people are so frustrating. I'm about to complain about how irritating I find all of this attention when I see a dark figure appear in the snow in the distance. My heart races and I feel an excited flutter in my belly. Hassen. He's waiting for me.

But then a second figure appears, and my excited flutter dies. Oh. Not Hassen. It must be Lila and her group returning. I'm excited to see my sister again, but at the same time, I feel a niggle of dread. While she's been gone, I've been hitting it with the guy that kidnapped her.

That's going to be hell to try and explain.

I worry that I should feel guilty. What Hassen did was wrong, but now that I know him better, I don't hate him. I'm not happy with his actions in the past, but I've also behaved like a jerk myself. I was kind of an asshole when we woke up, and I've continued to be an asshole up until recently. Heck, Marlene won't come out of her cave when I'm around, and Stacy still cringes like I'm going to throw something at her again. I get annoyed with their reactions to me, especially now that the guys are all acting like I suddenly became hot shit overnight. I shouldn't be judged by how I acted when I was stressed out and afraid . . . and I wonder that I've been judging Hassen all along.

After all, one reason why I hold him at arm's length when it comes to our relationship is because of my sister. Because I don't want Lila to be disappointed in me. I'm all mixed up and I'm not sure how to handle things.

I wait at the entrance, hugging my cloak close to my body as the party moves closer. A few others trickle out of the cave and move out to greet them, but I hang back. I hate that I feel like I don't know how to be around my own sister anymore. I watch as she comes into view, her hair pulled into a braid, her face ruddy with cold. She's smiling broadly and has a large pack on her back, and she makes gestures with her hands as she scans the people emerging, looking for someone. Looking for me.

And then I feel like an asshole, because it's my baby sister. I love her. I step forward and raise a hand so she can see me, and Lila's face lights up with pleasure. I feel my anxiety abate and I wade out into the snow to greet her.

There you are, she signs as she approaches. *I was wondering if you were hiding!*

I make it to Lila's side and hug her close, ignoring Rokan. I squeeze her tightly, and she seems good. She smells like sweat and furs, but she looks great. I pull back and smile at her, then sign, *I didn't want to crowd you.*

You're allowed. She reaches for my hand and squeezes it, then signs, *You look great, by the way. How is everything?*

I'm good. I missed you. I realize that it's true. I've been keeping myself occupied with hunting—and Hassen—but now that my sister's back, it feels like a missing piece has slid back into place. For all that we're struggling to find our way here on this planet, she's still my best friend and my family. I need her.

But you look good, she tells me, and reaches for the straps on her pack, glancing at her mate. *I'm exhausted.*

Oh shit. I'm an asshole. She's walked for days now and has a bag full of fruit—that can't be light. I rush forward, signing, *Let me help.*

Both Rokan and I pry the pack off Lila's back, and my sister stretches, then puts a hand to her back and grimaces. *I need to work out more.*

For some reason, this strikes me as hilarious. Work out? On an ice planet? Lila's already a twig. *Doofus,* I tell her, and loop an arm around her waist, ready to help haul her into the cave.

Rokan shoulders her pack and touches Lila's arm, a question in his eyes. She reassures him with a quick hand signal and a smile, and leans on me.

"I will take the packs in," Rokan says and signs. "Bring Lilah by the fire so she can rest?"

"Will do," I tell him. I don't even resent him at the moment. We both just want what is best for my sister.

By now, people are spilling out of the cave, and there are excited, raised voices in every direction. Bags are being distributed, and humans are flooding out, babies in arms, because they can't wait to see what kind of fruit was brought in. I weave through the crowd with Lila and head for the firepit. For the first time in possibly ever, there's no one sitting around it. I'm pretty sure they're all crowded out front. I park Lila in front of the firepit, at the best seat, and help her shrug off the top layer of her wraps. They're a little damp, and I spread them out on one of the poles set up nearby for such a reason. There's no tea bubbling over the fire, so I grab a tripod and string a pouch over it, motion to my sister that I'll be back, and fill it up at one of the multiple springs bubbling through the cave. There's a basket of spices and tea kept near the fire—Stacy's, probably—and I dig through it before finding tea and setting it up. I'm actually pretty proud of myself that I know how to do all that just from watching the others—now I just hope I'm not boiling my sister a tea made from meat spices.

I sit down next to Lila and sign to her again. *Are you hungry? Do you want something to eat?*

Just tired, she tells me. *I was fine until we saw the tribal cave, and then I lost all my energy.* Her smile is tired. *I'm glad to be home. You should be glad you didn't go. It was a fun trip but a hard one. I'm wiped out.*

Did you get a lot of fruit? Was your one-eyed friend there?

We did get a lot of fruit, but we also ate a lot of it and just harvested seeds and cuttings from the plants. We could not take all of it back. There's so much, it's incredible. We brought back as much as we could carry, but we buried some in a cache as well. We were so busy!

Sounds like it.

And no, no sign of my friend. It was just us there. She rubs her stomach. *I liked the fruit, but I would be happy not eating any more of it for a while. I never thought I'd say it but I'd prefer raw meat right now!*

I laugh, because that's not something I expected to hear, either. *Are you going full sa-khui, then? Eating raw?* I know that's how the sa-khui prefer their meat, and some of the more daring humans have taken it up, but not me. I like my steak well-done and not fresh out of something's gut.

A shy look crosses my sister's face. *It's not that I like the thought, but I've been having cravings for the past few days . . .* She stops and clasps her hands together, and I see her eyes are shimmering with tears.

"Oh my God," I breathe aloud, and then realize what I've done. She understands me, though, and laughs and nods. Lila's pregnant. I squeal with excitement and grip her hands in mine. She beams at me, and in that moment, I'm so utterly thrilled for my sister's happiness. I love that my shy, scared sister is just blossoming out here on this ski slope of a planet. It makes me tear up, too.

My sister's going to have a family and a baby, just like everyone else. I'm so happy for her, and yet . . . I still feel the sting of losing her. And I feel alone all over again.

Which makes me think of Hassen.

Which makes me think I should probably tell my sister I'm flirting with Hassen.

Okay, *sleeping* with Hassen.

Not that anyone's doing much sleeping.

I watch Lila's happy face. She wipes away her tears, beaming. We knew it would happen because of resonance, but still, to think about it and to actually have it happen are two different things.

You can feel it? Already? I touch my breast, thinking about the parasite inside me—the khui. I can't feel it, ever, though I have noticed that the mated couples purr at each other when they resonate. *Is it because of the khui?*

She shakes her head. *It's more of . . . what you don't feel.* Her cheeks color. *The resonance slows down. Plus, Rokan knows.*

He thinks he knows because he's a man?

No, I mean he knows. She taps her temple. *In his "knowing" sense.*

Oh, right. I keep forgetting that Rokan's a minor psychic of some kind. Maylak's cootie makes her a healer, Rokan's gives him spidey-senses, and mine? Well, mine kind of sits there like a lump. Which is probably a good thing. Not that I'm jealous of all the babies, but it feels weird and isolating to have the only inert khui out of the entire tribe. I mean, damn. Surely I've got something worth passing on to the next generation. Sometimes I feel like I need to go sit in the bad kids' corner with Hassen.

Annnnd yeah, I really need to tell my sister about Hassen.

I swallow the knot of worry building in my throat, and sign to her. *I'm glad you're back. We need to talk.*

Is everything okay?

I regret that I've said something. Like, immediately. The weariness on Lila's face seems to increase tenfold, and now she looks stressed. Am I stressing her out? I stifle the flash of irritation that I feel. I'm stressing *her* out? I've taken care of her ever since our parents died. I'm the one who's had to be in control. I'm the one who's had to choke back my fears and be strong. We're both in new emotional territory and I need to learn to be patient, which isn't one of my strong suits. But since I've already jumped the gun, I might as well plow forward. *You didn't see Hassen when you were walking back, did you?*

No, and I'm glad. I'm still not comfortable with him. Her expression hardens just a little.

Her words feel like a brick in my gut. Telling her about this was a mistake. It's too fresh. She won't understand. Heck, I'm not even sure I understand it myself.

Why? What is it? Lila looks concerned. *Has he been bothering you? He's supposed to be exiled as punishment.*

He's not bothering me, I gesture back. *It's just . . .* I pause, and then continue. *We've become friends.*

Her eyes widen with alarm. *Maddie, no. Don't be friends with him.*

It's okay, Lila. We talked about why he stole you. He's really sorry, and it wasn't that he was in love with you. He just wanted a mate.

And that's why he wants to be your friend right now! He's using you because you're available!

That's not it, I tell her, and then drop my hands. It's not, is it? I sought him out, not the other way around. Even as I tell myself she's wrong, I worry. Hassen was so desperate for a mate that he tried to steal one. And then here I come, flinging myself at him. Maybe it's not about me and him bonding and being friends as well as fuck buddies. Maybe it's just about him trying to grab himself another mate.

I think about the fact that he more or less proposed to me after we slept with each other, and decide not to share that with my sister. Actually, I decide I'm not going to share a lot with my sister. The look of horror she's giving me tells me plenty. *We're just friends,* I sign. *Don't freak out.*

You need to stay away from him, sis. I lived with him for weeks. I know what he's like. He's impatient and overbearing and . . . She waves her hands in the air, clearly at a loss for words. *He is not a good man! I don't want him taking advantage of you!*

Oh, that is so *cute.* Considering that I took advantage of Hassen the moment he decided to hang out with me, my sister has the wrong one pegged as a predator. *Seriously, we're just friends. I just wanted you to know, okay? So there wouldn't be any surprises.*

I'm going to speak to Vektal and tell him that he's hanging around bothering you, Lila signs angrily. *It's not right.*

Don't you dare, I send back just as quickly, and her eyes widen at my vehement gestures. *Don't you say a thing!*

What is going on?

Nothing. Okay? We're just friends!

You didn't resonate, did you?

Fuck no! I just feel bad for the guy, all right?

How can you feel bad for him? He stole me! He tried to force me to be his wife!

Yeah, and he lost everything. Heaven forbid a guy wants to fall in love and take care of a girl. I stop myself even as I think it. Am I having Stockholm syndrome on my sister's behalf? Hell, is that even possible?

I'm really confused. I get to my feet. *I think I need some time to myself.*

But I just got back, Lila gestures, hurt in her eyes.

I give her a quick bear hug. *I know, and I'm a horrible sister. I'm sorry. We'll talk later, okay?*

She nods, mystified, and blinks her big eyes at me in that wounded way. I feel like an asshole. I'm abandoning my sister just as she got back from her trip so I can go talk to Hassen and try to figure out why I feel so mixed up. I should hang out with her. She hasn't been here for days.

You haven't been around her for days because you weren't invited, a seditious little voice in my head says. *At least Hassen wants to spend time with you.*

That decides it. *I have to go,* I sign to her, and pat her shoulder. I leap to my feet and head off, gathering my furs close to my body. There's an extra wrap by the entrance on a drying rack, and I snatch it and tug it around my shoulders. Everyone at the entrance is busy chatting and exclaiming over what's in the bags. No one's going to notice me if I sneak off, hopefully.

I move along the cliff walls, wincing with every crunching step, waiting for someone to yell at me to come back, to ask me where I'm going. No one does, though. They're too preoccupied with all the goodies Lila and her crew have brought back. I slip away, my steps hurrying despite the calf-deep snow, and crest a ridge. After that, I'm home free. No one's going to chase me now.

Time to find Hassen and get some answers. Or just vent at how confused I feel about my sister. And about him.

Really, I'm pretty mixed up over everything. I don't know if he's the person I should go pouring my heart out to, but right now I think he's the only one that will truly understand how I feel.

There's a copse of trees over the next ridge where we normally meet. I'll head there and see if he's nearby. I don't have a weapon with me, but it's not a far walk and I can wait for him. He's bound to come by at some point.

I hope.

Something feels tight on my face, and I swipe at my cheek. It's ice. I'm crying, and my tears are freezing on my face. Shit. Why am I crying? Is it because I feel like my sister's even more distant than ever? That I'm jealous of her and her happiness and the fact that everyone freaking loves her while I'm the town leper? Is it that I'm suddenly the one who needs looking after and I resent that? Is it because she hates Hassen and I feel like I have to choose between her happiness and mine?

How did this all get so complicated? I press my fingers to my cheek, warming the tears until they melt away.

CHAPTER EIGHT
Maddie

I wait at the trees for what feels like forever. It's probably only a half hour, but it feels like eternity. There's nothing around except snow and more snow. No animals, not much vegetation, and certainly no Hassen. The wind tears at my clothing and my exposed skin, and I feel very alone and small and vulnerable.

And lost. Lately I've been feeling very, very lost, and I hate it. I'm tired of feeling this way. I'm tired of feeling like everyone's got their shit together but me. Even right now, I'm out here in the wild with a damp wrap that's not keeping me very warm, no snowshoes, and no weapon. If that's not idiotic, I don't know what is.

My frustration mounts by the minute, and I'm just about ready to bail out and head back to the cave when a figure appears in the distance. I see big shoulders, horns, and lots of blue skin exposed, which means it's one of the sa-khui. When he starts racing toward me at a breakneck speed, I figure it's Hassen.

And stupid me starts weeping again. All the frustration seems to be seeping out of me in girly, wimpy tears. I hate that.

I'm not a crier. That's not who I am. I'm strong, damn it. I'm capable. I'm not . . .

Not like Lila. And Lila's happy.

And that just makes me blubber even more.

"Mah-dee!" Hassen races to my side, running his hands over my arms and then touching my face. "You are cold. Why are you out here? Who is with you? Where is your spear?"

"I'm here by myself," I say, swiping away the tears that keep freezing on my face. "I needed to talk to you."

"With no *weapon*? Mah-dee, you must think before you leave the cave! It is not safe—"

"I know," I cry out, swatting away his hands as he tries to cup my cheeks. "Okay? I know! I get it. I suck at taking care of myself. That's not exactly headline news." I dust away more of the tears that seem to keep coming.

He frowns down at me and puts a finger under my chin, tilting my head up. "Why do you cry? What is wrong?"

"Oh, you mean other than everything? *Everything* is wrong?"

"Why is everything wrong? You must tell me." He rubs a knuckle along my jaw. "I do not like to see you cry."

"Yeah, well, I don't like crying, either."

Hassen tugs my coverings closer to my body, and then his breath hisses. "Mah-dee, this is wet—"

"Yes, I know! I'm shitty at surviving. I know this! I just . . . I had to escape before the guys noticed me again."

He grabs me and hauls me into his arms, not in the romantic way that heroes carry fainting heroines, but like a mother carries her child. "I am taking you to the nearest hunter cave and we are going to get you something warm to wear, and then we are going to talk."

"Okay," I say in a sniffly, whiny voice. I put my arms around his neck and bury my face there, except when I do, I bang my forehead on one of his down-curling horns. Typical. Even Hassen's trying to kill me.

We're silent as he moves through the snow, heading unerringly for one particular cave that we tend to visit a lot. The walk seems like it takes forever, and by the time we get to the cave, I'm trembling with cold, the furs I'm wrapped in feel soaked, and I'm miserable all around. He ducks into the cave, shoving aside the screen over the entrance, and then gently sets me down. He rubs my arms and legs with his big, warm hands, stripping off my wet furs. The look on his face is full of anger, though, so I don't thank him. I don't think he'll appreciate it. He grabs one of the bundled furs and cuts the ties with his knife, then flings it around me.

I know I'm in the doghouse when he then moves to the firepit and begins to make a fire. If I'm cold enough to warrant a fire and then we have to replenish the fire-making supplies, I'm so going to get an earful from him.

"I'm sorry," I begin, but he shoots me an irritated look that makes me go silent again. Okay, if he's not in a talky mood, I'll just sit here and shiver. I clutch the blankets closer and feel pretty sorry for myself at the entire situation.

It takes a few minutes before the fire catches, but eventually there's a little flame going and Hassen scoops me up and drops me next to the fire like I'm a child. He adjusts the furs wrapped around me, tucking my feet under them, and then rests on his haunches, pausing to glare at me. "Why are you out in wet furs? Explain."

"I told you." I shift on the floor, a little uncomfortable at his angry scrutiny. "I had to sneak out when no one was paying attention."

"Are the others back? I thought I saw their tracks." His expression darkens. "Are they being cruel to you?"

"Only if you count trying to smother me with gifts and attention cruel, I guess." I wiggle my bare toes and dig them into the furry underside of the blankets, because, okay, it does feel much better than my snow-wet boots.

"Gifts? Attention?" As I watch, his mouth draws into a scowl. "Who is giving you gifts? Bek?"

"Not him." I shake my head. "Vaza gave me some tea, and every time I turn around, Harrec's trying to feed me, and Taushen's trying to be my new best friend. I mean—"

He growls.

I'm so startled by the sound that I stop talking. He actually growled. Just like a rabid dog . . . or a bear. "Are you okay?"

"Fine," he snarls at me. "Any others?"

"Any others what?"

"Any others courting you?"

"Fuck, I sure hope not." The thought makes me miserable. "I can barely sneak away as it is."

"No more sneaking," he tells me, tucking the furs closer. "It is clear that you cannot take care of yourself."

For some reason, that really hurts. I burst into fresh tears. "You asshole. N-n-now you s-s-sound like Lila."

He snorts and takes one of my cold hands and grips it in his, rubbing it to warm it. "Your sister has learned how to set a snare and build a fire. That is all. Do not let her words tear you down."

Actually, my sister never said those things. Lila is too sweet and kind. She would never willingly harm me. And so now I feel worse because I'm making Hassen think bad things about her. "She is my sister. She's just trying to look out for me because she wants me to be happy," I sigh. "And I'm not happy because I don't fit in."

Though I don't point out that I've been happy in the week that she's been gone, because it makes me feel worse. I don't want to think that I can't be happy around her. I need my sister in my life. I love her. I'm just not sure we're on the same page anymore.

When we first crashed here, I didn't panic too much, because I had Lila. I had to be strong for her. Now Lila doesn't need me, and the overwhelming feeling of losing everything is starting to mess with my mind. Now that she's back, I feel like I'm losing Hassen, too. I stare at him, hurting. This might be the last chance I have for a while to be alone with him.

I can't waste a minute.

I fling myself forward, grabbing at his vest. "Let's have sex."

"What?" He stares at me, incredulous.

"Right now. I want you." I push him backward, straddling his hips. I run a hand down his chest, desperation mixing with lust. I forget all about being cold, about being miserable, about my sister. All I want is this moment with him. I want him inside me, pushing deep, and making me think about nothing but him and pleasure.

Hassen hesitates for a brief moment, and then he grabs me by the hips, flipping us over. He claims my mouth in a hungry kiss, his tongue a searing bolt as it spears into my mouth. I cling to him, whimpering as his hands rip at my leggings. I tear at his, too, because I need his skin against mine. I need his body.

I need him.

His fingers push between my thighs. When he finds me dry, Hassen begins to rub a slick, slow path up and down through my folds. Oh God, yeah. It's amazing how he knows just what I need. I wrap an arm around his neck and kiss him with even more intensity, wanting to show him how good he makes me feel. I run my hands along his shoulders and down his spine, and when his tail flicks against my hand, I grab it and give the underside a rub.

He hisses, and it's like I've uncaged a wild animal. He's ferocious with hunger, and his fingers press into me, thrusting hard. I gasp and twist my hands in his hair, not sure if I'm stopping him or egging him on. All I know is that we need to come together before we both explode.

Then his weight is shifting on top of me, and he's pushing my thighs farther apart. It's stretching the seams of my leggings, but I don't give a fuck. I need him. I ignore the soft tearing sound of the leather bunched at my knees and kick at it. "Get these off me," I tell him. "I want to wrap my legs around you when you fuck me."

Hassen breathes my name, and his hand leaves my pussy—damn it—to help me get my leggings the rest of the way off. Then he's surging over me and I feel his cock press against my core.

"Yes," I tell him. Oh, yes.

He's not done torturing me, though. He slicks the head of it through my juices, then drags it up and down my folds, like his fingers were doing just a moment ago. I'm practically coming off the floor, it feels so amazing. All this because I touched his tail? I need to do it again. I reach for the wildly flicking appendage, and when I manage to snag it, he thrusts into me, and his spur settles against my clit. Oh, fuck. He doesn't play fair.

"Your cunt is so tight, Mah-dee," he tells me, rubbing his nose against my cheek as he slowly pushes deeper. "It is where I belong, is it not? Deep inside you?"

Dirty talk. Dear lord. I'm helpless before it. I cling to his tail, my other hand scratching up and down his side, looking for purchase. I want to touch him everywhere and make him feel as crazy as he's making me feel, but all I can do is wrap my legs around his thighs and clutch at his tail like a loon.

He pumps into me, and my entire lower half lights up. It's the combination of big, ribbed dick and spur that does it to me every time. By his third thrust, I'm clenching up around him and lights are flashing behind my eyes. By the time number six rolls around, I've gone over the edge, lost to the immediate and violent orgasm ripping through me. Of course, Hassen never thrusts just six or seven times. He goes a lot longer—sometimes I think it's just to see if he can kill me with his dick. At least, that's what it feels like—death by delicious orgasm. He covers me with his body, and I feel his bumpy forehead press to mine as he strokes into me, over and over again. Then he's coming, and I can feel the heat of his spend wash over my insides. He shouts my name as he comes, and I feel a ridiculously girly sort of pleasure hearing that, even as I come all over again.

Hassen rolls onto his back, and instead of moving off of me, he holds me in place, and then I'm lying on top of him, his cock still deep inside me. Our bodies are slick where they're joined, and I can feel his come on the insides of my thighs. He holds me close, though, panting, and gently brushes the hair off my brow. The look on his face is pure contentment, and for a moment my heart squeezes and I wish he wasn't the asshole that kidnapped my sister. I wish there was no baggage between us and he was just another faceless hunter in the mix. Then maybe I wouldn't be so reluctant to pleasure-mate.

But I suppose if things were truly like that, we never would have come together in the first place. Because Hassen would have gone on the hunts with the others, and I would have still felt like lonely, lost Maddie. Funny how the only time I don't feel lost is when I'm with him.

He plays with a few strands of my hair and then raises his hips in what feels like a slow, delicious thrust. "Do humans mate in this position?"

"Yup." I put my hands on his chest and prop up. He feels hard and ready to go again, which is insane, considering he just finished a minute or so ago. "If you can think of it, humans have tried it."

"Mmm." He twines my hair between his fingers and then regards it, the gold stark against the blue of his skin. Then his gaze focuses on me. "Tell me more about the males bothering you."

I skim my hand over his chest, teasing his rock-hard nipples. That's one sa-khui trait that's taking some getting used to—nipples you could scratch glass with. But it's strange, because on him, they seem right. "It's not important."

"And your sister?"

I don't want to think about Lila. I'm too confused when it comes to my sister. "She's not important, either." I rock my hips over him. "Right now, all that is important is you and me."

His eyes gleam, and on that, I see we are both agreed.

Hassen

I haul a large dvisti carcass over one shoulder as I head toward the tribal caves. The large kill is more than duty—it is a peace offering and a show of strength all at once.

This day, I will go to my chief. I will show him that I am a strong, capable hunter. I will tell him of the tireless work I have done to feed the tribe, of the many caches I have filled while in exile. I will tell him of the endless traps I have set and let him see that I am a strong and worthy hunter. Despite spending my days with Mah-dee, I have been hunting at night to ensure that I do not slack; now, when I feed the tribe, I feed not just companions and family, I feed Mah-dee.

It has been two long days since I have seen my mate, and I keenly feel every moment. Even though I made her swear not to go to the trees and wait for me, I still check there regularly, just in case. My Mah-dee is passionate and loving . . . but she does not listen to orders well. But she has stayed away, and I must believe that it is because the cave is full once more. She cannot slip out to see me.

I expected this.

I did not expect to be gutted by it. Even now, the ache of her absence gnaws at me. My mate should be at my side, in my furs. She should be in my arms at night, pressing her small face against my chest and holding tightly to me. I should be at her side, giving her more lessons on how to hunt and take care of herself, and comforting her when she is sad. The fact that I cannot be there for her makes me crazed.

I think of Vaza, and Harrec, and angry, fierce Bek—are they comforting my Mah-dee? Offering to dry her tears with gifts?

I bare my teeth as I think it, and my steps speed up.

Today, I go to my chief and demand he end my exile. The brutal season will be here in a few hands of days, and I want to make a cave with Mah-dee. She is my mate, even if we do not resonate, and I must care for her like any good hunter.

It does not matter if Mah-dee is not convinced. I will not give the others time to persuade her otherwise. If she is not yet sure, I will use my cock, and my tongue, and my spur to convince her that she is mine.

And I will do whatever Vektal asks as long as he gives her to me.

There are a few tribesmates out in the snow near the front entrance to the caves. I raise a hand in greeting as I pass Tee-fah-nee and Salukh. They are digging new rows of holes in their strange fascination with growing things. Hemalo and Kashrem have their skins spread out on the snow, scraping away as they converse. Sessah and Farli play with her pet dvisti a short distance away. Nearby, I see Bek at the front entrance of the cave, taking morning guard duty.

I narrow my eyes at the sight of him.

Even though Bek was not named by Mah-dee as one of her suitors, I am wary of him. He has shown interest in the humans before. I head toward him, cutting through the snow. Farli sees me and waves, then races after her pet as it scampers away. The others do not pay attention. Good.

Bek nods at me, eyeing the carcass over my shoulders. "Good kill. Lots of meat on that one."

"I am a good hunter."

He shrugs, leaning against the cave wall. His arms are crossed over his chest, and he idly scans the grounds, watching over all. When I do not leave, he turns back to me, a frown on his face. "What?"

I lift my chin at him. "A better hunter than you."

His eyes narrow at my challenge, but he does not move. His tail flicks, an outward sign of his annoyance at my words. "You have been out in the snows too long. It has addled your mind."

"I am the best hunter of the unmated males," I continue. "The most worthy of a mate."

Bek snorts. "Is that why you approach me? You think I chase after the angry, yellow-maned one?" He shakes his head and gazes off into the distance. "I am done with humans. She is all yours."

His bitter answer pleases me. I grunt acknowledgment and pass him, heading into the cave. Bek has been warned. Now I must let the others know of my intentions: Taushen, Vaza, Harrec, even quiet Warrek, if I must. The elders—save Vaza—have not shown much interest in the human females, but I will ask around. If they must be chased away from my Mah-dee, then I will snarl at them as well.

I enter the cave and wait a moment for my eyes to adjust. The central fire burns bright despite it being early morning. A few of the humans frolic in the waters of the spring with their kits, and I see their mates talking nearby. Stay-see is by the fire, and as I watch, her mate kisses her cheek and then lopes off, heading deeper into the cave. Vektal and his mate, Shorshie, sit with Li-lah near the fire, and off to the far side of the bathing pool, Kemli is talking to Claire and Jo-see, gesturing at their bellies and laughing. A few others move in and out, busy with tasks. It is a good morning, and the cave is bustling with people.

Too many people. I do not see Mah-dee.

Sevvah and Aehako approach as they see me enter. "So much meat!" Aehako exclaims, rubbing his hands together. "You spoil us, Hassen."

I fling the kill onto the ground before them. "I do my duty. Have you seen Taushen and the other hunters?" It is early enough that I should be able to catch them before they go out on the trails. I need to find them to warn them away from my female.

"Taushen and Harrec are getting arrowheads from my mate," Sevvah tells me. "Do you need more, too?" She gets out her butchering knife and eyes the kill, then gestures at the legs. "Grab it by that end, Aehako. We will need to smoke a good deal of this before it goes bad. Warrek brought in two quill-beasts at first light, and we have too much fresh meat."

I grunt. It is a slight admonishment. When the weather is good, we bring back smaller kills and cache the larger ones for the brutal season. I am showing off by bringing in such a large kill, and wise, motherly Sevvah knows it. I touch her shoulder. "My thanks for taking this on."

"We will make good use of the meat." Her eyes are bright with amusement. "Should I be worried for Taushen and Harrec?"

"I will set them straight."

"Oho," Aehako says with a grin, kneeling by the dvisti and hefting it into his arms. "I would like to be there to see that."

"Hush," Sevvah says, batting at his arm. "Tell your sweet Kira we need her help with this meat."

He grins at her and drags it away, over to one of the rocky, jutting shelves along the wall of the cave set aside for the messier tasks.

Sevvah just gives me a curious look and then follows him away. She will not stop me, even though it is clear she has guessed my motives. I do not care. Let the others wonder. It will not matter. I just need a bit of time to convince both Vektal and my Mah-dee that she belongs with me.

I head for Sevvah and Oshen's cave, but I do not make it farther than a few steps before Rokan bumps into me. I snarl a warning, pushing him backward. "Watch where you walk!"

Rokan blinks, and his eyes seem clouded. "Eh?"

"You nearly stepped on my tail, friend." My irritation turns to concern. "What troubles you?"

He glances around the cavern, and his gaze settles on his mate for a moment, before turning back to me. "My apologies, Hassen. I am . . . not myself."

"What is it?"

"Nothing . . . yet." His frown deepens and he rubs his neck, casting a worried look at the entrance to the cave. "Is the weather bad?"

I shake my head. "Many clouds and fog but no snow."

"Fog?"

I shrug. "The air is thick today." Sometimes it is; sometimes it is not. It is not worth worrying over. I am not like Rokan to fuss over the weather. Hunting must be done, even if the clouds are thick with snow.

Rokan rubs his neck again, then drops his hand. "Nothing seemed unusual to you?"

I frown at him. "I do not understand. Speak plainly."

A hand touches my shoulder, and Vektal—my chief—appears at our sides. He gives me a nod of greeting. "I would speak with you, Hassen."

"And I, you." My snarls to the other hunters will have to wait a short time.

We walk a few steps away, still in the main cavern. I glance over where Rokan is standing, but he is clearly distracted and not paying attention to us. I wish that I had a private cave of my own where I could talk to Vektal, but that is my reason for being here today after all.

I want Mah-dee in my bed. Forever.

Vektal's expression is stern as he gazes at me. "You brought in a large kill." His words are mild, and I know he is leading up to his real questions.

"I did," I say, unashamed. "There are many more mouths to feed now."

He nods slowly. "Taushen says that you kept to the trails near the cave while the hunters were gone."

I cannot hide my scowl. Taushen is more observant than I thought. "Many of the caches close to the cave are full, thanks to my efforts."

"I did not say you were not doing well. I am pleased with your efforts." But he does not smile, and his expression is not an easy one. "But I would know your reasons for staying so near to the cave."

"The brutal season will be upon us soon," I say, plunging forward. I must get to my request before my chief hears more sour words from others. "I want my exile to end."

"That is not your choice. It is mine."

"You would not leave me alone through the brutal season!" I am shocked—and heartsick—at the thought. Even one night alone feels endless. I cannot imagine being by myself through the continuous, heavy snows of the brutal season, unable to leave my cave. Unable to see anyone.

Unable to stop the others from courting the mate I have chosen . . .

"I did not say that," Vektal continues. His voice is low, and he glances over as a distracted Rokan wanders past, touching the cave walls. "That is why I wished to talk to you. So you could explain yourself."

"There is nothing to explain. I have nothing to hide. I want to return." My hand curls into a fist, and I clench it over my chest. "I am truly sorry for taking the female Li-lah. I am happy that she and Rokan have resonated, and I no longer wish to claim her as mine." Even saying it aloud, it feels wrong. The day I stole Li-lah away feels like so long ago, even though it has been less than two full turns of the moons.

I am a different hunter than that grasping, desperate male. I have seen what I have to lose. And I have found someone else . . . someone endlessly stronger and braver and far more clever. Someone that sees me and comes to me with her worries and her tears. Mah-dee is my family now. She is *my* mate.

So I continue. "I wish to take the female Mah-dee as my pleasure mate and take a private cave for ourselves."

Vektal's expression grows hard. "Leave the humans alone."

I shake my head, my teeth gritting with frustration. I can tell that he does not like that idea. His shoulders are stiff and his tail lashes—much like mine is lashing. "I am not forcing her. Mah-dee and I have mated. She wants to be with me." I say it, and at the same time, I hope desperately that it is true. That Mah-dee would not turn me away if I had a cave to share with her. That she would welcome the chance to be my pleasure mate. "She carries no hate for me."

"You stole one sister and tried to force resonance." Vektal's nostrils flare. "Because you did not wish to wait for it to happen. You endangered her life. And now you wish to mate with the other sister? Are you mad? Has being in exile made your brains turn to meltwater?"

"She wants to be with me," I grit out.

"Did you ask her? Or did you just demand it like you did with Li-lah?" His expression is incredulous. "Hassen, your exile is light because the tribe needs all its hunters. But we do not need you harming the females. Do I need to exile you completely? Must we shun you entirely?"

Anger flares in my mind. He will not listen. "It is not the same. Mah-dee is not the same as Li-lah—"

"So you will not steal her?"

"Maybe I should," I snap. "If you will not give me a cave so I can take her as my mate, maybe I should steal her and go far away for the brutal season!" Even as the words tumble forth, I know they are a mistake. Vektal's expression grows dark and angry.

I know I have lost. I know he will not listen to me now. Maybe not ever. Mah-dee is slipping from my grip and I am helpless to do anything about it, all because I was an impatient fool who stole away a crying female I did not even like.

"You must leave," Vektal snarls, gesturing at the cave entrance. "I do not wish to see your face until—"

Nearby, Rokan staggers backward, and he nearly crashes into us. That is the second time in the last few minutes, and I grab his arm to steady him.

He jerks away, and his eyes are wild. His face is bleached of color and he stares past me. "Out of the cave! Everyone out of the cave!"

CHAPTER NINE
Hassen

Everyone turns and stares at Rokan, confused.

"Out of the cave!" Rokan roars. He surges forward, stumbling through the center of the cave and heading for his mate. Li-lah has her back to him and is still hand-talking to Shorshie, unaware. As I watch, Rokan scoops her up and races for the entrance.

A second later, Maylak staggers out of her own cave, her kit at her breast. Her hand is at her brow and there is pain in her eyes. "My chief, I am worried—"

Her words are drowned out by a loud pop. Then another. Then it is like an endless stream of pops, and it becomes a roar so loud that I clap my hands over my ears. I can hear one of the humans screaming, but the pressure in my head is so bad I cannot tell who. There is a deafening boom, and I can hear nothing but a ringing in my ears. The world has gone silent.

We stare at each other in surprise, shocked. A few others are emerging from their private caves, confused and startled. I see Vektal's lips moving, but I cannot hear his words. He gestures at me, speaks, and then points at the entrance. Then he races for his mate, who is getting to her feet by the fire, holding a crying kit who makes no sound I can hear.

Does he wish me to get everyone out of the cave, like Rokan said? Rokan with his strange sense? Who knows everything? But what does a loud sound mean—

The ground shakes beneath my feet.

No, it's not shaking as much as it's shifting. The entire cave is shifting. I see Vektal reach out to brace Shorshie, Talie held tight in his arms. He shouts something, then gestures at the entrance.

Out of the cave, Rokan had bellowed.

Something is wrong with the cave. The ground continues to shift under my feet and I look down to see cracks forming in good, solid rock. Impossible. The rock shifts beneath my feet again, and I nearly lose my balance. It is not safe to stand. As I look up, the walls of the cave seem to shake around me. A loud rumbling grows through the ringing of my ears and then I see the ceiling buckle. A chunk of rock falls from overhead.

Out of the cave.

It is all happening so fast. There is no time to think.

Mah-dee. She is in here somewhere.

Through the roar of the shaking cavern, I can hear people screaming. Kits are crying. Rocks are tumbling through the air to land at my feet. Nearby, I see a rock slam into Jo-see, knocking her to the ground. Haeden bellows in fear and scoops his mate up, his expression wild-eyed. Vektal throws a blanket over the fire, smothering it, even as the others race for the entrance. The need to escape is overwhelming.

The cave—our home—feels like a trap.

Mah-dee must be found. I stagger forward and a falling rock hits my shoulder. A sharp stab of pain moves through me, but I ignore it, just like I ignore the stone under my feet that is shifting and moving apart, and stumble forward.

Where is she?

I crash into Farli as I head down the back tunnel. She's sobbing, trying to carry her pet dvisti. Its leg is at an awkward angle and the creature is biting her. She says something to me, her expression devastated and full of fear, and cringes when the entire cave shakes even harder, debris raining from above.

There is no time to think. I cannot leave Farli, but I must get Mah-dee. I must be fast.

I take the dvisti from her, hauling it into one arm and then slinging her over the other, and race for the front of the cave. I dodge boulders that were not there seconds ago and race over fallen rock, while the air fills with dust and the cavern continues to shake. Farli squirms against me, but I ignore her movements. There is no time for her to complain. There is no time.

I make it to the entrance of the main cave and there are a few people gathering in the snow a short distance away, coughing. I set Farli down and then hand over the dvisti. She asks something, but I cannot hear it. My ears are still ringing and painful. "Mah-dee," I tell her, then bolt back into the caves, because I must find my mate.

I push through the people streaming out of the cave. Mah-dee's yellow mane is not amongst them, and so I must keep searching. I head deep inside again, only to find the passageway I pulled Farli from now blocked by a tumble of stones. "Mah-dee!" I shout, but I cannot even hear my own voice.

I push at the rock blocking the passage, but it will not move. I cannot get to Mah-dee's cave. I snarl in frustration, flinging my body against it even as rocks tumble down around me. I am not leaving this cave without my mate. If she dies here, I will die with her.

A hand touches my arm.

I look over, but it is Hemalo, not Mah-dee. I am disappointed.

He gestures at the rock and indicates he will help me lift it. Good. Even though he is a leatherworker and not a hunter, Hemalo is big and strong, his arms bulging with thick muscle. He can help me move these rocks. I nod at him and move to one side of the boulders. He takes the other side and we succeed in moving the first one, but others roll into its place. Rocks rain down around us, and Hemalo gestures again. *Hurry,* his movements are saying, and there is stark fear on his face.

I know how he feels. My mate is in there, too.

We move faster, grabbing at the next giant rock and managing to roll it down the tunnel. More rocks slam into my back as I work, but I ignore them. Bruises do not matter if my mate is trapped. I will find Mah-dee and free her. I must.

Hemalo heaves his big shoulders. More of the rocks tumble free, burying our feet and covering us with dust. I kick the stones aside, and as I do, I feel the floors shiver again. The entire earth feels as if it is coming apart, and my stomach clenches with unease.

"Mah-dee!" I scream again.

In the midst of the shaking and the rocks falling, I think I hear something. I look up at the top of the pile and see small human fingers wiggling through a tiny gap in the rocks.

Relief rushes through me, and I surge up to the top so I can touch her fingers. She clings to my hand and then a moment later pulls away, and I can see her eyes through the narrow slit. There is blood on her face, and dust, but she is alive. Her fingers pluck at the rocks, trying to remove them. Then she gestures.

Trapped.

I know the hand-speak word. I nod. "I will get you out," I yell, even though I am not sure she can hear me. "I have you, Mah-dee!"

Hemalo and I double our efforts, and a few moments later, the gap is wide enough for someone to crawl through. I put an arm through, reaching out for Mah-dee. To my surprise, she pushes a bruised Asha forward. Her shoulder looks wrong, and she takes my hand so I can pull her through the narrow wedge. I hear her scream with pain when I tug her forward, even though I am gentle, and Hemalo bellows below, anguished over his mate's distress. It seems to take forever, but then Asha and her long limbs are free, and she falls into Hemalo's arms.

I do not stop to see if they are all right; she is his now. He will take care of her. Instead, I push my hand back through the rock, reaching for Mah-dee. Her small hand grasps mine, and then she's wiggling forward, trying to nudge her body through the small hole. I tug on her arms, hauling her forward, but her clothing snags, and I can feel the rocks tearing at her skin. She cries out but taps my arm, indicating I should keep pulling.

So I do. I give one last mighty heave, and her leathers tear in my hands, and she spills into my arms, sending us both tumbling to the ground.

Mah-dee. I cup her face and press quick, fevered kisses to her exposed skin. I do not care that she is bloody and filthy. She is alive and whole. Her hands clutch at mine, and I press her close to me.

The earth gives a mighty shake again, and I feel her stagger. New rocks fling themselves at us, and the cavern groans loudly enough that even my ringing ears can hear the danger. I must get Mah-dee out of here.

Wait, she signals to me.

I shake my head and grab her, carrying her out of the hall. She can tell me more when she is safe. I race out of the collapsing cavern, noting with alarm how much of the perfect circle of the tribal cavern has collapsed on itself. The floor near the bathing pool is a yawning pit, and the chief's cave is buried entirely behind a massive slab of fallen rock. I can see no signs of Warrek's small cave that he shares with his father—that end of the cave is destroyed completely. Even as I stare at the destruction, the floor shifts and rises ahead of me, turning into a cliff. I lock my fingers onto the ledge and haul both of us, Mah-dee clinging to my back, out of the cave and forward into the snow.

Outside, there are people everywhere. Kemli strokes Farli's hair, weeping, and I see humans clinging to their mates. Now that I am outside of the cave, I can hear kits wailing in distress, and more than one mother has her tunic open to nurse her child. Maylak is bent over Jo-see. The tiny human is puking in the snow, her mate stroking her back, her face swollen and bruised. Hemalo has Asha gently laid out in the snow, stroking her limbs and cradling her against his chest.

Someone is screaming. A female. I can hear her, but my ears are painful and I cannot make out what she is saying.

Vektal is nearby, stalking through the small clusters of people, touching each arm. The devastation of the cavern seems to match the strain on his face, as if he takes this all personally. He is our chief, and we are his responsibility. I know how he feels. These are my people. This is my home. To see it destroyed . . . it tears me apart inside.

And yet, Mah-dee is safe. She is safe, and nothing else matters.

I set her gently in the snow and press another kiss to her face. She wraps her arms around my waist, squeezing me tight, and then looks around. *My sister,* she signs. *Where?*

I gaze out across the churned, filthy snow. There, in the back of the group, sitting with Leezh and Raahosh, are Rokan and Li-lah. I guide Mah-dee over to her, and the sisters embrace, Mah-dee falling into Li-lah's skinny arms. Rokan has a pinched look on his face, his eyes hollow. He stares at something past me, and then jerks to his feet.

I turn.

One of the human females is stumbling forward. She screams something, and others pull at her arms as she surges toward the cave. She has a brown mane, and I can see a kit strapped to her back, like a pack. One human female carries her kit like that—the one with the food and the smiles for everyone. Stay-see.

Mah-dee waves to get my attention and then signals, *I think someone is still in the cave.* Tears streak down the mud on her face.

My tribe. My people. I nod at her and head forward, moving to Stay-see's side. Others are coming forward, pulling at her, trying to get her to sit, to calm down. She screams something again, and I realize it's her mate's name. Pashov. Her face is red from yelling, and she plunges forward, only to have Shorshie grab her and hold her back. Stay-see claws at her, desperate.

Pashov is still in the cave. In the tunnel where I found Mah-dee, perhaps. I turn and look at the cave again. The entrance is collapsing. If Stay-see goes in, she and her tiny kit will be crushed. I think of the rocky ledge I pulled myself and Mah-dee over. Stay-see does not have long enough arms. And if Pashov is not out . . .

Rokan and I both rush forward at the same time. I stop him,

gesturing he should go back to his mate. He has a female and a kit on the way. The tribe needs him. I am just the exile.

And I know where Pashov might be.

I hear Mah-dee scream my name, the sound garbled and painful in my ringing ears. I run forward, back into the collapsing cave, heading for the tunnel. All around me, the floors shake and move, and my heart races. There is no sign of anyone. Of anything. Everything we had is gone. I think of the humans huddled in the snow outside, clinging to their mates, and my worry spikes. The humans are fragile and must be kept warm. Just because they are out of the cave does not mean they are safe.

For now, though, I must save Pashov before his mate tries to come in.

A large rock tumbles from the cliff, lodging itself against the entrance of the cave. Everyone takes a step back, alarmed. All except for Stay-see. She pushes against the hands holding her, crying. If we do not bring her mate back, she will go in after him, so I must do it, and it must be now.

I head in, ignoring Mah-dee's screams. The cavern looks worse than when I left it a few moments ago. There is not much time. I jump back down to the portion of the floor that has fallen, and down into the tunnel that housed the new caves. My heart aches at the sight. Everything my people had . . . gone in a flash.

The tunnel is full of rocks once more, no sign of the gap that I pulled Mah-dee through. I climb the pile and use both arms to dig the rubble free, because I must make it large enough for my body and I must do it quickly. I am able to reopen a small portion of the gap after a few long moments of digging, and peer through. There is no hand waiting to be grabbed, and I can see nothing and no one. It is completely dark.

Pashov's home is not down this tunnel, but there is a storage cave. I can find it in the dark, provided it is still there. I make the gap bigger, shoving aside rocks even as more tumble overhead. It feels like a losing battle, but in my mind, I see Stay-see's devastated face. I see Pashov, my friend, who always has a smile and a fresh spear when he runs across me on the trails, even though I am exiled. And I cannot stop. I will not leave until he comes with me.

I lost my family to the khui-sickness. My tribe is all that I have. My tribe and Mah-dee. And now that she is safe, I must make sure all of my tribe is safe. I work faster. When the hole is large enough, I crawl forward and push my body through. The rocks scrape at my chest, tearing at the plates covering my skin. I manage to make it through to the other side and slide down the enormous pile of rubble. The dust is thick, but there is also light, trickling in from the ceiling in one of the caves, and there was no light there before. The roof has collapsed. The entire cave is coming down, and I feel another pang of grief.

It is difficult to walk with so much stone and debris in the tunnel, and I see Dagesh's cave is completely collapsed. Haeden's, too. Mah-dee and Asha's is in better condition, and my heart thumps with relief at the sight, knowing that she is safe. Farther down is the storage cave, and my worry spikes at the sight of it. The entrance, always narrow, is little more than a hip-high wedge. I crawl in, looking around, and there is more light trickling through. The baskets here have been crushed, the food so carefully stored away now destroyed. There is a bundle of neatly bound furs at my feet, and I grab it, tossing it back into the tunnel. The females will need them in order to stay warm.

I see no Pashov, though. No one is here. There is nothing but rock and dust. So much dust that it chokes me.

I turn to leave, to check the other caves, when I step on something soft. I lift my foot, thinking it to be more furs.

It is a tail.

I suck in a breath and drop to my knees, clawing at the fallen rubble surrounding me. In the dim light, I did not realize there was enough rock to cover a body. I see it now, hints of Pashov's tunic buried under dust and debris. I dig him out and pull my friend free, flipping him onto his back. His head lolls, limp, and there is blood everywhere. One of his horns is completely crushed, and his brow is swollen.

He is dead.

Grief pounds through me, and I clutch my friend close to my chest. He is a good hunter. Strong. Always kind and calm. He has a mate and a kit. This should not be his fate. I howl my anger and loss to the caverns, but the sound hurts my throbbing ears. He deserves a good burial, my friend. One with the proper mourning songs and goodbyes. If I leave him here, he will have nothing.

Yet how can I take him out of the cave and present his mate with his body? It seems wrong.

I run my hand over his face to close his eyes. They are not open, though, and out of curiosity, I hold my hand under his nostrils. Warmth brushes against my skin, followed by a bubble of blood.

He is breathing.

Pashov is alive, but barely.

I must get him out.

I haul myself to my feet, even though my body is aching with pain. His limp weight is heavy, and I worry about injuring him more. I manage to drag him along to the hole I have made in the rubble, and fling the furs forward before trying to push him through. Sending him through feetfirst is difficult on my side, but I cannot send him through the other way and have him land on his wounded head. The tremors in the ground now are mere shivers, and the hole is not filling back up, which means I am able to slide his body to the other side. I crawl after him once that is done, and the rocks feel wet with blood. I do not know if it is his or mine.

By the time I slide out to the other side, my strength is failing. I am surprised at myself—I am a strong hunter, capable of traveling all day and completing any number of difficult tasks with ease. I cannot be tired now. Pashov needs me. Mah-dee needs me. I must get out before the ground begins to shake again. I picture Mah-dee's face and imagine her weeping like Stay-see if I do not come out of the cave, and it gives me the strength to get to my feet. I take Pashov into my arms and carry him down the tunnel, and then must heft him onto the lip of the ledge that used to be floor before hauling myself up after him. I pick him up again, because the ground is trembling once more . . . or I am. It does not matter—I can see sunlight and what is left of the opening of the cave.

I stagger out into the sunlight, my friend in my arms, and there, my strength collapses. I drop to my knees, my head ringing. "He is not dead," I say aloud, then remember I cannot hear myself, and likely no one else can hear me, either. I lift my head, searching for Maylak.

Someone collapses against Pashov—it is his mate, her hands moving over him. Her high-pitched screams sound like painful whines in my ears, and my head feels thick. I cough, and it seems like I cannot pull in enough air.

But then Maylak is there, and she is kneeling next to Pashov. And I am relieved, because that means he will be saved. She can heal him. Make him better. I want to comfort Stay-see with these words, but it feels like too much effort. All of my strength was used up to get him out of the cave. Even getting to my feet feels like a monumental task.

A hand extends in front of me. I look up, and it is Vektal. My chief. His face is grim and he is filthy with dust, but I can see the thanks in his eyes. I nod and let him help me to my feet, only to stagger forward a few more steps into the snow.

Gentle, cold fingers touch my hand, and I realize I am still clutching the parcel of furs. They are taken from me, and then the fingers touch my face, and I look into Mah-dee's worried eyes.

I pull her against me and rest my brow on her shoulder. It feels so good that when I fall asleep, I do not even care.

CHAPTER TEN
Maddie

I stroke Hassen's brow as his head rests in my lap. He seems to sleep better when I touch him, so I run my fingers lightly over his forehead, over and over again, tracing his brows and trying to ignore the fact that it's cold and I hurt and the world just kind of upended itself before breakfast.

Everything is . . . well, it's crazy. There's no other way to describe it.

The tribal cavern is gone. The big, hollow donut of a cave with the pool in the center and the cute little rooms for everyone to sleep in is completely demolished. It's like the entire cliff collapsed in on itself. Someone told me once that the cave was probably hollowed out and made bigger by the elders when they crash-landed here, and I'm guessing that all those alterations to the rock ended up making it brittle. Then again, maybe it was the power of the earthquake. The ground still trembles now and then, reminding us that nowhere is safe.

I'm . . . surprisingly chill about the entire thing. Which is weird to me. It's terrible and awful, but we're alive. We'll figure something out. Maybe I'm adapting quickly because I so recently arrived here. My world changed entirely when I woke up out of that pod to find big blue aliens hovering over me. That was a shock. This is sucky, but it's small potatoes in comparison.

Hassen's all right, and my sister's all right, and that's all that matters right now.

I caress Hassen's cheek while he sleeps. He looks like one big bruise, the poor guy. There's a gash on his forehead, and he's covered in scrapes. One shoulder has a jagged, shallow cut, but he's mostly dusty, I think. I've been gently washing him clean as he sleeps, doing my best not to disturb him. I worry that he's sleeping, but I'm hoping it's just the shock of adrenaline wearing off and that his surge of energy knocked him out and not something more serious. If it's a head injury . . . The healer's busy, and I don't know when or if she'll be able to help him.

I look over where Stacy is huddled near her mate's side. Pashov is still laid out where Hassen put him down. She has his hand gripped tightly in hers, eyes hollow. The baby on her back is wailing up a storm, fists waving in anger. There are a lot of babies wailing, actually. Some parents, too, but I can't blame them. Maylak still has her hands pressed to Pashov's chest, her eyes closed and her expression one of intense concentration. She's been doing that for a while now, and her face is starting to look hollow with exhaustion.

No one steps in. No one can. There's only one healer, and so we all have to be patient and hope for the best. No one wants to be the person that calls her away, because then what if Pashov dies? I don't know him well, but I know Stacy, and I've seen them interact. He clearly adores her and their baby, and they seem happy.

Seemed, I guess. I stroke Hassen's cheek again.

Pashov's injury is severe, and the realization that Stacy might soon be a widow is a sobering one. I see others clinging to their mates, so I'm guessing it's hitting home for everyone. Haeden sits on the snow with his mate cradled in his lap, holding her protectively. Nearby, Rokan is hovering over Lila, constantly touching her as if he needs to make sure that she's all right and unharmed. She's untouched by bruises, one of the few that made it out of the cave before the rocks started falling. And I feel nothing but relief at that. I'm so glad, because I don't know what I'd do if it was Lila stretched out under Maylak's hands, unmoving.

Or Hassen.

The thought creeps into my mind, and I shiver. Hassen went into the cave to save me. Both Asha and I had been sleeping when it all started, and it took me a few seconds to realize that what had woken me from sleep was the sound of gunfire. Which was weird, since there are no guns here. But then the ground shook, and I realized something else was going on. By the time Asha and I crawled to the entrance of our cave, it was too late—the hall had been blocked off by falling rock. For a few awful moments, I'd thought we were dead. No one was going to come for us. We're not the most popular people in the tribe after all, and neither of us have mates that would look for us. We didn't know what to do.

But then Hassen *came* for me.

Not just that, he dug me out, risking his own life. And he saved Asha, too. I mean, sure, maybe Hemalo was there, but all I could see was Hassen. He's the one that risked himself to save me. And the look in his eyes was so intense and so fiercely protective that I felt . . . scared. Breathless and scared all at once, because I'm worried that I'm falling for the guy and I shouldn't. I can't choose between him and my sister.

I do know that what I'm feeling for him is becoming less and less casual as time goes on. Maybe it took a cave-in to realize just how much he's coming to mean to me, but when he went back in for Pashov, I wanted to scream and stomp my feet. I wanted to hold him back and not let him go, because it was dangerous.

And I'm pretty sure I didn't breathe until he emerged again.

I stroke his brow thoughtfully, studying him again. He's breathing evenly, and I relax a little. He's fine. He is. A little banged up, but whole. And a bit of a hero after saving Pashov. I hope Vektal takes notice. I look around at the scatter of people out in the snow, and Vektal and Georgie both are going around to each little clustered family, checking on them. Someone's building a fire right in the middle of things, which seems ridiculous, but then again, what choice do we have? We don't know if it's safe to go back into the cave, and a lot of us aren't dressed for being outside for a long period of time. The chief and his mate are doing what they can to calm people, but there's so much to be done. I can still hear babies crying, and the stack of furs that Hassen brought out is sitting in its bundle, unused. Nearby, Farli's weeping and hugging poor Chompy, who looks like he has a broken leg.

Everyone's in shock.

I think of Hassen, and how he didn't hesitate to risk his life to rescue Pashov. I could be helping. Maybe it's time I stop looking at myself as a victim. I'm stranded here, but these are good people, and I'm happy. It feels weird to say that while staring down a disaster, but I am. I have Hassen as a friend, and my sister is here, and I'm fed and looked after. And I can be more than I have been. I can do more than the minimum to stay alive.

I don't have to crawl in my bed like Asha and wait for the world to pass me by.

I can help.

I'm not in shock like the others. Some are banged up. Some have dried blood in their ears, and I wonder if the explosive bang of the earthquake busted a few eardrums. Nearby, Tiffany is shivering alone. I look for her mate and see Salukh standing near the healer, comforting a weeping Kemli and her mate, Borran. His parents. I've forgotten that Pashov is one of their sons . . . and Farli's big brother. Poor Farli. She's been a good friend to me, and she's freaking out. This must be so awful to a teenager.

Oh man. I can do more than just sit here and smooth Hassen's brows while he sleeps. I pull the fur wrap off my shoulders and bundle it into a pillow, then gently ease his head down onto the ground. Lila grabs at my hand as I get to my feet. She's been crying, her face shiny with icy tears. *Where are you going?*

I'm going to help, I tell her. *Do what I can.*

She nods and dashes at her cheeks, then squeezes her mate's knee and gets to her feet, facing me. *What can I do?*

God, I love my sister. How have I never realized how brave she is, just on a day-to-day basis? I reach out and give her a quick, impulsive hug. I still have my family. I'm good, no matter what. When I release her, I sign, *Can you pass out those furs?*

She squeezes Rokan's hand and dashes away. I watch him jerk to his feet and then stop, as if he plans to go after her. There's a tormented expression on his face, as if he wants to smother her with protection and has to stop himself. "Can you watch Hassen for me? Let me know if he wakes up?" I ask him. He's silent, and I realize he's got blood in his ears, too. I tap his arm and sign my question, and he nods.

I immediately move to Farli's side, just as Stacy's baby starts to wail louder. I kneel next to Farli. She's a hot mess, a large slice on her cheek, dirty from the cave-in, and her arms are covered in strange welts. "Are you okay?"

She turns teary eyes toward me, clinging to her pet. "My brother—"

"He's going to be fine," I assure her, keeping my voice calm and comforting. Funny how my bartending skills are coming into play now. Farli's not a sad drunk, but I know how to soothe and make it seem like I'm in control of the situation. "Let's take a look at your pet, okay?"

She squeezes him tighter, and Chompy bleats and bites at Farli's arm, leaving another raised welt. Poor kid. She's so freaked out she hasn't even noticed. I gently pull him from her stranglehold, and he hobbles away a few steps, bawling. She immediately starts sobbing again. Shit. I'm no veterinarian, but his leg is clearly broken. With so many people banged up, there's no way the poor healer is going to take a look at a pet. "We need to splint his leg. So he doesn't walk on it. Can you get me a stick or a pole of some kind? A bone?"

Farli blinks at me, then sucks in a deep breath. "B-bone?"

"Yes. While your brother is getting healed, we're going to fix Chompy, okay?"

She nods again, then slowly climbs to her feet. She wobbles a little but seems to recover when her pet bleats and moves a little closer, cautious. "I think Hemalo and the others were tanning . . . earlier . . ." Her lip wobbles.

"Okay, good. See if there are leather strips and a nice, sturdy bone. We'll get him good as new, I promise."

She wanders away, and the little dvisti limps after her. At least she's moving and out of her stupor. I'm going to have to figure out how to brace a dvisti's leg, but one thing at a time. Stacy's baby wails even louder, and I head over there, because I can't listen any longer and not do anything.

Asha seems to have the same idea I do, because we both arrive at Stacy's side a moment later. She's got Maylak's infant in her arms already. "I've got this," I tell her, and touch Stacy's shoulder. "I'm going to take care of your baby, okay? You just stay here by your mate's side."

She doesn't seem to hear a word I'm saying. Her entire body is focused on Pashov, her gaze flicking back and forth from the healer to her mate's swollen, bloody face. He . . . doesn't look good. Neither does Stacy, actually. She's trembling, and I don't know if it's from fear or cold. I pull the baby out of his backpack-like wrap on her back, and he flails his hands, smacking my jaw and screaming at me.

"It's all right, little buddy," I tell him, jouncing him. I'm about as good with babies as I am dvisti, but hey, time to learn a new skill. "We're gonna get you warmed up, okay?"

I look around for my sister with the blankets, and as I do, Ariana comes up to me, sniffling. She has an extra baby blanket with her, hugging her child close. "I grabbed several of Analay's blankets when we ran out," she tells me. "Do you need this one?"

"You're a lifesaver," I tell her, and she smiles through her tears. "If you see my sister, can you tell her to bring Stacy a blanket? I think she's cold."

Ariana focuses on Stacy, and her expression softens, and then she looks at me again. "My Zolaya went to a nearby cave to get some supplies. I'll give her mine until he gets back."

"Good thinking," I tell her. She hurries to Stacy's side, removing her fur cloak and putting it gently around Stacy's shoulders.

I wrap Pacy in the fur and tuck him against my hip. His butt-wrap is wet, and I tug it off, then swaddle him in the blanket again. Going commando might not be the best thing for a baby, but it has to beat sitting in your own frozen pee. He calms down a little, hiccupping, and I bounce him on my hip, making faces at him. Okay, one problem down, and now I need to find Farli again. I look out over the scatter of people. A few are moving toward the fire, and I see Kira and Aehako standing near a man kneeling in the snow. He's cutting at his horns and grabbing handfuls of snow and rubbing them on his face. Weird. His grief is palpable, though, and my heart clenches. We lost someone. I look over at the healer, but she's still working on Pashov. Not him, then. I quickly glance over at Hassen, just to reassure myself, but he hasn't moved. Someone else, then.

Farli comes back to my side, a long bone in her hand. "Will this work?"

I nod absently. Pacy babbles something and smacks my shoulder. I grab his tiny hand in mine. "Who's that, Farli?"

"Warrek." Her lip trembles, and her eyes fill with tears. "He is grieving. His father, Eklan . . ." She shakes her head. "He was old. Maybe he was not able to get out in time. He was kind, though. I liked him."

One dead. Warrek's pain tugs at me. "Who is he good friends with? Can we find him and have him go sit with him? He needs all the support he can get right now."

"He has been teaching Sessah how to hunt and cares for him as if he is his own son. Perhaps him? Or Hemalo? They are close."

"Both are good. You run and tell them to go help him out. That he needs friends right now. Give me the bone and I'll work on Chompy."

"The chief . . ."

I look over where Vektal was last. He's moved on to Marlene and Zennek, wrapping a length of leather bandage around Zennek's arm, which looks to be broken. "He's doing the chief thing. I'm sure he knows. Right now we need to pull together and just do what we can, okay?"

She nods at me and races off. Chompy staggers after her for a step or two, then bleats. I snap my fingers at him, and he turns back toward me. "Come here, lil' buddy. Me and my baby friend here are gonna make your leg all better. In theory." I make kissy noises at him like he's a dog, and he wobbles over to my side. Poor little guy.

I kneel down in the snow and try to figure out how I'm going to bandage a dvisti's leg while Pacy yanks at handfuls of my hair and babbles nonsense in my ear. Something moves at the corner of my vision, and I glance up. It's Lila. She stops waving and then makes an exaggerated gesture. Look. She points off into the distance.

I look.

And gasp.

There's a plume of smoke rising in the distance. It's like a finger pointing into the sky, leaving a smear of dirt as it goes. A volcanic eruption. I think of the hot spring inside the cave. It's not the only one. Maybe this entire planet is a hotbed of tectonic activity and that's why there are so many hot springs.

It explains the noises. The earthquakes.

This one doesn't look close—it seems very, very far away, farther even than the distant mountains—but I know ash can travel far. I've seen the news. What I don't know is what it means for us.

I can't help but worry. Life is hard here already, and the brutal season everyone keeps talking about is nearly here.

What are we going to do?

"I bet it's the island," Josie says near the fire. "Remember, I told you it was all green? Maybe it was warm enough to keep plants growing there because of all the volcanic heat."

"If that's the case, it's gone now," Georgie tells her in a tired, dull voice. "I don't know if anything would survive that explosion."

"*Vol-kay-no?*" little Esha asks. She's resting against Claire's rounded belly, sucking her thumb.

"It's a big fiery mountain," Josie explains. "The fire is in its belly and it flings itself out with smoke."

"And ash?" Esha asks.

"Lots of ash," Claire says, picking a fleck out of Esha's smooth black hair.

As the day has gone on, the scatter of people has slowly flocked together. Most are clustered near the fire, and the crowd has grown bigger as the hunters have gone out to the nearest hunter caves and brought back supplies. A few have ventured back into the rubble of the old cave, but there's not much to be salvaged that isn't under a ton of rock. Everyone has furs now, and a few hasty half-tents have been erected with spears and leathers to keep out the worst of the wind . . . and the ash.

We're *covered* in ash.

At first, we thought it was just dirt from the cave, but when the snow around us got progressively filthier, we realized it was coming from the volcano. I don't know how long it'll last, but it's not too bad so far. Just enough to make you feel grimy and remind you that this planet isn't safe, no matter how comfortable you get.

I'm sitting by the fire next to Lila, sharing a blanket with her. Rokan is sandwiched in on Lila's other side, his arm around her waist, and I can feel his warmth radiating. It feels weird to want to cozy up to him, but as the suns go down, it's getting colder and colder. No one's ready to complain yet, though, so we're sucking it up. Today we're just existing. Tomorrow there will be plans for survival and strategy, but for now, we're just a wounded family leaning on each other.

Across from me, Georgie nurses her daughter, brushing her curls back from her horns over and over again. Her mate, Vektal, sits at her side, his posture strong and proud. Only his face shows the lines of worry and concern. He looks older and more tired as the day goes on. I'm glad I'm not chief—I'm not sure I'd want all of this on my shoulders.

Maylak and Pashov are both resting in a nearby lean-to. Stacy hasn't left her mate's side, even though he hasn't woken up. Maylak collapsed in exhaustion a few hours ago and is taking a much-needed nap, Kashrem providing his lap as a pillow for the healer.

Pashov's not doing worse . . . but he's not doing better, either, and Maylak has wiped herself out trying to help him. Everyone's cuts and bruises—and some have broken limbs—will have to wait another day. Others are pitching in and helping out, and baby Pacy is currently with Megan. Makash, Maylak's infant son, is with Liz.

In the distance, there are a few figures hunched over in the snow. They don't want to join the fire. One is Warrek, who is taking the death of his elderly father badly. He needs space, and

I don't blame him. Sometimes you have to work through things without people talking to you and asking you questions. Two hunters are at his side, offering silent companionship so he doesn't have to be alone in his grief. One of them is Bek . . .

And one is Hassen.

My Hassen. It feels weird to say that, but right now, I kind of feel like he's mine. He snatched me from the cave and saved me from certain death. And I realized as people gathered, flocking to family, that Hassen has none. He is one of the many that has no family surviving the khui-sickness from so many years ago. He's completely alone.

So I'm claiming him. He's mine now.

I watch his back as he sits a few feet away from Warrek. He's normally full of energy and life, but today he's moving a little slower, and that concerns me. I know it's because of everything that's happened and he's fighting a multitude of bruises and worry—everyone is. But I don't like to see it in Hassen. I worry about him.

He's also avoiding me. He woke up a few hours ago, scanned the tribe like he was mentally counting heads, and I felt it the moment he saw me. Goose bumps prickled all over my body. I wanted him to come and hug me in front of everyone, but his gaze went to his chief and then moved on. A few moments later, he got up and went to Warrek's side, and he's been there ever since. Poor guy. I'm also a little hurt that all I got was an eyeballing, but how can I bitch at a time like this? He's comforting a friend.

Okay, mentally I'll bitch, but I won't say a thing aloud.

I know it's rough right now. I know Hassen's on shakier ground than ever before, so maybe that's why he's deliberately avoiding me. He's an exile, and I'm the only single female left.

And with all that's going on, relationship stuff should be the least of our problems. But I still wish he was cuddling next to me by the fire, keeping me warm like Rokan is keeping Lila warm. And I know he has to be hurting, too. Not just physically, but mentally. Everyone is. You can only be strong for so long before you crumple on the inside.

I know this. When our parents died, I took over being both Mom and Dad to Lila so she wouldn't feel the lack. I pushed hard to be everything to her, and I think I ended up needing her more than she needed me. Maybe that's why I've struggled so much here on the ice planet while she's thrived. I'd made her my purpose in life, and now she no longer needs me, so I've had to find a new purpose.

I just . . . haven't entirely found it yet. And I'm worried that with Hassen, I'm latching on to a new person to make my "project," as horrible as that sounds. But I guess I shouldn't trust my judgment about relationships on a day when a volcano exploded and made everyone homeless. I'm probably freaking out and overreacting, the same as everyone else.

But I also can't sit here. I need to talk to Hassen, if only to make sure he's coping all right. Some of the sa-khui are completely losing their shit, and I don't blame them. This is all they've ever known, and it's gone.

I get to my feet, pretending to stretch, and then step away from the fire. Lila gives me a concerned look, but I wave her off. I'm restless and need to get up and move around. Everyone's all huggy by the fire, and while it's sweet, it's also making me feel lonely. I watch the three figures on the horizon and then move to the food and waterskins that have been gathered from the hunter caves. It's a lot of trail mix and dried jerky, neither of which I'm a fan of. Time to learn to enjoy them, though. I get a pouch of each and then hike through the ash and snow toward Hassen, Bek, and Warrek.

Bek gets to his feet as I approach, warning in his gaze. "Now is not the time. Go sit with the humans by the fire."

I look at Warrek's slumped shoulders, and my heart breaks for him a little more. "I brought food and water in case you guys were hungry."

At the sound of my voice, Hassen goes alert and turns around.

"No one is hungry," Bek says.

Hassen ignores Bek. He gets to his feet and approaches me, and as he does, I hold out the pouch of food and the half-frozen waterskin. Did I think Hassen was giving me a brush-off? I must be insane, because the devouring, hungry, possessive stare in his eyes as he looks me over? Yeah, that pretty much puts all my fears to rest.

He doesn't take the food, though. He just curls my hands around it and gives them a little squeeze. "You should eat."

I snort. "Pretty sure I can miss a meal or two. I brought it for you and your friend." I almost ask if Warrek is okay, but that's a stupid question. His home collapsed and his dad died. He's not okay. "Is there anything I can do to help?"

"You can go back to the fire," Bek says, surly. He takes a step forward and he's standing in front of Warrek. He's being protective of his friend, I get it. I'm not even annoyed.

Hassen is, though. He bares his teeth at Bek and pulls me protectively against him, his arm going around my shoulders. "Mah-dee is trying to help."

"It's okay. Really." I put a hand to his waist, and I don't know if it's to comfort him or me. "I just wanted to check on you guys. Make sure you're okay."

"You're cold," Hassen says, placing his hand over mine where I press it against his side. "I will come back to the fire and warm you. There are not enough blankets to go around—"

"No, stay here with your friend," I say in a soft voice. "He needs you. I didn't come to pull you away. I just . . . well, I don't know what I wanted." I'm just being needy and now is not the time. I'm kind of ashamed of myself for distracting them, and I feel like Bek's look of displeasure in my direction is sadly appropriate. "I'm just glad you're feeling better. Take it easy if your head hurts, okay?"

Bek gives me an incredulous look.

Okay, yeah, I feel stupid even for suggesting it. Everyone is hurting. Everyone is injured. No one has the luxury of taking it easy, and I'm making a mess of things. I give Hassen's side a squeeze. "I'll talk to you in the morning, okay?"

"You are cold—"

"I'm fine, really. I'll go sleep with Lila and Rokan."

He growls low in his throat. "Next to Lila."

I laugh, because I guess that did sound weird. "Yes, next to Lila. I promise." On impulse, I take his hand in mine and lift it to my lips, and kiss his knuckles. His hands are torn up from digging earlier, scabs and scratches everywhere. I smooth my fingers over his skin, wishing I could help. "I'm going to go back to the fire now. Just say something if there's anything we can bring you, all right?"

And I leave and turn back to the fire, to my sister, and the tribe. I'm not exactly sure I fit in there, but I know I'm not needed up here on the ridge. I'm just intruding. I feel Hassen's gaze on my back as I go, and I have mixed emotions about that.

On one hand, I'm ashamed that I went and bothered them. On the other hand . . . I'm relieved that Hassen needs me and wants to be with me. It's his sense of loyalty to his friend that is keeping him at his side.

I can't fault him for that. I know all about that sort of thing, I muse as I head back to my sister's side.

CHAPTER ELEVEN
Hassen

I go to Mah-dee in the middle of the night. My people are piled into the snow, huddled together under the makeshift awnings, doing their best to avoid the wind and the ash it brings with it. Mah-dee's yellow mane is easy to find even in the darkness, and she sleeps on the edges of one blanket, her sister on the other side. She shivers even in her sleep, and I am filled with protectiveness at the sight of her. I should be here warming her with my body. Let the chief snarl at me in the morning. He is busy right now keeping his mate warm, their kit snuggled between their bodies.

Mah-dee needs me.

Bek remains at Warrek's side after I am gone. My old friend is silent in his grief, but I am glad he has company. I went to him because I know what it is to lose family. I lost mine to khui-sickness and grieved alone. Bek lost his parents then, and even now, I suspect he grieves the loss of Claire. His silent company will be a comfort of sorts, even if Warrek will not realize it for some time.

I shrug my cloak off my shoulders and lie on the ground next to Mah-dee. The snow does not bother me. The wind is a bit crisp, but the weather is still pleasant yet. I try not to think about the fact that it will turn in less than a moon's time. I try not to think about all the supplies in the storage caves, crushed. I try not to think about the fact that we have no place to live. I try not to think about old Eklan, or Pashov, who has yet to awaken. I try to ignore the low weeping of Pashov's mate.

Instead, I focus on Mah-dee. I pull her against me, and she turns immediately against my chest, nestling close. I wrap her in my cloak and hold her tight. My cock aches with the need to be inside her, but it is reflex only and easy to ignore. Right now, all I want to do is feel her pressed against me and know that she is safe. I tuck her head under my chin, wrap my arms around her, and try to sleep. Tomorrow will be a difficult day.

Even when I close my eyes, though, I can hear Stay-see's broken sobs. I do not sleep for long, and when I do, I dream of Mah-dee, trapped behind rock. I see her fingers reaching through the hole, trying to get to me. I wake up covered in sweat, my hands knotted in her hair as if I am trying to cling to her even in my slumber.

Mah-dee sleeps on, though. Unaware of my nightmares, she drools against my chest, and her breath rumbles out of her.

I hold her until dawn. At least, it should be dawn. Instead, the light is dull and ominous. The clouds overhead are thick and dark, and more ash continues to fall. I worry that Mah-dee is breathing it in, and cover her head as she sleeps. We will need to make masks for everyone in the tribe, I think, until the ash stops falling. It is yet another thing that must be done. My heart aches at the thought of just how much work is ahead of us.

I sit up slowly, making sure that Mah-dee is bundled against the cold, and look around for Vektal. My chief is standing in front of the collapsed cave, his arms crossed. From here, I cannot read his expression, but I know what he must be thinking.

I rise to my feet, noticing that ash cascades off my body as I do. It is a concern, but then again, what is not? We have no home, no supplies, and there are so many small kits and fragile human females that we must work even harder to keep all fed. I would not change it for anything, but it weighs heavily on my mind.

I approach my chief, passing by Aehako, who is stoking the fire. Raahosh is stringing his bow, readying to go out on the hunt. Others are rising, and I hear the gurgle of more than one kit being fed. Today, we must have solutions. And I must be one of them, exile or not.

"My chief?" I ask, coming to his side. "What can I do to help?"

He turns away from the cave to look at me, and there is stark grief in his eyes. His jaw is set in a grim line and he nods at me. "Hassen. Are you injured?"

"I am well enough." I can hear now. My limbs ache, but my bruises are fading. Nothing is broken. "Tell me what to do and it shall be done."

Rokan approaches, and Salukh, too. Taushen is nearby and gets to his feet. Even Hemalo, who is not a hunter, has a spear in his hands and comes forward.

"We cannot stay here," Vektal says. "The cave is ruined."

"Can we go inside? Salvage what we can with a bit of digging?" Salukh asks.

Vektal shakes his head. "I have been standing here watching and I see rocks continue to fall inside. One more shake and anyone inside could be killed. We cannot risk it."

"We must have supplies," Hemalo says. "What can we do?"

"We need a place to live and for the females and kits to be safe," Vektal says, rubbing his chin. "But I worry the South Cave will be just as bad as this one."

"Then the elders' cave?" someone suggests. "Or the cave that the females landed in?"

"The caves by the salty lake?" another adds.

"Too many sky-claws," says Taushen. "The females would never be able to leave the cave entrance."

Vektal nods slowly. "I hear all of you. And I have many concerns, but right now, we must find a place that is safe for our people for the brutal season. If that is the South Cave, then we will go there. If it is not, then it must be somewhere else. We must check them all out to see which has survived the earth-shake. We can send hunters out to each one and see if they have survived. If it does not look safe to enter, do not go in." His expression is grim. "I lost one tribesmate yesterday and am close to losing another. I do not wish to lose more."

"Where to first?" I ask. "The elders' cave? Har-loh and Rukh are there."

Vektal's mouth flattens. "If they live, yes. For now, we will take the tribe to the elders' cave. Rokan, you and Li-lah go to the fruit cave you found and see if it remains. Raahosh, go with Taushen to the caves by the salt lake and check for sky-claws and to see if they are safe."

"I will bring my Leezh," Raahosh says. "I can protect her from the sky-claws. But I will not leave her behind when it is not safe."

Vektal nods grimly. "I understand. Taushen will go with you anyhow. Haeden, take Jo-see with you and go to the South Cave to see if it has survived. Harrec and Ereven, go to the original cave of the humans. The one where my Georgie and the others came from. See if it has survived or if it has been completely buried."

"I cannot take my Claire," Ereven says, pained. "She is heavy with my kit."

"I will go," Salukh says. "Tee-fah-nee and I can go with Harrec. Let Ereven stay with his mate."

Vektal turns to me. "I must stay here with the tribe. The hunters with the youngest kits will stay with the tribe and hunt for them. I need more hunters that can go to the farthest of storage caves and bring back everything they can. The farthest-flung caves must be checked, and if they are viable, bring back all furs, weapons, supplies, anything we will need. Bring the gear to the elders' cave. We will make that our home for now. Bring back all that you can. Hassen, you take the caves to the north. Hemalo and Asha can check the caves to the south. Bek can go to the west, and Vaza to the east."

I nod my agreement, but even as I do, my heart sinks. It is a good plan, and yet . . . the farthest-flung caves to the north are deep into the mountains. The others will be closer to their families and return that much faster. My journey is a long one. It will take many hands of days to travel that far, and returning will be that much slower, weighed down with sleds of supplies. I will be separated from my tribe—and Mah-dee—for a long time.

But it must be done. My tribe needs every hunter . . . and I am just the exile. The rule-breaker. Why should I not go to the farthest caves? I have no family waiting here for me. "I will go."

"I want to go with Hassen." Mah-dee's voice cuts through the air. She marches forward, bundled in furs, and comes to stand in the midst of the hunters. Some are smirking with amusement, but others look irritated.

The expression on Vektal's face goes dark. "Mah-dee—"

"I want to help," she cuts in. "You're sending out all the single guys, right? Send out the single lady, too. Hassen's been giving me lessons and teaching me to hunt, so I can help out. He can keep teaching me in the field, and I can help him bring supplies back."

"You do not need to help, Mah-dee," I tell her, though I would like nothing more than to have her with me. My heart thumps in my chest at the thought. "It will be much walking. It is not always safe."

"Because staying here is safe?" She gestures at the rubble-covered cave. "Nowhere is safe anymore. I'm capable. Let me help."

"You can go with Bek," Vektal says. "His journey is shorter."

Bek makes a grunt that sounds like irritation.

My fists clench at my sides, but my chief is right. My journey will be the longest to travel. She will struggle.

"I don't want to go with Bek," she says evenly. "He's not the one that's been teaching me. Why can't I go with Hassen? Because he's the guy that kidnapped my sister? You think I don't know this?"

"Mah-dee," I say in a warning voice. "Listen to your chief."

She moves to my side and reaches up and pinches my cheek. "That's cute. You trying to give me advice on that." She winks at me to take the sting out of her words and then turns to Vektal. "I want to go with Hassen. We're a good team, and I can help out. Two people bringing back supplies is better than one."

Vektal puts a hand on Mah-dee's shoulder. "You truly wish to do this? You wish to go with him?"

"What, you think anyone could make me go somewhere I don't want to go?"

This time, Rokan snorts.

"Can you keep up?" the chief asks her.

"I can and I will." Mah-dee's ash-smeared face is stubborn but determined. "You don't have to worry about me."

Vektal turns to me. "You will keep her safe."

It is not a question. I nod. "I will protect her life with mine."

Vaza steps forward, gesturing at me. "He is exiled!"

Vektal's expression grows bleak. "My friend, we are *all* in exile now."

Maddie

I swear I'll be fine, I tell Lila and give her hands another squeeze of reassurance.

She pulls her hands from my grip, a troubled look on her face. *If you want to help, you can come with us,* she tells me, every movement of her body indicating her worry. *You don't have to go with him.*

I want to go with him, I tell her. *He's my . . .* I pause in my signing, trying to think of the best way to put it. *Friend,* I decide on. *He doesn't have anyone but me, and I want to be with him.*

Her brows draw together, and I can tell Lila is trying hard to understand. *You don't hate him?*

I shake my head. *I hate what he did, but I don't hate him. Do you?*

She thinks for a minute. *I guess I am the same. Those weeks with him were awful, but he didn't mean me harm. And I have Rokan now. But . . . is it safe?*

He's not going to try to hold me captive to force resonance, if that's what you're asking. I'm pretty sure the thought would make Hassen break out in hives at this point. He's seen what he has lost with his tribe, and it's affecting him greatly. Plus, I know him now, and I like to think that we're better friends than that. He wouldn't pull that sort of stunt on me.

No, that wasn't what I meant. Rokan says it's a long journey. I worry it'd be hard on anyone, and we humans are a little more fragile than the locals.

It might be, but I can't stay here and gather dust. I flick my ash-covered hair, hoping she catches the joke. *And I'm just an extra mouth to be fed if I go with the others to the elders' cave. This way, at least I can help.*

But . . . Hassen?

Hassen, I agree. *He's been a good friend to me, believe it or not.*

I trust your judgment. Lila's expression is sad. *But I'm still going to worry about you.*

Oh, I'll worry about you, too, I sign to her. How can I not? She's my baby sister, and it doesn't matter that she can take care of herself and she's got a mate to watch her back. I'm always going to worry and want to take over and help out. Maybe that's how she feels about me, too. The anxiety and resentment I've been feeling toward Lila's happiness is gone. It's weird, but I've been slowly figuring out that if I need something—emotional support, friendship, even breakfast—I have to take charge and get it on my own. It's not going to fall in my lap, and people aren't going to make excuses for me being a shitty person. If I want things to change, I have to make them change. I just hate that an earthquake had to demolish our home in order for me to realize that.

Change is good. It's not always easy, but it's good. And it's time I made a few changes.

I'll see you back at the elders' cave, I sign to Lila. *I love you. Don't get killed, okay?*

I'm going to a fruit cave, she signs back, her smile wry. *It's not dangerous.*

Not unless the entire horde of metlaks has moved in there, but I don't say that. I don't even want to put it out into the universe. *Just be careful anyhow.*

I will. She pauses in her signing and then gives me a curious look. *Is . . . something going on between you and Hassen?*

Why do you ask?

Because I'm deaf, not stupid? Her mouth quirks with amusement. *I just know he can be pushy.*

And I can't? I tease back.

True. I guess if anyone can tame him, it's you.

The thought of taming someone leaves a bad taste in my mouth. Taming implies that I'm going to "fix" him. Break him to my will. And that's not what I'm interested in at all. I like Hassen just like he is—impetuous and overbearing, sure, but it's because he cares too much. He feels things too keenly. And I don't want to break that. *We're going on this together as friends,* I tell my sister. *If we end up more than that, you will be the first one I tell.*

Fair enough. She pauses in her signing and then grabs me in a fierce hug.

And I hug her back just as tightly, because this can't be the last time I see her. It won't be. I can't even think that or I'm going to start crying.

But Lila has to go her path, and I have to go mine. I can't let Hassen go out on his own. Not now, not when he needs someone at his back the most.

CHAPTER TWELVE
Maddie

Hassen and I set out a short time later with only a single small supply pack. There's not much to pack in there, other than an extra waterskin or two. All the rations are left with the tribe. We have two spears and a knife, but everything else is going to have to be made from scratch as we journey. Extra sleds, extra blankets, you name it—we're going to have to create them. And with every item we're not bringing along, I realize that this is going to be one motherfucker of a journey. I'd bitch about it, but I can't say that our journey is going to be any rougher than anyone else's. I look back at the tribe, gathered in a tight cluster, and I'm pretty sure I can still hear the wailing babies. There are a few people carrying a makeshift gurney for Pashov, who still hasn't awoken.

Nobody's got it easy right now. We just have to suck it up.

We walk, heading north. I want to turn around and hug Lila one last time, but I know she's already taken off with Rokan. I would like for Hassen to hold my hand, but we're both carrying spears and still close enough that the tribe would see . . . but it doesn't mean I don't wish for it, just a little. Snowshoes and clothing and furs are hard to come by, and with many humans needing them, all of the existing ones are spread thin. The wrap I have is light and not good for more than keeping out the wind, but we'll get more furs at the nearest cave. My snowshoes are rickety and feel fragile, probably because they were made from "extra" parts on an existing, sturdy pair. We'll reinforce them when we find more bones and leather. I remind myself that it could be worse. I think of Pashov, carried by the others, and poor Stacy, who is in a zombielike state of fear . . . and I feel lucky. Hassen's safe. Lila's safe. Lila's mate is safe. We're good.

More ash is falling, and the borrowed wraps I'm wearing aren't particularly warm, but the hike gets the blood roaring, and I'm soon panting and sweaty despite the chill in the air. It's overcast, thick, stormy clouds making it seem dark even at mid-day. There's more ash falling than snow right now, and I keep my mouth and nose covered, like I've seen the others doing. Surely it can't go on longer than a few days. I just have to suck it up. More troubling is the fact that the ash is getting into everything—considering that getting fresh water is as easy as scooping some new snow most times, I'm a little worried.

Even more troubling is just how silent Hassen is as we travel. He's courteous to me if I ask questions, and helps me free my snowshoes if I trip. He offers me a hand when I struggle going down a hill. But he's so very quiet, and the expression on his face is grim.

I worry about him. There's no determination in his step, no confidence. He's going through the motions, but there's nothing there. I can't tell if he's upset at me, or just upset at the world. I don't know if he's in shock or if he's grieving for Eklan like Warrek is . . . but I know there's something wrong. My heart aches for him. And even though I'm quickly getting exhausted and this is just the first afternoon in what promises to be weeks of a journey, I'm still glad I'm here, because he needs someone. He can't go through this alone.

Until he reaches out and tells me what is bothering him, though, I'm going to let him have his silence. Sometimes you need to be in your own head to process things, and nagging him won't help. Plus, it's taking all of my energy just to keep up. I bend my head and focus on putting one snowshoe in front of the other, following his tracks.

We make intermittent stops throughout the day, pausing to cross a stream or to check trails. We see a herd of dvisti in the distance, but don't go after them. I'm guessing we're going to have enough to carry home without adding more to our load. As the day wears on, my feet ache and my teeth chatter with cold, but I don't complain. I do, however, scour every passing cliff in the hopes that we're going to find a hunter cave and stop soon. I have to keep going until Hassen gives the word, though. I'm supposed to be helping rescue the others—I don't know what kind of rescuer I'd be if I can't even keep up with the preliminary hike.

And I don't want him to change his mind and turn around so he can take me back to the others.

There's no sign of either sun in the cloudy, angry skies, but I do notice it gets progressively darker as we travel. We veer off an easy trail through a valley to climb up a steep hill, and I want to bitch, but I figure there's a reason we're suddenly taking the hard road. When I see a cave entrance in the distance, a hint of a screen covering it, I sob with relief. There are a few rocks tumbled around the entrance, but it otherwise looks whole and undisturbed.

Thank God.

It hasn't occurred to me until just now that there might *not* have been a hunter cave nearby. That they might not have survived the earthquake, either. Man, we are in such deep doo-doo.

We approach it, and I inwardly cringe, expecting Hassen to turn this into a teachable moment. That I'm going to need to check the cave out, build a fire, do inventory, and I'm so damn exhausted that it makes me want to cry at the thought. It has to be done, though, so I need to suck it up.

But he only touches my shoulder absently. "Wait here. I will inspect the cave."

And that worries me, too. Because it's not like Hassen to coddle me. Normally he teases me, makes a few jibes at my bad observational skills, and then shows me the right way to do something after letting me attempt it a few times. He's not even trying. And okay, maybe now isn't the perfect time for lessons, and I'm grateful, but I also worry that this is just more proof that Hassen's retreating.

He can't retreat from me. I need him. He needs me. I can't let him push me out.

Hassen disappears into the cave and returns a moment later, waving me in. I enter the darkness and feel for a wall. The rocks here are a little jagged—probably freshly ripped apart by the earthquake—and I'm a little careful as I move inward. "Do you want me to make the fire?"

"I have it. Sit down."

I should argue, but I don't. I drop to the ground, and once I do, my feet scream with pins and needles. They feel like blocks of ice, and my boots are soaked. Actually, I'm pretty sure all of me is. I huddle on the ground, hating that I'm so weak. That I can't keep up. That I want to help and I'm going to end up being a liability after all.

The fire flares after a moment, and then I see Hassen's features light up as he begins to feed it fuel. I look around the shadows of the cave. It looks to be well stocked, a stack of rolled-up furs in one corner, and baskets of supplies along the walls. One end of the cave looks a bit rocky and collapsed, but otherwise it's large and comfortable, with the ceiling high enough that Hassen can stand fully, and enough room for both of us to move around easily. Some of the hunter caves are quite small, but this one's roomy. That's both good and bad—good because it's nice to stretch out, and bad because it takes that much longer to warm up.

Well, I can sit on my half-frozen ass, or I can help. I get to my feet and adjust the screen over the entrance so no gusts of wind threaten our tiny fire while it's being stoked. Then I head to the furs and begin to unroll them, making a bed. There are three large bundles, which means we have enough for two people and two separate beds . . . but I hope it doesn't come to that. "Mind if I get undressed?" I ask him. "My clothes are soaked."

He grunts. "Hang them by the fire so they can dry."

Not his chattiest moment. Doesn't even comment on the fact that I'm about to get naked. That's fine. I'm not feeling particularly sexy at the moment, just tired and cold. I peel wet layers of leather off my body and strip down to the leather band that serves as a terrible bra. I'm now bare-assed, and I wrap one of the thick furs around my body like a toga before spreading my clothes by the fire. He doesn't even glance my way, just continues to feed bits of fuel into the flame.

I feel my chest give another painful squeeze. He's depressed.

I can't blame him—the sa-khui had a devastating setback. He's allowed to be emotional, but right now we have to be strong. Lots of people are depending on us to bring back supplies to help with the brutal season. We can't fail them. I don't think he wants to fail them, either. I think he's just . . . struggling.

Instead of lounging in the nice, warm, furry bed I just made, I haul my toga over to the baskets and pick through the neat leather pouches stored inside. Soapberries, spices, something that looks like dried bait, fishing hooks made of bone . . . and another basket has some of the heinously spicy trail mix that the sa-khui love so much. I'm so hungry it looks good even to me. I pull out the pouch of it and move to Hassen's side, offering it to him. "Here. Eat."

"You eat. You need your strength."

"Oh, I plan on eating. But there's enough for both of us, and I doubt you've eaten since the cave-in. So dig in, my friend." I shake the pouch at him, letting the contents roll around in what I hope is an enticing manner.

He ignores it, staring at the small fire again.

I swallow my sigh and put the food aside and wrap my hands around his arm, hugging his limb to my breast. He doesn't push me away, but he doesn't respond, either. "Wanna talk about it, big guy?"

"I should send you back."

"'Scuse me?"

Hassen feeds another bit to the fire with his free hand. "This will be a long, hard journey. You should not come. You should stay back with the other human females."

"Let's just pretend I'm not hearing this sexist crap and let's talk about what's really bothering you." I stroke his arm. "Because you are clearly not okay."

"Okay?" he echoes, voice flat. "My people are homeless. My friend could be dying. The brutal season is coming. I am very much *not* okay."

"Yeah, I don't know anything about losing everything," I snap back.

He looks over at me, startled. His mouth sets in a grim line, and he pulls his arm from my grip. I think he's going to get up and push me away, but instead, he wraps me in his arms and squeezes me tight against his chest. He's not comforting me— he's clinging to me like I'm his lifeline.

I hug him close, stroking my fingers along his back. "I know it's hard right now, but your people are strong and resilient. They're going to get through this. If the home cave is gone, we'll live at the elders' cave. If not there, then somewhere else. It'll get figured out, and we'll survive."

"I . . ." He pauses, clearly struggling with emotion. His hands grip me tightly. "All this sorrow, this despair, it reminds me of before." I want to ask what *before* he's talking about, but he continues. "With the khui-sickness. My family . . ."

Oh. I slide my fingers along his skin under his vest, trying to comfort him with my touch. "You lost them."

"I lost everything. I despaired greatly for a long time, and I see all this, and I feel myself going back to that dark place." He takes a deep, ragged breath and holds me even tighter, and I can practically feel his chest ridges leaving an imprint on my cheek as he hugs me against him. "I need to be there, to help them, and Vektal sent me away." His voice breaks, and I can feel the tension in his body.

He's struggling so. My poor Hassen.

I pry myself loose from his choking grip and sit back, cupping his face so he has to look at me. "Hassen," I say softly.

"You know Vektal didn't send you away because he didn't want you around, right? He's sending you away because you're the best man for the job. You don't have to worry about babies or a mate or a mom that needs help. Maybe it sucks that you got picked for what's probably the least fun task out of all of them, but you're the best guy for it. It's not a slam against you, it's a compliment."

"He chose me because I am alone," Hassen says bitterly. "Because the tribe does not care if I live or die."

"Because you'll come back with the supplies and he doesn't have to worry about you," I correct firmly. "And you're not alone. I'm here right beside you."

"You should have stayed with your sister."

"Why? She doesn't need me." I tilt my head, studying him. "You don't need me, either, not really. I'm not going to lie—I'm probably going to be shitty company on this trip. I'm going to be slow as molasses, and I'm not very strong. But you do need a friend . . . and I can be that for you."

He covers the hands I have on his cheeks with his own, and then lifts my hands to kiss each palm. "Are we just friends, Mah-dee? You know you have my heart."

I feel a little flutter in my belly. I want to tell him that he has mine, except . . . I worry about my judgment. Am I just clinging to him because he needs me? Is he latching on to me because he wants someone? Anyone? But I can't turn him away. Not when he's clearly hurting and I want to comfort him.

So I'll skip the words for now. They can come out later . . . if at all. I move forward and press my mouth to his, kissing him. I move my lips against his, caressing and tender. I want him to know that, in this moment, he's absolutely loved and needed. I tease my tongue against his, and I can feel his breathing quicken as I twine my arms around his neck.

I want to show him just how much I care. Show him how much he's needed. That he's not disposable in my eyes.

I kiss his mouth sweetly for a moment longer, and then give a gentle little push to his chest, indicating he should lie backward. He does, watching me with hot, avid eyes. I move his leather vest aside, exposing his chest, and sigh with pleasure at the sight of all that hard muscle. Blue is officially my favorite color for a delicious, taut chest and perfect pectorals.

"What do you do, Mah-dee?" he asks, voice husky.

I just smile at him and lean down, pressing a kiss to his chest. I want to make him feel special, and I know just the way to do it. I nibble along the hard, plated ridges covering the center of his chest. I imagine it isn't as sensitive as other parts of his body, but judging from the way his breath is rasping, it's still pretty exciting to watch. I'm getting excited, too. I'm doing this for him, because I want him to feel good . . . but I like doing it. Touching him turns me on, and I can feel my pussy pulsing in response to his arousal.

I kiss lower, moving in a direct line down his front. I don't want there to be any guesses as to what I'm doing—I want him to realize and to anticipate. I flick my tongue down the hard line of his six-pack abs and scrape my teeth along his skin. He tastes a bit like sweat, and ash, but he also tastes like Hassen, and I love it.

"Mah-dee," he rasps as I lap at his flat belly, heading for his navel. "You . . ."

"Shhh." I kiss lower. "I'm concentrating. You don't want to ruin my concentration, do you?"

His pained groan tells me that no, no he does not. I dip my tongue into the depression of his belly button, tracing it before moving ever downward. I have a very specific destination in mind, and I can tell he's guessed it by now. If he hasn't, the fact that I put my hands on his loincloth and tug on the strings should tell him everything.

A couple of pulls on the ties and he comes unwrapped, like it's my birthday. Leathers fall backward, and then I see his big, delicious, oh-so-ridged cock thrusting into the air. His spur draws my attention, and I drag my fingers over it in a gentle caress before I grip his length in my hand and give him a tug.

Hassen's head goes back, his fangs bared in a hiss of pure pleasure. I love the sight of that. With a smile, I stroke his cock again and then lower my head to give him a kiss.

He howls my name in response.

I giggle, dragging my lips over the head of his cock, wetting them with the pre-cum that's sliding down the rounded tip. "I guess you don't have to worry about being quiet out here, do you? It's kind of fun to be noisy, isn't it?" And I lick him, making sure to drag my tongue slowly over the crown.

"Mah-dee," he pants. "My heart." He reaches out and caresses my face while I have fun sucking on his cock. "Just when I think you cannot give me more pleasure, you astound me."

Sweet guy. He hasn't seen anything yet. I wrap my fingers tight around his length, squeezing, and pull him deep into my mouth. I take as much of him as I can, letting his length slick along my tongue. He goes deep, and his girth feels massive. I loosen my jaw, working him deeper, until he butts against the back of my throat and triggers my gag reflex. I release him, and he groans again, impossibly turned on by my actions. Yeah, I'm probably blowing his mind right about now.

It's pretty fun, gotta admit.

I take him deep again, sucking hard, and this time I don't gag. This time, I start to hum "The Star-Spangled Banner." It's a trick I learned from a friend when I first started bartending, and she told me all about how wild it made her boyfriend. The humming increases the vibration in your throat and tongue, and it feels really, really good to a guy. Maybe not quite as good as a prostate tickle, but I don't know if Hassen's ready for that sort of thing yet.

What I do know is that he likes the humming. His big hand touches my hair and then flexes, pulling back. It's as if he's wanting to push down on my head and is afraid of hurting me. I hum louder, working him with as much saliva and hand motions as I possibly can. He's so big, and the ridges are so distracting, that it's hard to take him as deep as I want, but he doesn't seem to mind. Over and over, I pump him with my mouth, humming that patriotic little tune as I do. I can feel his body tightening as I launch into the climax of the song, but he's not there with me. Not yet.

So I give the underside of his spur a little tickle. I figure if it's anything like my nipples, gentle rubbing on the underside will make him as crazy as that sort of thing makes me.

His body jerks. The breath explodes from his lungs, and the hand goes down on the back of my head, holding me on his cock. I lose control of the song, but it doesn't matter. He lifts his hips, pumping, and then a moment later, my mouth fills with hot jets of come. He shoots so far down my throat that I barely taste it, and I hold still, squeezing the base of his cock to milk him. When I can swallow no more, I jerk back, my mouth flooding with the last of his release, and I cough a little as my throat works.

"Mah-dee," he pants, a starstruck look in his eyes. I love the way he says my name like this, after he's come. Like I just made his world all better again, with only my mouth.

I cough-swallow the last of his load, rather ungracefully, but the way he's gazing at me, he doesn't care. "Sorry," I wheeze.

"I should not have come in your mouth," he says, pulling me down against him and cradling me against his chest. He holds me like I'm the most precious thing in the world, and I cuddle up against him and love it.

"That was kind of the plan," I tease, snuggling closer. "I wanted to make you feel good."

"You did." He is silent for a moment, and then adds, "Can I make you feel good?"

"I didn't do it for quid pro quo," I tell him. "I just wanted to give you some pleasure."

"Quid . . . ?"

"Reciprocal. Shit, you probably don't know that word, either." I think for a moment, then trace a circle on his yummy, yummy abs. "I didn't do it because I wanted you to do the same to me. I did it because I wanted to make you feel as wonderful as I think you are."

"I enjoy licking your cunt, though," he tells me, and one finger trails up my arm and then traces a circle around one of my nipples, sending a shiver through my body. "Surely you would not deprive me of such joy?"

If it can make him forget the world for a few hours, I suppose I must "bear the burden" of having my pussy eaten out. Darn. "Wouldn't dream of it, big guy."

CHAPTER THIRTEEN
Hassen

TWO WEEKS LATER

"You are slow today," I mock my mate as I crest a large hill. "Pick up your feet. We have far to go."

Behind me, Mah-dee grumbles something under her breath about *ahs-wholes* and makes a hand gesture that tells me she is not pleased with me. She does move faster, though not fast enough to keep up with me.

I just chuckle at her response and gaze down across the snowy plains. Mah-dee makes a lot of angry noises, but she tries very hard, and she never gives up. I might tease her about her speed, but I would never leave her behind. Having her company on this trip has made the bleak worries in my mind fade. She is very strong in spirit, my Mah-dee. If she does not have an answer, she will make one. To her, there is no crying over what has happened, only the need to come up with a solution. She is good for me. When my sorrow over my tribe threatens to overwhelm me, Mah-dee sets my head to rights.

My heart has chosen wisely, even if my khui is silent.

I scan the snowy terrain, looking for changes. I have gone

this way many times in the past, but much of the landscape looks different after the earth-shakes. Two more have happened in the last few weeks, but then things grew silent. The ash has tapered off, and the snow is clean again, the skies clearing once more. It almost feels normal.

Mah-dee arrives at the top of the hill, her breath quick pants. She moves to my side, her hand tugging at mine. "What are we looking for?"

"Dvisti. Metlaks. Sky-claws."

"No, no, and helllll no," she proclaims, moving a little closer to me. "I've eaten enough of number one to last me the rest of my life, and number two and three are big nopes in my book."

"Then your *boohk* is lucky. There are none that I can see." That is another strange change after the earth-shake. While the dvisti have been plentiful, I have not seen a single sky-claw, and metlaks are infrequent. While I am glad that the sky-claws have moved on, I worry that there is something I am missing. This is metlak territory. We should at least see traces of them.

"How does it look?" she asks me. "Compared to before? Any big changes? Maybe that's why there's no one around."

"No changes," I tell her, studying the distant cliffs. There are fewer valleys the closer to the mountains we get, and the land spreads out, smooth and white. We are nearing the edges of familiar territory. Farther north, and we will be close to the strange, flashing cave where Mah-dee and Li-lah were found. I will not go that far into the mountains; there are no hunter caves that deep into metlak territory. They keep to their hunting grounds, and we keep to ours.

"I see a cave over there," she says, pointing off into the distance. "Is that our next stop?"

"There are two caves in this area," I tell her. "That one, and then one around that bend." I point in the opposite direction, to the distant cliffs.

"I've got a bit more juice in me," Mah-dee says, adjusting her furs tighter around her head. "We can go to the distant one before we call it for the night."

I touch her hood, wishing I could caress her mane. I feel a swell of affection for Mah-dee. My heart. She is strong and pushes herself to her limits because she wishes to be a good partner. Her pack would be as big as mine if I let her, but I watch out for my mate and make sure she is not straining herself. "It is our last stop."

"Our last stop . . . overall? Really?" She looks up at me, surprised. "Then we start the journey back?"

I nod. For many handfuls of days, we have visited cave after hunter cave, checking for supplies. Some of the caves were completely gone, crushed by rock. Some were untouched. A few had some damage, and one or two had been raided by metlaks and no longer had anything usable. Mah-dee has been scribbling charcoal marks on a skin—"taking notes," she says. We leave the supplies in each cave, taking only what we need for immediate survival. Once we have stripped the farthest caves of their goods, we will travel back along the path we came from, and clean out the caves as we go.

Here, at the farthest caves, we will need to hunt something sizable for the bones and large skins to stretch to make sleds. A big one for me, and a smaller one for Mah-dee. I would drag both behind me if I could, but I suspect my fierce, yellow-maned human would not like that much. Just thinking about her reaction makes me smile.

Being with her has been . . . joyous. There is no other way to describe it. If I was alone, I would be full of despair, worrying over my tribe. But with Mah-dee, she forces me to think logically. To trust that the others are safe under the chief's care, and to focus on the task at hand. To her, there is no problem that cannot be fixed.

This journey has not been so lonely with her at my side. I wake up each morning with her in my arms, and I go to bed each night in a different cave, but with Mah-dee's hands tucked against my chest. We mate most nights, but sometimes she is too tired, and that is fine, too. It is enough to hold her close and inhale her scent. It is enough to hear her laugh, or to see the smile cross her funny human face.

When she is with me, I think that even the destruction of the cave is not so bad. It is not something that will destroy us. We will survive and go on. Mah-dee has started her world over. Lilah, as well. Each human female who found herself here in the snows of our planet, far from home, has started their worlds over. The sa-khui can do this, and be stronger for it.

Mah-dee teaches me this every day.

"So how far are we from the ocean?" Mah-dee asks, shielding her eyes from the sunlight. Today is one of the first days that the suns have broken through the dark gray clouds, and the sight of them has made both of us happy. Sunlight means no more ash. No clouds and no earth-shakes mean things will return to normal soon . . . and the brutal season will remain at bay for one more day.

O-shun means great salt water to her. I remember this. I point at the spiky mountains on the horizon. "On the other side. Did you want to go?"

"Can we cross those?"

"Not easily. We would go around. Take the long way. It will add another two hands of days to travel." I think for a moment and then add, "My hands, not yours."

She wiggles four fingers at me and grins. "I'd like to see what the ocean looks like here, but we should probably get back to the tribe as soon as possible. I guess now's not the time for a detour."

"True. I would still go for you."

"You're sweet," she says, squeezing my fingers. "You can just tell me about it instead. Is it blue?"

"Is what blue?" I begin to head down the far side of the hill. The snow here is deeper, and I turn back and offer her my hand so she can descend easily.

"Is the ocean blue?" She grabs my hand and tilts her snowshoes, like I have shown her.

"No, it is green."

"That sounds gross. Like a dirty swimming pool. Maybe I'll just pretend it looks nice since we're not going to go see it."

"You would not want to swim," I caution her. "The shore is very rocky and would tear at your feet. Plus, there are many things that live in the water that could eat you in a bite."

"Charming. I love this place." Her tone is dry. "So where are we? Close to where you found me and my sister?"

"Closer to the mountains. We would need to journey for another day or two in order to reach it."

"Good. I really don't want to head in that direction." She shudders, and I feel the tremor in her hand. "Sometimes I still have nightmares about those little green dead guys and what might have happened if the ship hadn't crashed."

I squeeze her hand tightly in mine. I do not like to think about that at all.

Mah-dee pauses at the base of the hill, pretending to adjust the straps of her pack. I have learned these little tricks; she does not want to tell me that she is tired, so she checks her things. Sometimes it is her shoes, sometimes her pack. I wait patiently, pretending not to notice that she is breathing hard. Every day, she gets stronger and can go for longer, but she is still new to this life. It will take time, and even then she will never be as strong as a sa-khui female. Humans are delicate.

It is good that I am strong and capable, because I can take care of her. The thought gives me fierce pleasure.

"Hmm." Mah-dee's steps cease their crunch in the snow.

I stop and turn. "What is it?"

"Thought I saw something. What's that over there?"

I look around, but I do not see what she refers to. "What?"

"Over there. I thought I saw the snow moving."

I look where she gestures and see nothing but rolling hills and more snow. A cluster of many snow-covered bushes is visible at the top of a small mound, but other than that, there is nothing unusual. I turn to ask Mah-dee what it is that bothers her . . . when one of the bushes moves.

It is not a snow-covered bush at all . . . but a metlak.

And it is not just one, but several. At least two hands. As another bush moves, I realize that it is three hands, maybe more. And they see us. They are hunting us.

Metlaks normally avoid sa-khui, and are chased away by anything bearing our scent. They are cowardly creatures . . . but they are also hungry. I think of the hunter caves we found that were raided, the contents destroyed and the supplies eaten. If they are brave enough to go to our caves, they are brave enough to attack me and Mah-dee. Perhaps they see our packs and think we have food.

Mah-dee is in danger. A cold chill moves over me, and I scan our surroundings. Even if I take her to a hunter cave, there will not be enough time to make a fire to chase them off. We must do something, and fast.

I turn and grab Mah-dee by the arm, hauling her along. "We must go."

"Where are we going? What's wrong?"

With my free hand, I yank one of the spears off my back, pulling it free from its bindings on my pack. "Those are metlaks, and they are coming after us."

She jogs at my side, trying to move fast, but the snowshoes slow her down. "Should we try to talk to them? Lila says they're intelligent—"

"They are hungry," I tell her. "And unpredictable. I do not want to risk it. We are going to walk faster and hope they do not follow us."

It is a stupid hope, but right now, it is all I have.

Mah-dee quickens her steps, and I can hear her breath huffing. "Should I get out my weapon?"

"Yes."

"Oh, fuck."

"Not right now," I tell her, scanning the distant cliffs as we hurry toward them. If we get to the hunter cave fast enough, maybe I can hold them off long enough for Mah-dee to make a fire. The metlaks hate fire and are easily frightened. Mah-dee is not fast with a flint, but perhaps today . . .

She stumbles, a small cry escaping her. I stop in my tracks, turning to help her up. "Are you all right?" She struggles to get to her feet, nodding, and one of her shoes flops around her ankle, the leather ties broken.

"My shoe," she pants. "I can keep going." Then she stumbles again, crying out, and her hands cling to my arm. "Okay, might be my ankle, too. Leave me, Hassen—"

I do not even let her finish. With a growl of anger, I grab her into my arms and sling her over my shoulder, ignoring her cry of protest.

I will not leave Mah-dee behind. I will die first.

With my spear as a walking stick, I jog slowly toward the cliffs. They come ever closer, and despite the gentle weight of Mah-dee on my shoulder and her squirming, I am able to move faster. "Are they still coming?" I ask Mah-dee as I plunge forward.

"Oh yeah," she says, her voice wobbling. "Also, I might be sick if we don't slow down. Your shoulder's hitting my stomach—"

"Then be sick," I tell her, and speed up.

"Okay," she says faintly. "Should I get out a weapon?"

"Yes."

"Fuck."

"Not right now," I tell her again, distracted. I am closing in on the distant cliffs, and they look . . . different. The rocks are tumbled here, the snow mounded. The earth-shake has affected this place, too, and I worry that the hunter cave will not even be there. Desperation makes me move faster, and I head toward the overhanging cliffs and the shadow they cast. We are close. As we approach, I can see the shadow of the cave in the distance, and I double my steps, hurrying. I must get Mah-dee to safety. If I can block the entrance of the cave with her behind me, I can hold them off for longer—

A shattering sound.

The snow beneath my feet disappears. I yelp in surprise, and Mah-dee screams as we tumble through the air. I fling my spear aside and curl my body around hers, trying to shield her—

We land. I fall onto my back, and despite the soft snow, the wind is knocked from my lungs. Blackness dances behind my eyes, but fades just as quickly, and I feel Mah-dee groan as she pulls herself off of me. "What . . ."

I struggle to sit up. It is dark here, the shadows protecting us from the sunlight above. I look up and see we are in a crevasse, the ground above us split open. A layer of ice must have covered it somehow and I broke through, plunging us down here. Snow is piled around us, and the cliff walls scale far above my head and Mah-dee's. As I look up, I see a metlak peer over the edge.

Mah-dee sucks in a breath, touching my arm.

The creature hoots at us, then grabs a handful of snow and flings it in our direction. Others appear at its side, agitated. They skirt the edges of the crevasse, glaring down at us and screaming their anger, but none approach.

"I don't think they can get to us," Mah-dee says. She looks over at me, worry on her face. "Are you all right?"

I sit up, looking around for my spear. It is several arm lengths away, and I get to my feet slowly, testing my body. "My tail is bruised," I say, rubbing it. "But I will live."

She giggles.

I scowl at her. "What is so funny?"

"Just you . . . rubbing your ass while we're stuck in a pit."

"It is not a pit," I tell her, glancing around, trying to determine what exactly it is. It is almost like the ground has an open wound and we have fallen into it. I am not entirely sure I like it.

"A canyon, then. We have them on Earth."

I look up. "At least it has stopped the metlaks." They throw handfuls of snow down at us as if responding to my words, but do not move otherwise. They will not come down to us. I do not even know if they can. We are at least two body lengths below them, maybe more. I eye the rocky walls. I will need to climb them to get out and lower a rope to Mah-dee. But that is a problem for later. "We are safe for now."

She shudders. "There is that. I guess we just stay down here until they leave."

I glance around. The canyon is wide enough that several hunters could walk abreast, but a herd of dvisti would not make it through. As valleys go, it is extremely narrow. It winds in a zigzag, and I wonder where it goes. I grab my spear, rub my tail, and then pick up my fallen pack and sling it over my back. "Since we are down here, let us see where this goes."

Mah-dee looks up, where the metlaks watch us from above. "Yeah, I guess we might as well." She pulls her broken snowshoe off her foot, then the other one, and fixes her boots before hopping to her feet. "Snow's not very deep here. That's good." She takes a few crunching steps forward and holds a hand out to me.

Her hand is cold, and I make sure to wrap my fingers tight around hers.

"We're going to be okay, right?" Her voice is small.

Her worry makes my heart ache. She is normally so confident, so assured. She has kept me strong in many dark days. I must do the same for her. I turn and bring her hand to my mouth, pressing my lips to her knuckles. "I will not let anything harm you, Mah-dee."

"I know. I just . . . I'm a little rattled." She gives a nervous laugh and glances back at the still-watching metlaks. "Those things are creepy."

"Stay close to me."

"Not a problem." She pulls her hand from mine and puts an arm around my waist. "I'd rub your sore butt for you, but I'd rather get away from the metlaks before we fool around."

I grunt, not entirely sure how to take that. "Let us see where this takes us, then."

CHAPTER FOURTEEN
Hassen

We head into the narrow canyon. It is dark here, almost like walking through a long, winding cave if it were not for the narrow strip of sky above. I keep an eye on the walls of the canyon, in case there is a place where it is shallow enough that the metlaks can get to us. So far, though, the walls grow taller with every step farther into the canyon we take. Soon, the walls are so tall that five males standing atop one another would not be able to get to the surface . . . and I would not walk away from that fall with just a sore tail.

Mah-dee cocks her head as we walk, admiring our surroundings. "This place is kind of cool."

A strange comment. "Of course it is cooler. We are in a valley. It will not be as warm as where the suns touch the snow."

She laughs. "No, I mean, it's nifty. Not cold. It reminds me of the Grand Canyon back at home, except, like, it's purple and blue instead of orange and red. Was this carved by a river?"

"Eh, I do not know." I study our surroundings. I have never considered that. All I know is that here the cliffs almost close overhead like teeth. In some areas, the walls of the valley close in tight and it almost feels as if you are walking in a cave tunnel. "Stay close."

"I'm close. Any closer and I'd be grabbing on to your tail and rubbing against your ass," she grumbles behind me. "Though you'd probably like that."

"Save it for later, when we are by the fire."

"Flirt."

I grin with amusement at her words. Perhaps I am flirting. I like to tease Mah-dee. She teases back, unlike her sister, who cried and wept if I so much as looked at her. Not for the first time, I curse the day I grabbed the dark-maned sister instead of the yellow-maned one.

It is quiet as we walk. Our footsteps crunch on the snow, but Mah-dee quickens, moving to my side and slipping her fingers around my belt. "There really isn't as much snow down here," she says. "You'd think it'd all fall in and pile up, except it's not. Maybe this canyon is protected from the weather. Look up." She gestures, and I obediently glance upward. "One side of the canyon looks higher than the other. I bet it protects the bottom from a lot of the weather."

"Perhaps." I pull her closer against me. "It will be all right, I promise."

"I know. I'm with you." She looks up at me, and there's a small smile on her face. "Everything's okay when we're together. You realize that, right?"

I feel a surge of affection for her, along with intense possessiveness. Mah-dee is *mine*. No female has ever been as strong, as smart, as clever, as sweet, or as giving. No female is as perfect for me as her. I think of Li-lah and her weeping, and curl my lip with disgust. I was a fool. "I will keep you safe," I vow to her.

She smiles up at me. "I know."

"No, you do not understand." I stop and put my hands on her shoulders, turning her toward me. This feels . . . important. It feels big. She must listen to me. I must spill to her how I feel. "You are my heart, Mah-dee. Without you, I am nothing. You saw me as an exile and still took me to your furs. You are kind and giving."

Her cheeks flush with color. "Hassen, you make it sound like charity—"

"Was it not giving?"

"I wasn't thinking about giving! I was thinking about how I wanted to sleep with you!" Embarrassment shows on her face.

"You chose me out of all of the males in the cave. You could have had any of the unmated hunters. Instead, you pick the one that you should hate the most." I cup her face in my hands. "What did you see in me?"

"You just . . . looked like you needed a friend. And I did, too." She puts her hands over mine. "No, it's more than that. I needed to connect to someone. I felt alone, and lonely, and I felt like . . . well, that you would understand. That you would know how it felt to be surrounded by people and still feel adrift." Her fingers brush over my skin. "No one else could relate. And it didn't matter to me that you were the guy that stole my sister. Well, okay, it did matter a little, but I needed to know how you felt. If you were in love with Lila, I wouldn't have approached you."

My lip curls at the thought. "In love with Li-lah? Never."

"Which is why I wanted you. You made a mistake, but that doesn't mean you should be punished forever. And maybe I'm looking at it with rose-colored glasses or something, but I know what it's like to lose your shit during a bad moment and then have people keep throwing it in your face over and over again." She smiles wryly.

"I . . . have no idea what you just said."

She chuckles. "I figured as much. Just know that I see beyond your actions to the person underneath, okay?" She pats my hand. "You're good people. Don't ever forget that."

I feel a warmth in my breast, and smile down at her. Mahdee sees the true me. It makes me so . . . happy. For the first time in a long time, I feel content with my place. If I am exiled, so be it. If I have lost the trust of those I care for with my actions, as long as I have Mah-dee, I can live with it. Perhaps I will never get over the shame of disappointment, but it will not destroy me. My mate will not let it. I feel a rumble of pleasure in my chest that I have such a female at my side. "My mate," I tell her softly. "What would I do without you?"

Her eyes go wide. "Your mate?"

"You have been since the day you claimed me." I stroke my thumb over her soft, strange, pink mouth. "There is no other for me. There never has been."

"Not even my sister?" Her voice catches.

I snort. "Your sister is my greatest mistake. I do not think I have ever even liked her."

Mah-dee bites gently at my thumb when I stroke it over her mouth again. "You might want to learn to like her, since she's my family."

"Because she is your family, I will *tolerate* her."

Mah-dee giggles. "That is a terrible thing to say, and I shouldn't laugh."

"You should laugh. You should laugh all the time. I love to hear it. It makes me happy." I lean in closer. "You make me happy."

Her smile dims a little. "It feels awful to be so happy when things are so rotten for so many. Can I . . ." Her expression changes to one of worry, and she clutches at my vest. "Oh my God. Do you feel that?"

"What?" I feel nothing but the warm, content rumble in my chest.

"I think it's another earthquake!"

The panic in her voice makes me pull her protectively against my chest, and I hunch my shoulders over her smaller form, trying to shelter her with my body. We are not safe here in this slice of the ground. "I have you."

A long moment passes, and I wait to feel it. I feel nothing under my feet, though, just the warmth of her pressed against me, and the tickle of her mane against my chin.

She stiffens against me and then pulls back, a frown on her face. "Okay, this is going to sound weird . . ." Her hand presses to the center of my chest. "But you're rumbling. Baby, do you have indigestion?"

I do not ask what she means. Now I feel it, too. The building, slow thrumming in my chest that is spreading warmth throughout my body. I . . . dare not hope.

I drop to my knees and press my head to her teats, listening. Hoping.

"Oh," she breathes, just as her chest begins to resonate. "Oh. I think . . . I think the ground isn't shaking. I think it's me."

"And me," I tell her, utter joy racing through me. I hold her tightly, burying my face against her as I listen to her khui begin its song.

It is singing to *me*.

And I am singing back.

"Oh my God," Mah-dee says, her voice faint. "Is this what I think it is?"

"Let it happen," I murmur to her, stroking her back. "We are meant to be, Mah-dee. Even our bodies know it."

"I . . . guess they do." Her hands go to my mane, and then she touches my cheek, caressing my face. "I love you, big guy. You know that, right?"

I nuzzle at her teats, wishing she were not wearing so many layers of furs. I want to hear the song in her chest as loud as the one that is rumbling through mine. I want to feel her warmth. I want to lick at her nipples and taste the juice of her cunt. I am hungry for her with my entire body. I *need* her. Right here. Right now.

I push my hand under her tunic and then into the waistband of her leggings. Her small squeak of surprise is drowned out a moment later by the moan of pleasure she lets out when my fingers brush over her curls. She is wet with need, the scent of it perfuming the air and making my mouth water. "I must taste this," I groan, shoving at her leathers. "Get on your back for me, Mah-dee, so I can taste your cunt."

She whimpers, sliding to her knees. "Should we? The metlaks—"

"—cannot get here. They are far behind." Far enough, at least. I lock an arm behind her legs and one behind her back, maneuvering her onto the ground. The moment her yellow mane spreads out in the snow, I pull at her leggings, dragging them down her hips. I am desperate for her. The resonance hums through me, its song more powerful than anything I have ever imagined. How do others fight this? I cannot take another step without pleasuring my Mah-dee. I will die if I do not have her now.

I ache to bury myself inside her, and war between tasting her sweet folds or pushing myself deep into her and feeling the tight grip of her cunt around me. Has it been hours since we last mated? It feels far too long. It feels like forever.

Mah-dee's soft moan of need decides for me. I must pleasure my mate. *Now.*

I push her legs into the air, using the leather of her leggings as a handhold. Her thighs spread before me, damp and flushed a delicate, soft pink. Between them, her cunt gleams wet for me. *For me.* I growl with pleasure and bury my face there. She squeals with surprise, and I feel the tremor moving through her body when my tongue drags over her folds. The taste of her has never been more delicious. Ravenous, I brace my arm on her thighs and redouble my efforts, pleasuring her with my mouth and my tongue. She cries out and wiggles against me, muttering things like *fuck* and *yes* and *you nasty thing* and *just like that.* All the while, her juices run down her thighs and over my tongue, and the resonance in her chest sings as loudly as mine.

"Even your cunt tastes sweeter," I rasp between hard, insistent laps of my tongue. "How is this possible?"

"Don't know," she chokes out. Her hands wrap around one of my horns, and she pushes my face farther into her cunt. "Don't care. Just . . . keep . . . going."

An easy task—I am ravenous for her. I push my tongue into her core, stroking it in and out as if it were my cock. She cries out, and her thighs quiver against my arm.

"My clit," she demands.

I push my tongue into her again, and move my hand between her thighs. I rest my thumb on her third nipple and rub it as I drive deep.

She screams, clutching at my horns, and I feel her cunt quiver tight, trying to lock around me. The need to be inside her grows unbearable, and I snarl as I push my leathers down, releasing my aching cock. When I sit up, she cries out in protest, but then I am sinking into her, and her protest chokes into another moan of my name. Being inside her, resonating? My eyes close. There is no sweeter pleasure. I grip her hip with one hand and thrust deep.

This is my home. Mah-dee is my home. Here, inside her cunt, it is where I belong. I pump into her again and feel the walls of her tighten around me, holding me like a fist. I want to thrust into her forever, to feel the slick channel of her gripping my cock, but resonance is overwhelming me. I feel my sac tighten, and then I am exploding into her with wild thrusts, pumping her full of my seed as it pours forth with brutal intensity. She whimpers my name, her cunt clenching tight, as I thrust into her over and over and over again.

Even when I am spent, my seed slicking out of her and down her thighs as I pull my cock free, I am still hard. Still resonating with need. I rub at my humming chest, both pleased and a little alarmed at the fact that I could take her again even now. And again.

And possibly again, over and over for the next few hours. Or days. No wonder Rokan did not emerge from his cave with Lilah for days. The resonance need is overwhelming.

"Okay." Mah-dee slides her legs together slowly, her movements languid. "I can't believe we just did that."

"Resonance? It is my heart's greatest desire."

"No, you big goof." She props up on her elbows. "I can't believe you just threw me down in the snow and nailed me. And it was awesome." She glances up at the steep cliffs overhead. "You don't think the metlaks are still watching us, do you? That might put a damper on the memories."

I shake my head. "They give up on their prey easily." I move over to her side and pull her against me, tucking her body against my chest. "Unlike me."

She snorts, sliding a hand under my vest and stroking my back. My khui immediately begins to hum loudly, and I feel my need for her rising again. "All of this was just . . . unexpected," Mah-dee tells me. "I never thought . . ."

"All of the other humans have resonated." I hold her tighter to me, imagining if she had resonated to someone else. The thought makes me want to tear out the throat of anyone who so much as looks at her. *Mine.*

"Yeah, but I'm not exactly . . . the mom type." She shivers against me, and her hands go still. "Do you think we just made a baby?"

"Not yet." Not if my need is any indication. I still hunger for her just as much. I am not sated in the slightest.

"But that's how this works, right? We resonate until there's a kid?" She sounds worried. "I don't know about the timing here . . ."

"Because I am exiled?" It hurts me to think that she might be disappointed.

Mah-dee punches my side. "No, you dummy. Because we're *all* exiled. Everyone's homeless. It's not just you. It's all of us. You can't be exiled from the cave—there is no more cave." She presses her cheek against my chest, and her leg twines around mine, a movement that makes my cock ache with the need to bury myself inside her again. "I just . . . don't want to be a burden in a time when everyone's going to pull their weight. I don't know if you have noticed, but I have a bit more weight than most."

Her words make no sense. "Your weight is nothing to be ashamed of."

"Isn't it?"

I look down at her face. Is she mad? "You are sturdy. You are strong. You are healthy. Why should I care?"

"Um, because it takes more to feed me? Because I require more leather than Josie for a new tunic?"

She *is* mad. "Jo-see eats more than two humans. Does that mean we should get rid of her?"

"Well, no—"

"And Farli will soon be taller than all of the human females. Should we get rid of her?"

"Now you're just splitting hairs—"

"I love your sturdy human body," I tell her, leaning down to kiss her pink mouth. "I love your soft thighs that wobble when I sink into you. I love your big teats that bounce when my cock is inside you. These things change nothing. If you were Jo-see's size, I would care for you in the same way I do now."

"That's good, because I'm pretty sure I'll never be Josie's size." She is smiling as she looks up at me. "I'm pretty sure one of my boobs is bigger than her head."

"It just means you will be able to feed our kit much milk."

"I'm pretty sure boob size doesn't have anything to do with milk production, but okay." Her arms go around my neck, and she looks up at me with big, worried eyes. "I'm still not sure how I feel about being a parent. Half the time I'm not even sure I can take care of myself."

"I will be with you," I tell her. "We will do it together."

"We'd freaking better!"

I roll her onto her back again, parting her thighs. Her khui begins to sing louder. The question in her gaze is silenced as I rub the head of my cock along her drenched cunt and then push into her.

"Again?" she asks weakly, and I can feel her body quiver deep.

"Again," I agree. "Over and over again, for the rest of our days."

Then she says something about *Jay-sus* and a wheel before her legs go around my hips once more.

CHAPTER FIFTEEN
Maddie

I'm kind of an impulsive girl at heart, but after four rounds in the snow, I pat my new "mate" on the back and tell him we need to get moving. My leathers are wet from the snow, I'm cold, and I'm getting hungry. I'm still horny—thanks, cootie—but I'd also like a fire before nightfall.

Hassen helps me fix my clothing and takes an extra fur out of his pack, bundling it tight around me. He steals a few kisses as he does, and I can't get mad. I'm a little worried about the future, sure, but mad? No. It's strange, but everything feels . . . right. Like this was meant to happen. Maybe the reason I've been drawn to Hassen all along is because we've always been meant to be together.

Great, now I sound like one of the aliens.

I press a hand over the purring in my breast. It's so strange. I thought it might feel weird, but it's kind of comforting, actually. And the sex? Okay, the sex is off the charts. Maybe the timing on the whole resonance thing could have been better, but

I don't think I'd ever be one of those who sat down and said, "Yes, I'm ready to be a mom."

Then again, resonating to each other when we're in danger and homeless? Still could be improved.

"You are quiet," Hassen says, bending down to fix my boots. "Do you have regrets?"

He keeps asking me things like that, and it makes my heart ache every time. Does he think he's such a terrible person to be mated to? That I'm going to wish I wasn't mated to him? "Not a one. I'd choose you over anyone else in the tribe any day."

Hassen rises to his feet, a hint of worry on his face. "And your sister?"

"She'll deal. I don't think she hates you, big guy. I just think she didn't want to be your girlfriend." I smile up at him. "Which is good, because this would be kind of gross otherwise."

"The thought of mating with your sister makes me ill."

"Good."

"To think I came so close to making a mistake . . ." He pulls me against him in a swift hug. "I am glad it is you, Mah-dee."

"I'm glad it's me, too." I squeeze him back and then peer down the winding path in the crevasse. "You think we'll find an answer down this path? Or are we going to have to go back?"

"There is one way to check." He pauses and looks at me. "Do I need to carry you?"

"What? Why?"

"Because you are weak from mating? I have felt your legs trembling each time I pushed into you."

"Oh my God. No dirty talk while I'm trying to be serious, please." I press my knees tight together because just hearing that is turning me on. "And I can walk. I'll let you know if that changes."

He takes my hand in his and holds me tight. He does take my pack from my back, and I let him, because I am a little tired, if I'm admitting it to myself. Being boned within an inch of your life by a seven-foot-tall blue dude taxes the stamina, all right. But I'm not complaining.

The gorge we're in widens the farther we go. The area we dropped in was maybe twenty feet across. Here, it could be a hundred. "And all of this has never been here before?" I ask him.

Hassen shakes his head. "The earth-shake has opened the land."

"Or maybe this was under the ice all this time and the ice was just too thick?" There's very little snow dusting the path down here, and it feels weird to imagine all of this just magically appearing.

"Perhaps." He steps ahead of me, just a little, and grips his spear in his other hand. "We will be cautious in case there is more ice."

Oh, I don't like to think about that. If we fall through a second layer of ice even deeper, I don't know how we're ever going to get out. I gaze up at the steep canyon walls. I'm not exactly sure how we're going to get out of here as it is if the metlaks are still back there, but one thing at a time. Hassen won't let anything happen to me . . . or our baby.

I touch my stomach. A baby. Holy crapping balls. I'm terrified and excited at the same time. Even more immediate and wonderful, though, is that I have Hassen. We're mated—at both a physical and a spiritual level. Our bodies know we're meant to be together. I'm not alone anymore, and neither is he. I'm in awe.

I might also be a little high on endorphins, but whatever.

"So do you want a boy or a girl?" I ask him as we walk. I have to admit I'm not paying attention to our surroundings—

snow and rock, rock and snow—as much as I am watching his profile like some sort of dreamy teen girl. He's really the handsomest guy on the planet. My cootie is smart.

"I would be happy with either. All I want is for our kit to be healthy . . . and to look like you," he adds after a moment. "But if I chose, I would pick a girl."

"Oh? Don't most guys want a son that takes after them?"

His thumb strokes my knuckles as we walk, distracting me. I can hear the purring in his chest almost as loud as mine, and I'm wondering if this means we're about to have round number five in the snow. I doubt we've even walked a mile yet . . . but I'm kinda okay with that. "I would like a girl," he tells me, pulling me from my dirty thoughts. "Because our tribe has had so few for so long. I would like others to experience the joy I am feeling at this moment." He glances over at me. "And I would like for her to have your yellow mane."

"I'm both flattered and a little appalled that you want our baby to look like me and yet you're ready to give her away to some guy before she's even a cell in my womb."

"Not just anyone," he tells me, footsteps crunching in the snow as we walk. "He would have to prove himself worthy of her. And if he is half as lazy as Taushen, I will knock him upside the head with my spear."

I giggle. That's more like it. "Is Taushen lazy, then?"

He scowls. "He is young and would rather spend time talking to Farli than check his nets."

So basically he's like every other teenage boy. I smile to myself. "Let's get back to our baby. What kind of names do you like?"

"Whatever you want to call her. Since the human females have arrived, my people have been combining names." He pauses in his steps, a frown on his face.

I pause, too, content to be at his side while we take a small break. I'm thinking about names, mentally twining them. "Like Madsen? Or Hassie? I gotta admit that I'm not a big fan of Hassie, and my real name is Madeline, not Maddie, so I guess that changes things—"

"A ship."

It takes me a moment to realize he's not suggesting we name our daughter Ass-hip but is saying *a ship*. "What do you mean, a ship?"

He points ahead, an incredulous look on his face. "There is a ship down here."

The hairs on my neck prickle. I still don't know what he's talking about, so I look to where he's pointing. I see nothing but rocks up ahead, and there's no sign of alien spacecraft. All I see is more stone, a fine layer of ice covering the portion of the cliff that he is pointing at.

Then, I see it.

Not a ship, of course. I think his barbarian mind hears the word "ship" and assumes "cave" or "place where people live." It's not a ship. It's stone, but it's neatly stacked, square stone that curves along the cliff wall, with more trailing along the curve in the path ahead. It reminds me of one of those Indiana Jones movies where the hero looks up and sees the entrance to a forgotten city in the jungle.

Except this isn't a jungle. It's an alien planet. And I didn't think anyone lived here but us.

CHAPTER SIXTEEN
Maddie

It's so weird to round the corner in what is an uninhabited crevasse on a deserted, icy planet populated with nothing but other
crash-landed aliens . . . and realize that there was someone else
here before you.

Long, long before you.

I reach out and touch one of the even, neatly stacked stones
that make up the crumbled wall. At my feet are more even
stones, covered by a thin layer of ice and debris. Cobblestones.
These stones stretch ahead, and as I let my gaze move, I see more
stones, more cobbled road . . . and then ahead, I see buildings.

Tucked against the walls of the crevasse are a bunch of squat
stone buildings. They're square and even, lining a street, and if
I ever had any doubts that this stuff was man-(or alien-)made,
those have been firmly put aside. Someone lived here. Someone
lived here a long time ago . . . or is living here now.

"This isn't a ship," I tell Hassen. "It's a city."

He frowns, trying to digest this word. "It is a place that people live? Like a tribal cave, but in the open?"

"Right."

A tribal cave in the open is right on the money. It's not a city like I know of, with skyscrapers and suburbs. This is a Paleolithic city of some kind, tucked along the walls of the rocky canyon. The cobbled road underneath my feet stretches out and leads to neat rows of small, squatty-looking brick buildings with no roofs. They're square and set in neat rows along the streets, almost as if someone took a grid and placed them all exactly where they needed to be. The size of each one is uniform, about as big as a bedroom back at home, and farther down the street, the buildings get bigger, one the size of a house. Still no roof, though.

It's all very strange. It's like all the roofs disappeared and so . . . everyone left? But that makes no sense.

"I don't know that anyone is here." I don't see anyone moving around, and the feeling I get is one of . . . stillness. Quiet. Emptiness. In a place this big, surely there would be some noise. I stop in my tracks and start counting buildings.

I stop when I get to forty, because, okay, that's a lot of buildings. There's more than that, but it tells me plenty—this was a settlement of some kind. Is a settlement. "Could it be . . . metlaks?"

At my side, Hassen makes a sound of disgust. "They do not create things. They do not live in ships."

"Cities."

"Cities," he amends.

"And your people didn't build this?"

"If they did, would they not live here?"

Yeah, I guess they would. It doesn't seem natural to leave behind a perfectly good city. "So where did they go? Unless they're here and we can't see them." I think of the metlaks that were stalking us earlier, and draw a little closer to Hassen, spooked.

"There are no tracks," he tells me, gesturing at the path before us, then turning and waving a hand at the trail we've left behind us. "If there were people, we would see traces of them."

"I know. Logic says there's no one here, but . . ."

He nods. "I feel the same way." He releases my hand and cups his mouth. "Ho! Is anyone there?"

His shout echoes off the canyon walls. It's eerie, but effective. After a moment, I'm pretty convinced we're alone here, too. I get brave enough to take a few steps forward, looking up. Sunlight spills in from above, but the walls are sheer and I don't see any paths or handholds. No one's coming down from this direction.

So while this is wild and strange . . . it also feels a little safer than I expect. "Do you think we should stay here tonight?"

"Here . . . where?" Hassen looks at me curiously. "In one of the hollows?"

"I think those were houses, though I don't know where the roofs went." I shrug. "We could put a skin over a corner and make ourselves a little nest for the night. Explore the place and see what we can find. Maybe there's a hint as to where these people went."

"Are they all dead?" he asks.

"Good question." Eek, I hope not. "One way to find out, though. Shall we go exploring?"

Hassen looks troubled. "I . . . do not know. This feels like walking into a hunter cave left by a . . . a stranger. I do not know how I feel."

I guess strangers are a big concept to a guy that grew up knowing all the people on the planet. "It's going to be okay," I tell him, holding my hand out. "We'll check it out together. I'd rather see what's down here than go back up and face the metlaks."

He nods slowly, then takes my hand, his spear gripped tight in his other. "Let us see what we can find, then."

Whatever happened to the people of this little Stone Age city, it wasn't plague or famine or anything like that. We peek in on each house, and they're all empty. Every single one is completely body- and bone-free, which makes me feel better. I think I'd probably have turned around and faced the metlaks if we'd found a stack of bodies. It's all very quiet and peaceful, just . . . empty.

I think it's old, too, and I tell Hassen that. A few of the small "houses" have rotted bits of what must have been furniture. There's nothing left but a few frames and piles of dust that suggest stuff was here that didn't survive the elements. Everything is coated with a thin layer of ice, too. Even the floors. Each of the small houses is made the same, a perfect little square with an ice-coated dugout section that must be a firepit, and something that looks suspiciously like a kitchen area. There's a debris-covered cubby connected to each house that has grime and detritus caked into the ice, and I can't figure out what they're supposed to be used for . . . until I find one that has a hole in the floor, and then I get excited.

"These aren't Stone Age people," I tell Hassen. "That's a motherfucking toilet." I get down on my hands and knees, leaning over the ice-covered hole. "Give me your spear!"

"What are you doing, Mah-dee?"

"Looking for pipes," I tell him. He hands me his spear, and I jab the butt of it against the ice, cracking the thick layer after a few stabs and uncovering the hole. I peer into it and then drop a chunk of ice down the hole. I can't see anything down there, but despite the shadows, it looks like there are pipes of some kind.

Crude pipes are still *pipes*.

"These people had toilets," I tell him, excited. I get to my feet. The stone walls suddenly look a lot less crude to me. Romans had running water and pipes, didn't they? Maybe this is the ice planet equivalent of an ancient Roman civilization.

I'm going to ignore the whole Pompeii-Vesuvius equivalent my brain immediately draws. There's no lava here. The volcano was a jillion miles away. "This place is fantastic, Hassen!"

"Why is it fantastic?" He gazes at me, hard brows drawn down.

"Because *toilets*. That means running water somewhere around here. Let's go find it!"

He's mystified by my excitement, but takes his spear back and follows me as I dash around the icy remains of the city.

I'm not wrong—in the big house, there's a bright blue hot spring bubbling, the edges lined with squared pavers. It looks deep and smells stinkier and more sulfurous than the one back at the old cave, but it's fresh water. I glance around. "Maybe this was a bathhouse. Or a communal gathering spot." I see lots of benches and another hollow that's probably a firepit. "This place is so great!"

"Mmm."

I turn to look at Hassen. "You don't like it?"

"I do not like that there are people here, Mah-dee." He still holds his spear, alert. "How can people have lived here without the tribe knowing?"

"Maybe they're other sa-khui?" I rub my lip as I think. "Actually, that can't be right. You guys crashed here about three hundred years ago, and these ruins look way, way older. That means this planet was inhabited before you guys got here."

His mouth sets in a grim line. "What does this mean?"

"I don't know," I tell him honestly, rubbing my arms. "It could mean any number of things. It could mean that the people that lived here are long gone and we're the only ones left on the planet. It could mean that there are people living somewhere else, but far away. Maybe they didn't like how cold it was here and left."

"For Jo-see's island?" He snorts. "If so, they are gone now."

I wince at the thought of another tribe of people vaporized by a poor living location. "You might not be wrong. But we don't know. What I do think is that we should stay here tonight, and then we need to tell Vektal about it. This could be a place to live during the brutal season."

He looks around, clearly not seeing what I see. "Here?"

"Yes, here." I gesture at the pool of water. "We've got water. We've got plumbing, however frozen. We've got houses. Those are like caves. People live in them."

"There are no tops!"

"We can make tops," I tell him. "Roofs, I mean. We can make roofs for each of the houses. And look at this place!" I point to the high canyon walls. "We're snug here. I bet it doesn't get much snow. No metlaks are going to wander down here."

"No sa-khui, either. We fell down a hole," he says in a flat voice.

"Then we can make ladders. My point is, it's not the worst idea."

"And if the people that left come back?"

"I'm pretty sure they're not coming back, big guy." I look around at the empty, forlorn house, trying to imagine it full of people and furniture, with a bright fire burning in the big hearth. "I'm pretty sure they all left hundreds—or thousands—of years ago."

CHAPTER SEVENTEEN
Hassen

Mah-dee is right about one thing—the *howses* are warm.

We finish exploring and pick one of the smallest of the small, cuplike structures to spend our night in. Under Mah-dee's instructions, I use my spear and several of the extra furs we carry to form a tent over the top of the *howse*. We build a fire in the center, and she moves into my lap so I can wrap her in my furs and let my body heat warm her as the suns go down and it grows dark. Once the fire is burning, though, she does not need my warmth. The small structure of the *howse* means it does not take long for it to get warm. With the fire going, it is almost pleasant.

It is very quiet, not unlike the tribal cave when all the hunters are out on journeys. Perhaps Mah-dee is right and this will be a good place for our people. I think of her excitement over the *toy-lets*. Those are a good thing, she tells me. The hot pool of water like our bathing pool at home? Also good. That we can make these cuplike structures into small, warm caves for each family? This place is just waiting to be inhabited again.

Mah-dee is excited. She thinks the chief will be, too. She thinks we can spend the brutal season here and be happy.

But I hesitate. To me it is not *home*.

It is a cold, strange place that someone else has left behind. I do not know what to make of it.

I know this thinking is wrong. I ponder this as I stare into the fire and hold my mate close. The humans have adapted to our land, have they not? It is strange and frightening to them, and yet they have made the best of it. Perhaps it is time for the sa-khui to adapt to change, as well.

I rub my mate's arms as she drowses in my lap.

Perhaps I need to learn to be brave like my human. Mah-dee has been nothing but strong and confident since she awoke from the strange alien bubbles. When her sister cried, Mah-dee shielded her. When I stole her, Mah-dee fought the others and wanted to get her back. Mah-dee does not know how to quit. She does not give up, ever. And she sees everything—even this strange, empty place—as opportunity.

I need to be more like my sweet mate. Embrace the changes that come into my life, the way I embrace her. After my family's death, I lived in fear of more change. When I stole Li-lah and ended up with nothing, I thought change was bad. I thought I had made mistakes and regretted my choices.

But those choices—those changes—have brought me Mah-dee, and she is the greatest gift a hunter could ask for.

Perhaps this place will be as good for my people as Mah-dee is for me. I slide a hand over her thigh, feeling possessive.

My khui immediately begins to rumble, sensing my mood. In my lap, Mah-dee gives a little sigh of pleasure and leans back against me, exposing her neck to me. I nip at it and move my hand between her thighs, seeking her little nipple there.

"Mmm, what are you doing, Hassen?" Her hand moves to my mane, and she twists her fingers in it as she holds me close. Her back arches as I find the sensitive spot on her cunt and stroke it. "Oh. Is *that* what we're doing?"

"We are resonating," I tell her between kisses to her soft neck. "It will happen, and it will happen many times. Tonight, you are mine and mine alone."

"Completely alone," she agrees, and I hear a smile in her voice. "It's kind of weird, isn't it? To be in a home and not have other people around."

"Very odd," I agree. I miss the noises of a busy cave, but after being exiled, I am growing used to it. "But like you, I think it will work. And tomorrow, we will leave and begin our journey home so we may tell the chief of this place." My fingers stroke her slick, wet folds. "But first . . ."

"First," she agrees, undulating her hips against my hand. "First, we have *all* the sex."

Maddie

TWO WEEKS LATER

"Mush, big guy! Mush! You're slowing down and we're near the finish line!" I call out from my seat atop the first sled of supplies.

Hassen looks back at me, eyes narrowed. "You have been shouting that all morning."

"It's because you're not a great listener, baby." I smile brightly at him to take the sting out of my words. "Get your second wind and let's go! Or are you too tired? Do you want me to get out and help?"

"Stay where you are," my delightfully surly mate tells me. "You will need your energy for later."

Despite weeks of resonating, I'm still dorky enough to blush and get all turned on, too. I press my thighs together and try not to think about sex too much, because if that happens, my cootie starts to purr, and then his cootie starts to purr, and then we throw down in the snow like a pair of wild animals.

It's a lot of fun, but it's also put us behind schedule. With every day that passes, it gets a little colder and a little snowier, and I suspect the brutal season is almost here. That means less time to fool around and more hustle to get home.

Which is why I'm riding on a sled instead of pulling one behind me.

We've got two sleds with us: a larger one that Hassen pulls behind him, and a smaller one sized for my frame. Both are full of furs, food supplies, and dried dung for fire fuel. We've killed game and skinned and smoked meat as we've traveled, adding that to the pile of supplies so we don't demolish every hunter cave we run across. They're not completely picked clean, in case someone needs to drop in during an emergency, but they're definitely down to the bare bones. For now, though, getting supplies to the tribe is the most important thing, and since dragging a sled has left me far too exhausted every day for my mate's attentions, he's decided that we should tie both sleds together and I should ride on top while he pulls them. Which sounds ridiculous except . . . it works. And I'm not passing-out exhausted by the time we stop every night, which leaves us plenty of snuggle time.

My Hassen craves snuggle time.

Okay, I do, too.

"Around the next ridge," he calls to me as we head into one

of the many undulating valleys. "And we shall be at the elders' cave. Are you excited to see your sister?"

"I don't know if 'excited' is the right word," I tell him. "I want to see her again, but I'm also a little worried she's going to lose her lid about you and me."

I hear him grunt as he digs his feet into the snow, pulling a little harder now that we're close to our destination. "She will have to learn a safe place to keep her lid, then. I do not intend on losing you."

I stifle my giggle at his response. I love his sweet words, especially when they're mixed in with a complete lack of knowledge of human euphemisms. It's fun. Actually, everything about being with Hassen is fun. I love him. I love our crazy, passionate sex. I love the way he holds me tight like I'm the best thing that's ever happened to him. I even love our journeying together, though it's hard. I love everything.

I'm just a little worried that Lila's reaction to our resonance is going to crap on my happiness.

Because I'm really, really happy. I know I'm supposed to be full of despair or worried about the future since there's been a cave-in and people are injured and Warrek's dad is dead. I know there's a lot to stress over and this place isn't safe and my sister might never recover her hearing and I'm pregnant at the worst possible time with a baby who's going to be half-alien and . . . I'm deliriously happy. Like, crapping-rainbows-and-bluebirds-singing happy. And it's not just because I've been getting dick on the regular—though that certainly helps—but I love Hassen. I love our funny conversations and the way he cares about everything so damn much. I can't imagine life without him at my side.

My sister is going to have to cope, because I'm not giving him up.

I'm lost in thought, trying to figure out the best way to soft-pedal the news to my sister that I resonated to the enemy, when I realize that Hassen's steps are slowing. "Do you need me to get out and walk for a while, big guy? Because I can. I don't mind."

He doesn't respond, and I see he's gazing at something up ahead. I turn to look—

And gasp. My stomach tenses and my entire body feels like it's been dipped in ice.

We're still a short distance away, but from here, I can see something sticking out over the cliffs. Something with smooth black metal curves that are completely out of place in this jagged, snow-covered landscape.

It's the elders' cave. And it looks like it's completely on its side. Oh, shit. "Is that the . . . it has to be. What does that mean?"

"Hold on," Hassen tells me. I barely have a chance to do just that before he surges forward, his steps quick as he races over the rest of the distance, heading for the ship. I cling to the leather straps to anchor myself, worrying. If the ship is on its side, then no one can live in there. Heck, I don't know if anyone can even use the computers anymore. All of this worries me.

It's also a little discouraging because that means it's just one more place knocked off the list of potential places to stay for the brutal season. Now, more than ever, our discovery of the little stone village tucked into the canyon seems important. I know Hassen has his worries, but I think we'll be safe there. Certainly safer than out in the open.

We're both silent as we head into the valley, approaching the elders' cave. Even from this distance, I can see a spread of small, hide-covered tents clustered around a central fire. Smoke rises from it, and I can see people moving. That means the sa-khui are still here. Good. One worry-knot in my belly unclenches.

A few people approach our sleds, and I see Farli with her pet, who's no longer limping. There's Georgie, holding her baby as she approaches, and Bek.

"Ho," Hassen calls out. "We bring back supplies." His voice is careful and even, and I know he has to be stressing. His gaze focuses on Georgie as he sets down the handles for the sled. "Where is my chief?"

"He's out with Rokan and Lila," Georgie says, adjusting her daughter from one hip to the other. "They've got a big group out at the fruit cave picking everything they can before the storm comes in." She glances up at the skies and grimaces. "It's going to be a nasty one, looks like."

"The brutal season is upon us," Hassen says gravely. He moves to the sled and puts his hands out for me, and I let him help me down. "Is everyone well?"

"Well enough," Georgie says. She looks at Farli and Bek. "Can you guys take the sleds? Sevvah and Kemli are smoking some meat by the fire, and you can get their mates to help unpack things." She shoots a look at me, bouncing Talie. "It's been a long few weeks."

"I'll bet," I say, putting my arms out to take the baby from her. Talie's getting big, and Georgie looks exhausted. "So my sister's not here? The fruit cave still exists?"

"She'll be back tonight," Georgie says, handing over her kit. "We weren't sure when you guys were coming back, though she'll be excited to see you. And yep, the fruit cave is still mostly intact, which is good. I've been half tempted to pile everyone in there instead of out here in the snow, but there's not enough room."

"The elders' cave," Hassen asks, his gaze going to the ship, "it is . . . ?"

"On its side. Yeah." Georgie rubs her forehead. "Rukh and Harlow say they managed to get out just in time, but there's no way we can set up shop in there for the winter. We're going to have to find an alternative." She looks at the sleds, and a little of the tension eases on her face. "These supplies are going to help so much. I'm glad you guys came back when you did."

She sounds . . . defeated. That's not good.

"The South Cave," my mate asks, his expression growing increasingly bleak, "is it livable?"

"Gone." She shakes her head. "We'll figure something out. It's going to be okay." The smile she beams our way is tight and tired, and I'm guessing it's an answer she's had to give over and over again lately. Poor Georgie.

I squeeze Talie tight, and the baby just blinks up at me with big glowing eyes. Okay, I haven't been much of a baby person in the past, but now that I'm carrying my own (at least, I'm pretty sure I am at this point, if the law of averages is with me), she's suddenly fascinating and adorable. "Is everyone all right, at least? Everyone healthy?"

"We're making it," Georgie says, crossing her arms over her chest and gazing back at the small, scattered camp. "Maylak's exhausted herself trying to heal everyone, so we're making her take it easy for a while." She gives us a quick look-over. "If you've got any broken bones, they might have to wait—"

"We're okay," I say quickly. "Don't worry about us." I move a little closer to Hassen, wishing he'd put his arm around me. I know he doesn't dare because he's back to exile status and I'm off limits, but we're going to fix that. Somehow.

"Pashov," Hassen asks, a hushed note in his voice, "is he . . . ?"

"Good and bad," Georgie says quietly. "He's alive and recovering, but . . . his memory is gone. He doesn't remember anyone. Not Stacy, not his son, nothing. But his body? His body is healthy enough."

Hassen sucks in a breath. "No memory of his mate . . . ?"

"Give him time," I say, before Hassen worries further over his friend. "He'll be fine. I imagine even a healer can't fully fix a traumatic brain injury. He's got a cootie, and he's got people to look after him. He'll be all right. These things just take time."

Georgie just nods. "I hope you're right."

"May I see him?" Hassen asks.

Georgie turns and points at a pair of tents near the fire. "He's in the tent on the left there. Go say hello, but don't go into the other one. Stacy's taking a nap. It's . . . hard on her." Georgie shoots me a worried look.

God, I'll bet. Her mate nearly dying and then him not remembering her? With a small baby, too? And all of this other crap going on? She has to be going through hell.

Hassen steps forward, and then hesitates, looking back at me. There's so much pain and worry in his eyes, I just want to take it all away from him and absorb it.

I reach out and touch his arm. "You go ahead, big guy. Say hi to Pashov. I'll stay here and talk to Georgie for a minute."

He nods at me, and I see a possessive flash in his eyes. "I will be back."

"I'll be here. I won't go anywhere without you."

A ghost of a smile touches his face. He rubs a hand down his jaw, tired, then heads off for the small tent.

Georgie waits until Hassen is gone and then arches an eyebrow at me. "Should I ask?"

"You can, but I'm not sure how much I'm willing to tell just yet." I'm kind of glad that Hassen's and my cooties are being mutually silent, because I'm not sure how our resonance will affect things. "Is he still an exile?" I ask bluntly.

"That's not my call to make," Georgie tells me. "That's Vektal's. It's his tribe."

"Yes, but you're his mate."

"Yes, and Hassen stole your sister after being warned that exile would happen if anyone did."

"Yes, and that was a big goof on his end. He knows that, and he's sorry for it. And I'm sure if you put a bug in Vektal's ear, he'd be willing to listen to reason and lift the ban on Hassen."

"Why would I do that? Look, I like Hassen as much as the next guy, and overall, I think he means well. But I think he also showed a criminal lack of judgment."

"He acts before he thinks sometimes. You know, like when he went into the cave to save Pashov?" I can't help but throw that back in her face.

"Point taken."

"Being exiled is *killing* him, Georgie. He doesn't have a family—all he's got is the tribe. Not being able to be part of the team really hurts him, maybe more than most." She's not getting it, and I'm growing frustrated with her. I know Georgie's going to see things through her mate's point of view out of sheer loyalty. I totally get that, and I'm probably doing the same thing when it comes to Hassen. "He's proved his worth to the tribe, hasn't he? And what's the point in exiling him when everyone's homeless? Doesn't that seem unfair? After how hard he works to provide for this tribe?"

Her mouth purses, and she takes Talie back from my arms. "I wish it was that simple, Maddie, I really do."

"It *is* that simple. You can talk to Vektal. Make him see things our way."

The look on her face is hard. "You think my mate doesn't have enough to worry about? You think he's not killing himself slowly trying to fix everything for everyone? To be everywhere? To be the leader they need him to be? You think this is easy for him?"

"I know it's not. It's not easy for anyone." I'm not getting anywhere with her, and so I'm going to have to play hardball. If it means getting myself booted out of the tribe, too, so be it.

Hassen's my mate, and I'm going to stand by his side. I think of Lila and feel a little squeeze of anxiety, but I tamp it down. Even if they exile me with Hassen, we'll find a way to visit each other, my sister and me. We're family. They can't pull us apart.

Time to bring out the big guns. "So Hassen found something interesting while we were out," I say casually as she settles her daughter back in her arms. I deliberately leave out my part in things. I want my mate to get all the glory in this, because I don't want to muddy the picture. I'm going to get him back into this tribe, damn it.

"Oh?"

"Yup. And you're going to want to hear about it. It's a game changer." And then I wait.

She looks over at me, little frown lines appearing between her brows when I don't continue. "Well?"

I cross my arms over my chest and give her a look. "You going to talk to your mate about mine and letting him back in the tribe?"

"Depends on what you found. It'd better be pretty fucking good," she snaps, and I can tell her patience is at an end with me.

"Toilets, Georgie. We found toilets." And a whole abandoned city attached to it, but whatever.

Her eyes narrow. "Did you say toilets?"

"Yup. Did you say you'll talk to your mate?"

She stares at me for a long moment, and then flicks her hand, indicating I should continue. "I'm listening . . ."

CHAPTER EIGHTEEN
Hassen

I watch my mate from a short distance away as she hugs her sister, waving her hands with enthusiastic talking. I am glad her family is home and safe. She worries about her Li-lah, even though the human is in good hands with Rokan. I know Mahdee worries that Li-lah will be against our mating, but such talk is foolishness. Resonance is resonance. Li-lah might as well be angry at the snow that floats down from overhead for all the good it will do.

Our khuis have chosen, and it is decided.

Mah-dee puts a hand to her sister's belly and makes a gesture. Li-lah nods, and they hug again. Rokan stands near his mate, grinning like a happy fool, and I am pleased for him. Resonance has taken, then, and Li-lah is with kit. As I watch, Mahdee puts a hand to her own stomach and makes the same gesture, and then looks over at me.

My chest resonates, and I know hers must be as well. I feel a surge of pride. My mate is carrying my kit. Whatever may happen, whatever path the tribe takes, Mah-dee and I are linked forever.

Li-lah's mouth opens in surprise, and then snaps shut. She makes a few motions at her sister, and then approaches me, her hands out in a warm greeting.

And I am suddenly . . . ashamed.

I took this female from safety. From her family. All because I desperately wanted a mate and a family. I did wrong. Now, perhaps, I truly understand what I have done, and I feel sorrow. I drop to my knees and make the hand-speak. *Forgive me? I am a fool.*

All is forgiven, Li-lah signs back. *Welcome to the family.* She offers me a hand and, when I take it, gives me a hug. I hold her stiffly, looking over at Rokan in apology. The sisters do not care, though. Mah-dee gives a happy squeal in the next moment and then launches herself at me, all clinging arms and legs. I pluck her from the air and swing her around, smiling.

"We're good, big guy," Mah-dee tells me, wrapping her arms around my neck and placing a smacking kiss on my cheek. "My sister is the best."

Li-lah just watches Mah-dee with gentle amusement, and I am relieved that she accepts me as her sister's mate. We can move forward from here. I hold my mate close and am thankful for her, for her khui that chose mine.

Then the chief appears, his mate at his side. Shorshie has an anxious expression on her face, and she holds Vektal's arm. "Maddie? Hassen? Can we talk to you two once you have a moment? Vektal wants to hear what you found out on your trip."

"The ship—" I question, but Mah-dee claps a hand over my mouth.

"I got this," she tells me, and then I feel her tongue flick against my earlobe before she surges to her feet and beams a winning smile at my chief. Dazed, I watch as she links her arm around Vektal's free one and gestures at the campsite. "Let me tell you about a little slice of human history. It's called the Lost Colony of Roanoke . . ."

I pull Mah-dee protectively against my side as Vektal rubs his brow. The look on his face is tired, and my chief—who is the same age as me—looks many years aged with worry. Mah-dee's hands are on my knee, and she squeezes it to reassure me.

"And this place, you believe, was once the home of another tribe?"

Mah-dee nods. "It's an old city. We can head in, throw up some teepee-type roofs, and ride out the brutal season all nice and cozy. We've got a bathing pool, plumbing, storage, fresh water . . . the only thing that wasn't there was game."

"Game can be brought back," Vektal says. He looks at Shorshie, his mate. "We would need to send a party of hunters out to determine if it is safe to bring the tribe. I would need to go."

Shorshie squeezes his hand and nods. "I can hold down the fort here."

"Hassen and I can show you," Mah-dee says, and her grip on my knee grows tight. "But he's not going to show you anything unless you remove exile status from him."

This is not the first time my fierce little mate has brought up my exile to the chief. She repeats it often, letting him know how displeased she is. Did I not save Pashov's life? Did I not save hers? Did I not find a new place for the tribe to live? Am I not accepted by Li-lah? Did I not resonate to Mah-dee? She sees no reason for my exile to continue. I am both pleased at her ferocity on my behalf and worried that she will end up getting herself exiled along with me.

"Now is not the time to talk of such things," Vektal says. "My tribe is falling apart. We need to focus on a home, feeding everyone for the brutal season, and—"

"And another set of hands will help with that," Mah-dee says firmly. "You need Hassen."

"I do. But I cannot lift exile so quickly. I made a mistake in going easy on Raahosh's exile, because it let Hassen believe that he would not be punished if he stole a female. I cannot make that mistake again. My hunters must follow the rules, or no one is safe."

"But circumstances are different right now," Shorshie says gently. "I don't think anyone would begrudge you changing your mind. This isn't a normal situation. We have to adapt." She shares a glance with Mah-dee. "Perhaps you can give Hassen some of the more difficult, less desirable tasks throughout the brutal season as penance instead? So he is still punished and yet not banished from the tribe."

I hold my breath. If they asked me to clean and scrape the intestine of every filthy scythe-beak from here to the mountains, I would gladly do so if it meant I was part of the tribe again and Mah-dee was with me.

"And I hate to be 'that' asshole, but Hassen's not going to show anyone anything unless he's back in the tribe. And if he's not allowed back, I'm leaving with him," says Mah-dee.

"Now is not the time to push for such things," Vektal warns, nostrils flaring. "Pashov is still not well. Rukh is nearly feral after Har-loh got hurt when the elders' cave turned on its side. It is taking everything I have to convince him to stay with the tribe, that she is safe here. My tribe is in danger of starving. You cannot hold such a thing over our heads—"

He is right. I open my mouth to speak, to tell my chief I will go regardless.

"I don't care," Mah-dee says fiercely. Her hand grips my knee so tight I feel her nails dig into the plated ridges there. "It might not be the best time for you as leader, but Hassen has no choice. You've backed him into a corner."

"Hassen can speak for himself, can he not?" Vektal says sharply with an irritated look at me.

"He can," Mah-dee continues. "But he has the most to lose here. I do not. I'm going with him regardless. And if he stays exiled, then we're going to go live in the lost colony without you guys. So there." She pauses, and then grimaces. "I just realized I sound like a demanding two-year-old."

Vektal nods crisply. "My daughter is less pushy than you, and she is spoiled."

Shorshie laughs.

"Very well," Vektal says and looks at me. "Your fierce pleasure mate has convinced me. You will be given extra tasks throughout the brutal season as penance, but you are no longer in exile."

My heart is full of fierce joy. I want to grasp my mate and hold her tightly against me, but I force myself to nod stiffly. "I will do you proud, my chief."

"I need all of my people here. Your home is with the rest of us."

"Out in the snow," Mah-dee points out. "With all the other homeless people. Who are gonna have a new home because of him." When Shorshie shoots her an irritated look, Mah-dee raises her hands. "I'm not saying, I'm just saying . . . Hassen's doing you guys a solid. I'll let it go now. I just felt it had to be said."

Vektal gives her an exasperated look and then turns to me.

"Your first task will be to keep your pleasure mate under control."

And now it is my turn to laugh. "No one controls Mah-dee. She does what she pleases."

"Damn skippy," Mah-dee says, and then puts her possessive hand back on my knee. "As for this pleasure-mate nonsense, I suppose that's something else we need to update you guys on . . ."

EPILOGUE
Maddie

"I can't believe you're leaving me here!" I'm torn between wanting to punch Hassen in the face and cry into his leathers. "You cannot be serious!"

"You were the one that boasted to the chief that we resonated," he tells me, smoothing my windblown hair off my face. "Now you will stay here with the other pregnant females."

"Hoisted on my own braggy petard," I sigh. "Damn it." I bury my face against his chest. "You're going to travel fast, right?"

"We will run the entire way," he promises. "We can make it there in half the time."

"Good." I rub my cheek against his skin, breathing in his scent and listening to the ever-present purr of his cootie talking to mine. I will not cry. I will not. It's only a week or two. I'll get in some lonely sister bonding time, since Rokan is going with Vektal and Hassen. I should have kept my damn mouth shut, but I was just so pleased with the fact that Hassen was no longer exiled, and I'm proud to be his mate. I wanted to tell the world.

So I did. And now I get benched.

I suppose it's for the best. I slept like a log last night in our tent, too tired to even have sex with my big sexy alien mate. All the travel has caught up to me, and I suppose I need to take care of myself if I've got an official baby on board. But it doesn't change the fact that I'm going to miss him fiercely. I cling to him a little harder. "Make sure you show them the toilets, all right? That's a big selling point to Georgie and the others."

He chuckles and strokes my hair. "I will show them. I promise."

"And you'll stay safe?" I lean back and look up at him. He's so handsome in the early-morning sunlight, with his dark hair whipping around his face. I love his big craggy horns and his stern cheekbones and the way his fangs peek out, just a little, when he smiles down at me, like right now. "Keep an eye out for metlaks and all that?"

"I shall be the safest of hunters," he tells me. "Because I have the fiercest of mates to return to."

That's so cute. He thinks I'm fierce. More like pushy, but I'll take it. I curl my hands in his vest and decide to give him a little something to incentivize him. "And when you come home, I'll suck your dick so hard you won't be able to walk straight for weeks."

Hassen's eyes go wide. He glances around the busy early-morning campsite, then picks me up and begins to walk away from the others.

I squeal, clinging to his neck. "Where are we going?"

"Back to our tent. We have a few moments before the others leave." His eyes gleam with possessive lust. "And I need to make sure that my mate misses me as much as I will miss her while I am gone."

"This sounds like a bangin' idea," I tell him, breathless. My cootie is singing so loud it's sending vibrations all through my chest. "And then you'll go and race to the city and show everyone how awesome it is and how you saved the day."

"Yes," he says, ducking into our small tent. He immediately drops to his knees and lowers me onto my back, his hand going for my pants. It's amazing how quickly he can get them around my knees.

"And then you'll come back home to me and we'll start our happily ever after, right?"

"My happy does not wait for later," he tells me. "My happy is now. Here. With you. I need nothing else."

And as he lowers his head between my thighs, I have to agree. I don't need anything but my mate.

BONUS EPILOGUE

THE RETURN

Maddie

It has been nine days since Hassen went with Vektal, Harrec, and Raahosh to show them the ice village we found so they can decide if it's a good place for the tribe to settle.

To think—it only takes nine days for a woman to lose her damn mind. I always thought it'd take a bit longer, but nope, it's nine days. Nine long, ridiculous, lonely days. I scowl down at the rope I'm braiding out of leather straps, making sure to weave the plaits together properly. If it was just for me, I'd let the dang thing be ugly, but everyone in the tribe seems to pride themselves on their handiwork, and if someone tsks over my sloppy braiding, I might have to punch a bitch.

So I take my time, and I make my plaits neat and tidy because everyone here is nice and I'm the cranky one. I'm the bitch. It's not their fault I miss Hassen desperately. I weave one strand over another. The ache in my chest lingers, and every beat of my heart almost feels as if it's in protest.

I should be fretting over the caves and where we're going to live. I should be hovering over my sister, making sure that her new mate, Rokan, is treating her right. Instead, all I can think about is Hassen and his ridiculous smile, Hassen and his big hands as he holds me close, Hassen and the way his eyes light up at the sight of me, as if he's never seen anything so fucking fantastic in all his life. Hassen and the worry etched onto his face when the home cave collapsed.

Hassen and his utter devastation at being cast out. He's like me in that family is everything. Sure, we might say and do dumb shit, but at the end of the day, nothing matters more than those around us. We're similar in so many ways, he and I.

And right now he'd be teasing me to break me out of my funk. I glance over at Farli, who is helping me braid rope. We're making a ladder so people can still climb inside the tipped-over ship. The computer might need to be accessed, and it holds information that we can use. We have to have it in some fashion or another. So . . . rope ladders. I suggested it the other day, not really expecting anyone to listen to me, but Georgie loved the idea. Looking back, she might have "loved" it just as a project to keep me busy. I smirk to myself. Probably a good call.

Right now, though, Farli needs to be coaxed out of her funk. Her pet is no longer limping, but he stays close to her side. As for Farli herself, her sparkle has been dimmed a little with the recent events. Normally she's the most bright-eyed and bushy-tailed girl, but lately her eyes are full of sadness at losing the only home she's ever known. I can't do much to fix that part, but I've taken it upon myself to be the big sister to her like I am to Lila, and that means being chatty and exuberant even when I don't feel like it.

So I plaster a big smile on my face and lean over toward Farli. "You know, this reminds me of the time I dated this real weirdo named Chuck the Trophy Hunter. Have I ever told you about him? I picked him up at a bar one night when I was out drinking with my girlfriends."

"A bar?" she asks, curious. "What kind of bar?"

"You're thinking like a stick, but a bar is actually a place where you go party with your friends." Close enough. "Like when you guys have a celebration? You can go someplace and they have celebrations every night."

"But why? What would you celebrate?"

"Well, I was celebrating the end of the workday. But mostly I was there to drink up all their sah-sah." That elicits a giggle from her, and so I continue on with my story. I tell her all about Chuck and the wall of deer heads he had, and his love of taxidermy. How he dressed like he was a regal hunter and how I was drunk enough to go home with him despite the fact that he had sixteen rabbits' feet (I call them "hoppers" so she can get a visual image) on his key chain (which I also have to explain). Chuck was a loser, but not as bad as I'm painting him to be. I'm exaggerating the situation for comic relief, which feels a bit like an asshole thing to do. But each time Farli laughs, I feel a little bit better.

It's not as if she'd meet good ol' Chuck anyhow.

"But why would he carry animal feet around with him?" she asks, puzzled.

"They were dyed all different colors for fun, and they're supposed to be lucky. You carry one with you and rub it for luck."

Her face contorts with disgust. "It is not very lucky for the hoppers! And why would you rub a dead foot?"

"A question for the ages," I agree. "But that's not the worst part about this date . . ."

By the time I run out of stories of my old dating antics, the twin suns have gone down and the rope ladder is mostly finished. We put it away for the night and Farli heads off with Chompy to find him some food. I feel exhausted after being cheery and full of tales all afternoon. I sit in front of the tent I'm sharing with Lila and Rokan, watching others prepare food by the fire. I should get up and help, but Stacy's at the fire, determinedly cooking up slabs of meat with that focused expression on her face.

When she's got that look, I avoid her. She's got a lot going on.

Tired, I watch Stacy cook, and when Lila drops down to sit next to me, I can't decide if I want to scream in frustration or curl up in her lap and be comforted. I do neither, of course. I'm the big sister, and Lila probably needs comforting. I hug her tight and, with one hand, sign to her. *Are you tired?*

I'm okay, she signs back. *You look sad.*

I make a quick sign for *laughter,* giving her a wry look. There's so much I want to say, but I don't want to vomit it all on her. She's glowing, despite the bad situation. Being with Rokan has made Lila come out of her shell in ways her big sister could never help with, and I'm both proud and slightly jealous that he's better for her than I am. It also makes me want to hide all my aching loneliness. Lila and Hassen have a terrible history between them and I should probably hate him, and instead I miss him so much I can hardly breathe with it.

No one tells you that you feel half-dead when your resonance mate is gone. That the silence of your khui is worse than anything. But Hassen is coming back soon enough, and I'm probably just being dramatic.

Lila is watching me expectantly, though, so I straighten up and sign back to her. *I miss Hassen and I hate that. I never needed a man before and now I need him.*

A sweet smile blossoms across her face. She signs quickly back at me, excitement in her gestures. *The new village will be a win,* she tells me. *Rokan has a good feeling about it. So good.*

That's a relief. I'm not surprised, though. It's a tiny village in a sheltered place. It has freaking toilets. Ancient toilets but still toilets. All we need to do is just move in. It certainly beats living in tents, which is what we're doing right now. So yeah, I'm not too surprised about the village. So I nod at her. *Everyone says Rokan is always right. You should ask him how much longer.*

Ahead of you, she signs back with a grin. *Tomorrow.*

Oh. Tomorrow? My heart flutters.

I can make it to tomorrow.

Hassen

It is a long trip to the new *howses* and then back again. Raahosh is never particularly entertaining company, but with the cave-in, both he and Vektal are quiet and taciturn. Me, I am missing my new resonance mate and wanting nothing more than to return to her side. This means that Harrec, who has no mate to miss, thinks to keep the conversation going, even if he must do it all himself.

We pause at the base of a cliff where water flows from a heated stream and refill our waterskins. Harrec, ever the joker, stuffs the front of his tunic with mounds of snow and jiggles them like they are teats. "Since there are no human females left for me, I shall have to become my own female. What do you think?"

Raahosh stares at him coldly and walks away.

Vektal just sighs and shakes his head like a much put-upon father. "Just fill your skins, Harrec. Let us be going. The tribe is waiting for us and we are close now."

"He is grumpy today," Harrec comments, lifting the sides of his tunic and letting all the snow fall to the ground. "Vektal is acting more like Bek-tal." He grins at his joke. "Get it?"

Normally I would joke with Harrec and try to lighten the mood. Vektal can get lost in his responsibilities and forget that he has any personality other than chief, so he can be fun to tease, because he will at least laugh at himself.

Raahosh is a lost cause. I fear I am becoming one, because I cannot even crack a smile at Harrec's teasing. All I can think of is my Mah-dee. I want her sharp, tart words, not Harrec's silly ones. I want Mah-dee to cast sultry looks in my direction and swing her hips, knowing that I will chase after her. I want her pressed against me in the furs, sleeping and content in my arms.

I just want *her*. I want to learn all about her. I want to experience everything with her at my side, not Harrec and my worried chief.

"Hassen?" Harrec moves to my side and gives me a playful nudge. "Have I lost you to a mood full of dark clouds, too?"

Scrubbing a hand down my face, I shake my head at him. "My apologies, friend. I am not myself this trip."

"Who is?" He gives me a crooked smile. "But even bad days can be made better with a laugh."

Immediately, I feel shame. Here I am, moping about my resonance mate being back at camp, and Harrec has lost a father figure. Old Eklan had taken him in and raised him to be a fine hunter, and Eklan died in the cave-in. Harrec might not be showing his grief as Warrek is, with horn-etchings and songs of mourning, but Harrec has always hidden his emotions behind a laugh.

It does not mean that he is not feeling them.

I move to his side and take him in a hug. We embrace, and Harrec clings to me, his breathing hard and raspy. When I pull back and slap him on the shoulder, there are tears in his eyes. "Let us focus on the good things, or else I will weep the entire journey and I have no wish to do so." He gives me a hard thwack on the shoulder, his goofy smile returning. "Tell me what it is like, you great fool."

"Resonance?"

"No, to be so tall." He rolls his eyes. "Yes, resonance."

Kneeling down by the water's edge, I fill my skins, watching to ensure that no fang-fish come close. "It is beyond my ability to describe. My thoughts have been taken over by Mah-dee, by her yellow hair and her soft skin. By her smile and her thick, strong legs. It feels strange to wake up and not have her by my side. Everything I see, I think of how she would react, what she would say. My mind is completely hers, along with my heart and my spirit."

Harrec studies me. "For someone who has 'no ability to describe,' you speak quite a lot."

"Ha." I splash water in his direction, and he laughs, some of the mischief returning to his face. "Let us just say that my words are a poor description of how resonance makes me feel."

Even now it seems as if my words are a vague insult to how much I feel for Mah-dee. How overjoyed I am that we are more than just pleasure mates, we are mates in every sense. That we will have a family.

"I am happy for you, my friend. I know you have wanted a mate for a long time." He hands his skins down to me so I can fill them and pass them back. After a quiet moment, he adds, "Perhaps I will get lucky and resonate to your daughter."

I jerk up and glare at him, offended on behalf of a daughter that does not even exist yet. "That is *not* funny."

Harrec shakes his head, handing another skin to me. "I was not being funny. What else is there for me to look forward to, if not the next generation of women? There are no other females for me to resonate to. Perhaps Farli, but she will most likely resonate to Taushen. I will be one of the hunters that gets old alone. It will be me and Bek and Warrek sitting alone as elders, wishing for mates . . . I need something to look forward to, Hassen. Anything."

There is a hint of desperation in his voice. I understand it. I do. Yet at the same time, I feel a surge of protectiveness for my small family. "Not my child, then. Raahosh and Leezh have a daughter. You can set your sights on her."

Harrec snorts. "The kit of Leezh and Raahosh? You know that one will grow up wild. I imagine she would rather eat my liver than resonate to me."

We see the strange jut of the elders' cave high in the air before we arrive, the side of it visible over the nearest ridge. It is unnerving to see, and reminds me that everything in our world that feels safe and settled can turn in an instant. At the sight of it, Harrec grows quiet, lost in his emotions again.

Then we see the plumes of smoke and the tents.

I am the first to race over the hill, though Vektal and Raahosh are not far behind me. It does not matter that my pack is heavy and laden with supplies, or that I am exhausted from days of constantly pacing through the snows, avoiding metlaks and moving as quickly as possible. It does not matter that we hit bad weather while we were gone, spending some days with our heads down, bracing against the wind. None of that matters, because we are home.

Home—the thought is a jarring one. This place is not home, because home is destroyed. This is where we have temporarily set up so our females, kits, and elders can be safe while we figure out what comes next. There is no home anymore.

That does not slow my feet, though. The first strain of resonance hums in my chest and I touch it even as I race forward, because now my khui has returned to life with Mah-dee's nearness. Suddenly I am the one that is emotional, choking back tears as I race toward the campfires, toward a figure that is stronger and thicker than the others, with big teats and a bold yellow mane and my heart unknowingly clutched in her hands.

Her back is to me, but Mah-dee senses something and turns, and I can see her eyes widen as she spots us coasting down the slope of the hill, sending snow spilling in our wake. "Mah-dee!" I bellow. "Mah-dee!"

She makes a happy little shriek and races toward me, her arms out. "Hassen!"

I race toward her, my khui singing, and the breath sobs in my throat. She flings herself at me and I catch her before her feet can touch the snow. Her arms go around my neck and she peppers my face with kisses, whimpering as she does. My cheeks are wet with tears, because for the first time, I have something to come home to. I have a person, a family. I am missed.

It is all I have ever wanted.

Overcome with emotion, I hold Mah-dee tightly and breathe in her scent, trying to make the tears stop in their relentless trails down my cheeks.

"I'm here," she breathes. "I'm here. I'm here. Everything's all right."

"I missed you so much," I choke out, my face buried against her neck. "My Mah-dee. My sweet mate."

"Are you okay? Is everything all right?"

I nod, but it is not all right. I am overcome with emotions, the sadness of what we have lost hitting me fully. Our kit will never experience the home cave. They will have no heated pool to swim in, no warm, snug family cave to curl up in. No shared hearth to drop by and share in the community food. Those were the only things that kept me going even after the deaths of my parents.

We must have that again, I decide. It is not just about a *howse*. It is about our people. It is about looking out for each other.

I cup my mate's face in my hands and kiss her fiercely, even as she wraps her legs around my waist. "Let's go find a tent and fuck for hours," Mah-dee tells me, nipping at my lower lip. "I can't wait to have you inside me again."

I groan, because I want that. I want that so much. And yet . . . I think about Harrec and what he said. How he has nothing to look forward to. The need to be selfish and hide away with my mate wars with the need to be a good friend. "Mah-dee. You know you have my heart, yes?"

"Those don't sound like fuck-time words," she teases, then sucks on my lower lip, and my sac tightens so immediately my eyes threaten to roll back in my head. "What is it?"

Pressing my brow to hers one last time, I sigh and set her gently down in the snow. I hold her hands—her cold, cold hands with too many adorable fingers upon them—and press them to my chest. "I have waited so long to see you again. The sight of you waiting for me . . . it filled me with such joy, my mate."

She smiles, and a moment later arches her brows. "But . . . ?"

"But Harrec was with us on the journey, and Eklan was like a father to him. I want him to sit down with friends until he feels like himself again. I know what it is like to be lost in grief and have no one to turn to."

Her expression grows gentle. "You big softy. All right. We'll put off the part where I tie you to the furs and don't let you come up for air."

A strangled sound escapes me, because I want that very, very much. "I am a fool—"

"No, you're being a good friend and supporting someone in need. I don't have to like it, but I understand it." She squeezes our joined hands. "Where's he at?"

I press my mouth to her hand again, feeling desperate and at the same time overflowing with emotion for this female and her understanding heart. More than anything, I want to touch her, and yet there will be time for touches when we are alone. Right now a friend is in need of understanding, and he does not need to be alone. I smile at her and then glance around the scattered encampment. I raced for Mah-dee the moment I saw her, and Vektal and Raahosh did the same, heading for their mates.

Harrec has no mate. He has no siblings. Eklan took him in and treated him as a son when he was young and alone, but now Eklan is gone and only Eklan's son, Warrek, remains. The two are friendly but opposites in personality, and I do not think they will know how to comfort one another.

Sure enough, I spot Harrec at the edge of the encampment, standing awkwardly near Warrek, who is seated in the snow, his back to the rest of us. Warrek is yet deep in his grieving, making notches on his horns and pouring snow on his face as he asks the spirits of the ancestors to look after his father. Harrec reaches out to touch Warrek's shoulder but receives no response. Warrek simply ignores him, lost in his pain.

That will not do. Not at all.

Mah-dee follows my gaze and sighs. "Yeah. He's taking this hard. It's understandable, but he needs time." She nudges me. "Go get Harrec—Warrek, too, if he'll listen—and tell them we're putting on some hot tea and they should join us."

I turn and give her another fierce kiss, trying to convey how much my heart swells when she speaks, and how much she means to me. She gives my backside a swat and chuckles as I pull away. Even though it is difficult to pull away from my lovely mate, I walk across the camp to approach both Warrek and Harrec.

"Ho, brothers," I say as I approach. "My mate is preparing tea. Come join us at our fire."

Warrek ignores me, rocking forward as he mumbles to himself, lost in his grieving. Harrec gives me a grateful look, though. His expression lightens, as if he is simply pleased to be remembered. "Tea? Just tea?"

"And food, I imagine. Have you ever known anyone to serve tea without food?" I chuckle and move to his side, clapping a hand on his shoulder. "Come join us. The camp is cold and lonely enough and there is room for all at our fire. We can eat and relax until Vektal gathers the tribe."

Harrec rubs his hands together. "I could eat something."

"Then come, both of you," I say. Harrec trots through the snow, heading toward Mah-dee's tent, but Warrek does not move. I drop to a crouch next to him and squeeze his shoulder. "Will you come, my friend? Get some food in your belly?"

Warrek turns to me and there is a look of such pain on his face. His eyes fill with tears and he shakes his head. "I would stay here, alone. It . . . makes me feel closer to him."

We all grieve the lost in our own way. I remember when my parents died and how much I struggled. He will come out of it in his own time. Until then, all we can do is make sure he is fed. I will bring him a bowl of something hot so he can eat without leaving his spot.

Maddie

If my sister, Lila, is surprised at goofy, sometimes obnoxious Harrec joining us for a meal, she hides it well. She pours tea and signs to him politely, even though he can't understand her because he hasn't gotten the ASL download from the ship.

"She's asking if you want more tea," I tell Harrec, signing the words as I speak them aloud.

He holds his cup up to her and looks over at me. "How do I say 'thank you'?"

Well, at least he wants to be polite. I show him how to touch his chin in the sign for *thanks* and he repeats after me, earning a smile from Lila. She fills his cup in the pouch near the fire and turns to me, a questioning look on her face.

Hassen is being a big brother to him, I tell her with quick gestures. *He needs a friend right now.*

Big brother and big sister, no wonder you two get along so well, she signs back to me with a teasing look. *You and Hassen are similar in ways I did not realize.*

It is still awkward, I admit, thinking about how he kidnapped my sister because he was so desperate for a mate. *You're being very understanding.*

Maybe he stole me because he was feeling a lot of heightened emotion because of the khui and didn't realize it was attached to you, Lila suggests.

Such a diplomat, my sister. *Or maybe he made a stupid move and it will teach him not to make stupid moves in the future?* My words are harsh, but I sign them with a smile and throw in a bit of playful emphasis. Signing is about body language, too, and I make mine teasing and fun.

He has a kind heart like you, Lila replies. *But he is also quick and impulsive . . . like you.*

I can't even disagree. I've definitely got a loud mouth and a hot temper. I give her a wry look and jokingly sign, *Fear for our child.*

It will be the kindest, most headstrong child ever, she agrees, and gives a muted giggle.

"Your hand language is pretty," Harrec says, watching us sign to each other.

"It is," I agree. "It's like a dance with hands. You should learn it so you can talk to Lila. She'll appreciate having more people to chat with."

"I will," he says. "It has just been very . . . eventful recently."

It has indeed. "There's no time like the present," I tell him in a crisp voice. "No one likes to be left out of conversations, and my sister is a big part of this tribe, too. And there's a rope ladder so you can climb up into the ship and use the computer. It's on its side, but it's still working."

Lila taps my side and signs, *You've got the big-sister look on your face. Give him a break.*

I'm lecturing him, I know it. I just get defensive when it comes to Lila. Just because she can't hear him doesn't mean she should be excluded from conversations. Even when I speak aloud to others, I sign out of habit so she can feel included, and I've noticed others doing the same. Josie, bless her heart, has made it a point to get to know Lila and got the ASL language early on so she could befriend my sister. Others in the tribe haven't been as quick, and I mean to nag all of them before we leave the ship behind.

Because right now it's a prime opportunity to get the "language dump," and I don't care if the ship is on its side. If we travel to the new village, we'll be days and days away from the ship itself. Right now, we're at the base and there's no excuse for anyone who hasn't learned ASL yet.

Or as Lila calls it, Ice Planet Sign Language.

Hassen puts an arm around Harrec's shoulder. "I will go with you up to the ship later. Perhaps we can convince Warrek to go with us, yes?"

"Perfect," I gush, even as I hop to my feet. "That's lovely. Do that. More food?"

I feed everyone twice over. I'm sure some of it is because I'm anxious to hear what Vektal thought about the village, and some of it is because the big-sister part is kicking in and I feel the urge to take care of everyone. But then the food is gone and we gather near the main fire to hear Vektal's verdict on things.

Even though Vektal is speaking to all of us, I watch Hassen closely. His expression is intense, as if the fate of the tribe rests upon his shoulders, and I realize again just how much this group of people means to him. Hassen has no family so he projects all of his love and affection upon his entire tribe.

They don't realize what a gem they have in him, I think fiercely.

Vektal tells everyone that we will be going to the new village. That it will be our home, and we will pack up and head there tomorrow. There are no cheers, no excitement, just a lot of worried faces. No one's going to relax until they're safe in their new homes. But Hassen is full of delight, turning to me and beaming with such happiness. "They like our village."

"You knew that," I tell him, nudging his arm. "You traveled back with Vektal. Surely you knew what he'd decided?"

"Yes, but I also worried he would change his mind." He gives me a sheepish look. "That it was too perfect, and we would have to continue to hunt for a safe place for our people, one that I did not find."

And then he would be exiled again, since Vektal approved his un-exiling because we found the village. It's obviously something that's going to bother him for a long time. Poor Hassen. I want to stand in front of him and defend him if anyone tries to give him shit. Just let them try.

My mate turns to Harrec and claps him on the shoulder. "We should head to the elders' cave tonight, then. Make sure that you get the hand language. We can take anyone else that needs it, too, since we will be leaving in the morning. Can you ask around? See who else needs to go?"

Harrec nods and wades into the busy group. "Who wants to learn hand-speak with me so I can bother our chief in an entirely new way?"

Someone groans.

Hassen turns to me and runs his knuckles along my cheek. "It seems it will be a bit longer before we can have a few moments alone, my resonance."

"Do what you have to do," I tell him and tilt my face up for a quick kiss. "I'll get started packing. If you're back late, just wake me up when you come to bed."

He kisses my mouth, and then my nose, a surprisingly tender gesture for the big guy. "I would stay with you," he murmurs, "but I must rescue Harrec before someone tosses him from a cliff. His jokes have been grating on Vektal's nerves for days now."

"Go quick, then," I say with a laugh.

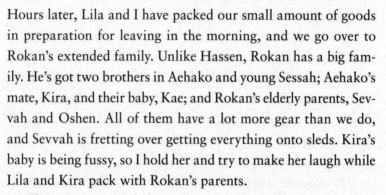

Hours later, Lila and I have packed our small amount of goods in preparation for leaving in the morning, and we go over to Rokan's extended family. Unlike Hassen, Rokan has a big family. He's got two brothers in Aehako and young Sessah; Aehako's mate, Kira, and their baby, Kae; and Rokan's elderly parents, Sevvah and Oshen. All of them have a lot more gear than we do, and Sevvah is fretting over getting everything onto sleds. Kira's baby is being fussy, so I hold her and try to make her laugh while Lila and Kira pack with Rokan's parents.

They're not excited about the new village. They're wary and afraid, and I've caught regal-looking Sevvah wiping her eyes when she thinks no one is looking. I want to scream and defend the new village—freaking toilets!—but I know this is hard for the people who have lived in the home cave all their lives. They've never known anything else, so change is scary.

By the time Kae is settled in for sleep and the last few bags of Oshen's sah-sah herbs have been packed away on a sled, I'm exhausted and Hassen still isn't back. I remind myself to be patient, that the computer that more or less shoves language into your head knocks you out cold, and it could be a little while before he returns. I want to fuss like baby Kae and pout that I don't have my mate, but I'm trying to be patient.

It's not a skill I'm particularly adept at.

Get some rest, Lila signs to me as she heads into our shared tent with her mate. *Early morning tomorrow.*

I'll be there soon, I reply and glance around the encampment again. Still no sign of him. I might as well get a bit of sleep, so I head in a few steps after her. It's a fairly large tent, with enough room for several people, but it's only been us the last few days. Rokan and Lila settle into the furs together, and I fluff my bed, adding a few of the bigger furs to make the sleeping pallet bigger for Hassen. For the last several days the tent has been full of supplies rescued from the caves, but now it's nearly empty and far too quiet. I lie in bed and stare at the shadowy ceiling of the tent, determined to stay awake until my mate comes back.

I don't, of course. I fall asleep right away.

I wake up a short time later to someone whispering and making noise by the door flap.

"Are you certain I am welcome?" Harrec asks, a miserable hitch in his voice. "I know you want time with your resonance mate."

"Of course you can stay in the tent with us," Hassen tells him. His tone is soft and full of understanding. "You know we do not mind. There is room for you, always. We might not be family, but you are my hunt brother and I am yours. We look out for each other. Where is Warrek? Should we bring him?"

"He is bunking with Bek and Maylak's family."

"Good," Hassen whispers, and my heart squeezes fiercely for him, because even now he's checking up on the others. Am I annoyed that Harrec is here because I want to jump Hassen and fuck the daylights out of him? Yes. But do I understand it? A thousand percent.

So I sit up in bed and point, my voice low. "There's an extra roll of furs by the door flap. Try not to wake up Rokan and Lila."

They nod and whisper, and Hassen shoots me a look of approval with his glowing gaze. Something tells me that Harrec's probably going to end up staying with us for a few weeks when we get to the village, and it's fine. Hassen needs to mother him like I mother Lila.

Harrec slaps at Hassen's hands as my mate tries to help him with the blankets. Harrec hisses at him. "I know how to make a bed, fool."

Did I say "mother"? I should have probably said "smother." I know I'm guilty of that when it comes to Lila, too. I bite back my amusement and pat the bedding next to me. "Leave him alone and come to bed, Hassen."

He doesn't hesitate. Just smacks Harrec cheerfully on the shoulder and then winces at the loud clap it makes in the tent. Rokan opens his eyes briefly, the khui glow in his gaze illuminating the tent before he rolls over and pulls a peacefully sleeping Lila closer.

Hassen grimaces and quietly tiptoes to my side, pulling off his outer layers of clothing. He smells a bit like sweat, but I don't care. He's back, and he's tired, and he's about to be in my bed. It's all I've wanted for the last two weeks. My khui hums a low, gentle song, and when Hassen slips under the furs and pulls me against him, I want to sigh with sheer happiness at how good he feels.

This is my home, I tell myself. I belong right in Hassen's warm, strong arms.

"Is this all right?" he whispers, low enough that only I can hear. "Harrec being here?"

"It's fine," I reassure him, and run my fingers over his skin. He's bare to the waist now, wearing only a loincloth to sleep in, and he's so fucking touchable. God, I love the way he feels. It's not just the soft suede of his skin but the muscles underneath, the way he moves, the way he purrs for me. He's delicious.

I keep touching him, over and over again, stroking and petting. "I missed you," I whisper, and press small kisses to his skin. "I missed you so much while you were gone."

"I missed you, too. It was as if my heart remained back here in the tent with you." Hassen cups my face, caressing it. "But I just woke you, my pretty mate. Go back to sleep. We can talk in the morning."

As if I'm tired now. My Hassen is here in my arms, and I've missed the sound of his voice, the rumble of his laughter. I've wanted to ask him so many things since he got back, but it never seemed like the right time. "Tell me about your journey. Was it a bad one?"

"It was . . . not good." His voice is no more than a whisper against my skin. "I do not want to think about it, though. It is over now, and we can focus on other things."

Fair enough, but I recall his worries about the site and need reassurance. "Did you see lots of metlaks on your journey?"

"Strangely enough, not as many as I expected." He twines a lock of my hair around his finger and rubs it. "The ones in that area are not used to us, I think. They did not like our scent. Perhaps we will get lucky and they will leave the territory. How are you so very beautiful, my mate?"

I press my lips together to stop from laughing aloud at the sudden topic change. "I'm glad you think so."

"I wonder how I am so very fortunate," he murmurs. "To

have the most perfect mate. I dreamed of you constantly while I was gone. It made the journey that much longer."

"I couldn't stop thinking of you, either." I kiss his skin, running my lips along his collarbone even as my hand steals down his waist. "I couldn't wait to touch you again."

I close my hand around the bulge of his cock. No surprise—he's hard underneath his loincloth. I want that thing gone, I decide, and tug at one of the strings holding the offending scrap of material over his hips.

"I picked out a hut for us," he whispers, running his hand through my hair as I undress him. "It is not near the center of the village. I want us to be able to be as noisy in the furs as we like."

It takes everything I have to bite back the chortle that rises in my throat. "I like that idea."

And I pull the loincloth free, wrapping my hand around the hot length of his cock.

His hand leaves my hair and skims along my jaw. "How . . . how is your womb?"

That makes me pause. "Did . . . did you just ask how my *womb* was?"

"I have never had a resonance mate before now. I have never put a kit inside her. So yes, I asked that." His thumb dips into my mouth.

I nip at it, amused. "Good point. And it's fine. We won't feel anything, babywise, for a long time yet."

"I cannot wait to meet my daughter."

"Or your son."

That makes him pause. "You think it could be a son?"

"It's too early to say."

There's a pause. I stroke my hand down the ridges of his

cock, lovingly tracing them with my fingers. Then, Hassen whispers, "Rokan would know. I can wake him up."

I give his cock a squeeze, making his breath hitch. "You are not waking up Rokan to ask about our kid when they're no bigger than a zygote. You're not going anywhere. My hand is on your cock and I'm going to fuck you because I've waited far too long to have you inside me again."

Hassen bites back the softest groan. "The others . . ."

"Are sleeping. So you need to be quiet." And I drag my hand up his length, teasing the tip just before I let him go. There has to be a hint of an exhibitionist in my system, I think, because I'm not bothered by the fact that there are three others sleeping across the tent from us. It's dark and we've got blankets. Everyone in the caves knew when someone else was fucking because sound carried and privacy was not that easy to come by. It's no different now, and we're freshly resonated. Of course we're going to be all over each other.

They're free to tease me about it in the morning. I simply don't care.

I push Hassen firmly on his back and slide my body over his, settling my hips over his pelvis. I've been waiting to touch him again, so I wore a long tunic dress to bed—and nothing else. I hike it up and rub my pussy against his length, letting him feel the heat of my body.

His breath hitches again and I lean forward, pressing my fingertips to his mouth. *Silent.*

He nods and slips his hands under my dress, grabbing my hips. Hassen lifts me up and then the head of his cock is pressing against the entrance to my body, and now I'm the one about to whimper aloud, because I've waited for this for *so freaking long.* I bite down on my lip, hard, as he sinks into me.

God, it's perfect. It's exactly what I needed. *He's* exactly what I needed.

I rock against him, feeling the strain of his big body under mine. He lifts me up by the hips again, then drags me back down. Our movements are slow and silent, because to go any faster would produce the telltale *slap slap slap* of flesh meeting flesh. We fuck at a leisurely pace, but there's an underlying hint of urgency, of knowing that we could wake the others at any time. It makes me wet and I clench tight around him, aroused that we're fucking within the shared tent. That we're stealing this moment for ourselves right under their noses.

It's naughty and irresponsible and awesome and I love each languid, deep pump of his cock into my body. I love the thrumming of our khuis, singing in unison. I love everything about this moment. We're one again, joined together, because this is how we're meant to be.

Hassen comes before I do, and that's perfectly all right. I press my hand over his mouth as he shudders under me, emptying into my body. When he's done and he can breathe again, I remain where I am, mounted atop him, his spur hitting me in all the right places, and I touch myself between my thighs until I climax, too. I'm not able to be as silent as he is, and a tiny, high-pitched sound escapes my lips.

It sounds so ridiculous that Hassen snickers. Aloud.

"Mmm?" Harrec says, lifting his head.

"Go back to sleep," is all Hassen tells him. "I was telling my mate a joke."

His mate can't answer. She's too busy being utterly mortified and trying to hold back laughter. If Rokan hears anything, he doesn't comment, just continues to sleep (or continues pretending to sleep).

I collapse atop Hassen, letting him pull the furs high over my head.

"What was that about being quiet?" he whispers.

"I tried," I tell him. "You're just too good at touching me."

"Yes, but you were touching yourself—" He can't finish the phrase because I have my hand over his mouth again.

It feels fun to grin in the darkness with him, though. To stifle our giggles and snuggle under the blankets. I know we should go to sleep. Tomorrow's going to be a big day and it's going to be both emotionally and physically exhausting to move the tribe to the new home.

But right now? This moment is perfect, and I'm not about to let it go. So I wiggle my hips atop Hassen and lean in. "When do you think you'll be ready to go again?"

"Hungry human," he murmurs, his eyes gleaming with excitement.

Hungry? More like absolutely insatiable when it comes to him.

AUTHOR'S NOTE

Hello there!

When I first mentioned that Maddie and Hassen would be getting together in teasers for this book, a lot of people railed at me: *Maddie should hate Hassen. Maddie should want nothing to do with the jerk who captured her sister! They will never work as a couple!*

Saying something "will never work" is like waving a red flag in front of a bull. I immediately try to think of ways to make it work, just because I am that contrarian friend. But I already knew that they would be perfect together. In this case, the old adage of "opposites attract" wouldn't be ideal. Actually, I don't know that a ton of my characters are complete opposites. I try to think of complementary pairings instead. Is that person shy and reluctant? Give them another introvert. Is this person a leader? Pair them with another leader. Someone needs understanding? Pair them with patience.

In Hassen's case, what goes well with bossy and overbearing (but means well) and is lonely?

Another bossy, overbearing, lonely sort: Maddie.

You might argue that Hassen isn't bossy and overbearing as much as he's selfish and thoughtless. And people can be a lot of things. We have layers, to reference a famous ogre. It is absolutely true that Hassen stealing Lila is selfish and awful and thoughtless, and he eventually realizes this. But if you look at it from his point of view, it's out of desperation. He urgently wants someone to love and cherish and to make a family with. He's so lonely that when Maddie and Lila show up, he sees this as his last chance at happiness and tries to grab it. In my head, it's a lot like a toddler squeezing a kitten too hard just because they love it so much. It's still a bad thing but done with the best intentions. Hassen just wants to take Lila away so he can love her and hug her and squeeze her. When she doesn't reciprocate, he realizes what a bonehead move he's made. He didn't think about how Lila would react.

(This is not me defending kidnapping.)

Maddie knows how he feels—not about the desperation that leads to kidnapping someone, of course, but about doing anything for family. She's very much ride-or-die with Lila . . . who is spreading her wings and no longer needs Big Sis. Maddie is feeling on the outs and looks for another person on the outs who'll understand just what she's going through.

Enter Hassen.

I also loved writing this story about these two in particular because they're not perfect by romance-novel standards. They're both stubborn; both can be jerks; both are overbearing at times. Maddie is crass. Hassen is kinda not the most clever of men. And I love that in this day and age, I can write a fat, sex-positive heroine who hooks up with a big, eager dummy who worships her. When I first started to read romances, every heroine had violet eyes and a waist that could be spanned with the hero's hands. The hero would be dark haired, smart, and wealthy and titled. Maddie and Hassen absolutely don't fit the bill, and that's what makes them so fun.

One large part of this story deals with the destruction of the home cave and the consequences of it, including Eklan's death. I think I mentioned Eklan maybe a half dozen times over the course of eight books. And yet people were devastated at his death in this story. I felt that if I was going to make big, sweeping changes, I also had to show consequences. I can't talk about how hard it is to live on the ice planet and never show anyone experiencing hardship. So I killed a redshirt . . . and got dozens of emails about how sad people were.

In actuality, I was going to make things much, much worse. I was going to have Ariana and several others killed off—both sa-khui and human—to show that life is dangerous, but I couldn't bring myself to pull the trigger. I'm too attached. Life is already hard enough (real life, not life on Not-Hoth), so why bring people down? At the end of the day, this is a happy series, a series that gives you warm fuzzies and leaves you with a (hopefully) good feeling. I want you to close each book knowing everything will be all right in the end. And it is, sort of. By the end of this book, they find a new home, which was inspired by the Lost Colony of Roanoke and the ruins of Skara Brae in Scotland. We'll have a lot more about the new home in the future. For now, know that your beloved barbarians are not going anywhere!

A huge, warm, fuzzy shout-out to my Berkley barbarian team. They really are the greatest and work so hard to make these books as perfect as they can be. Thank you to the fabulous Cindy Hwang and Angela Kim, Rita Frangie Batour, Jessica

Mangicaro, Stephanie Felty, Yazmine Hassan, and Michelle Kasper. Thank you again to Kelly Wagner for making Maddie thicc and flirty, as requested, and for Hassen's dopey, excited smile. I love this cover so much.

I hope you enjoyed the story and are looking forward to more to come. Barbarian on!

<3
RUBY

THE PEOPLE OF
BARBARIAN'S TAMING

THE CHIEF AND HIS FAMILY

VEKTAL (Vehk-tall)—Chief of the sa-khui tribe. Son of Hektar, the prior chief, who died of khui-sickness. He is a dedicated hunter and leader, and carries a sword and a bola for weapons. He is the one who finds Georgie, and resonance between them is so strong that he resonates prior to her receiving her khui.

GEORGIE—Unofficial leader of the human women. Originally from Orlando, Florida, she has long golden-brown curls and a determined attitude.

TALIE (Tah-lee)—Their infant daughter.

FAMILIES

RAAHOSH (Rah-hosh)—A quiet but surly hunter. One of his horns is broken off and his face scarred. Older son of Vaashan and Daya (both deceased). Vektal's close friend. Impatient and rash, he steals Liz the moment she receives her khui. They resonate, and he is exiled for stealing her. Brother to Rukh.

LIZ—A loudmouth huntress from Oklahoma who loves Star Wars and giving her opinion. Raahosh kidnaps her the moment she receives her lifesaving khui. She was a champion archer as a teenager. Resonates to Raahosh and voluntarily chooses exile with him.

RAASHEL (Rah-shell)—Their infant daughter.

HARLOW—One of the women kept in the stasis tubes. She has red hair and freckles, and is mechanically minded and excellent at problem-solving. Stolen by Rukh when she resonated to him. Now mother to their child, Rukhar.

RUKH (Rook)—The long-lost son of Vaashan and Daya; brother to Raahosh. His full name is Maarukh. He grew up alone and wild, convinced by his father that the tribe was full of "bad ones," and has been brought back by Harlow.

RUKHAR (Rook-car)—Their infant son.

ARIANA—One of the women kept in the stasis tubes. Hails from New Jersey and was an anthropology student. She tended to cry a lot when first rescued. Has a delicate frame and dark brown hair. Resonates to Zolaya. Still cries a lot.

ZOLAYA (Zoh-lay-uh)—A skilled hunter. Steady and patient, he resonates to Ariana and seems to be the only one not bothered by her weepiness.

ANALAY (Anna-lay)—Their infant son.

MARLENE (Mar-lenn)—One of the women kept in the stasis tubes. French speaking. Quiet and confident, and exudes sexuality. Resonates to Zennek.

ZENNEK (Zehn-eck)—A quiet and shy hunter. Brother to Pashov, Salukh, and Farli. He is the son of Borran and Kemli. Resonates to Marlene.

ZALENE (Zah-lenn)—Their infant daughter.

NORA—One of the women kept in the stasis tubes. A nurturing sort who was rather angry she was dumped on an ice planet. Quickly resonates to Dagesh. No longer quite so angry.

DAGESH (Dah-zzhesh; the *g* sound is swallowed)—A calm, hardworking, and responsible hunter. Resonates to Nora.

ANNA & ELSA—Their infant twins.

STACY—One of the women kept in the stasis tubes. She was weepy when she first awakened. Loves to cook and worked in a bakery prior to abduction. Resonates to Pashov and seems quite happy.

PASHOV (Pah-showv)—The son of Kemli and Borran; brother to Farli, Salukh, and Zennek. A hunter described as "quiet." Resonates to Stacy.

PACY—Their infant son.

MAYLAK (May-lack)—One of the few female sa-khui. She is the tribe healer and Vektal's former pleasure mate. She resonated to Kashrem, ending her relationship with Vektal. Sister to Bek.

KASHREM (Cash-rehm)—A gentle tribal tanner. Mated to Maylak.

ESHA (Esh-uh)—Their young female kit.

MAKASH (Muh-cash)—Their infant son.

SEVVAH (Sev-uh)—A tribe elder and one of the few sa-khui females. She is mother to Aehako, Rokan, and Sessah, and acts like a mom to the others in the cave. Her entire family was spared when khui-sickness hit fifteen years ago.

OSHEN (Aw-shen)—A tribe elder and Sevvah's mate. Brewer.

SESSAH (Ses-uh)—Their youngest child, a juvenile male.

MEGAN—Megan was early in a pregnancy when she was captured, but the aliens terminated it. She tends toward a sunny disposition when not abducted by aliens. Resonates to Cashol. Pregnant.

CASHOL (Cash-awl)—A distractible and slightly goofy-natured hunter. Cousin to Vektal. Resonates to Megan.

CLAIRE—A quiet, slender woman who arrived on the planet with a blonde pixie cut and now has shoulder-length brown hair. She had a failed pleasure-mating with Bek and resonated to Ereven. Her story is told in the novella "Ice Planet Holiday."

EREVEN (Air-uh-ven)—A quiet, easygoing hunter who won Claire over with his understanding, protective nature. Resonates to Claire.

AEHAKO (Eye-ha-koh)—A laughing, flirty hunter. The son of Sevvah and Oshen; brother to Rokan and young Sessah. He seems to be in a permanent good mood. Close friends with Haeden. Resonates to Kira and was acting leader of the South Cave.

KIRA—The first of the human women to be kidnapped, Kira had a large metallic translator attached to her ear by the aliens. She is quiet and serious, with somber eyes. Her translator has been removed, and she gave birth to Kae.

KAE (rhymes with "fly")—Their infant daughter.

KEMLI (Kemm-lee)—An elder female, mother to Salukh, Pashov, Zennek, and Farli. The tribe's expert on plants.

BORRAN (Bore-awn)—Kemli's much younger mate and an elder.

FARLI (Far-lee)—A preteen female sa-khui. Her brothers are Salukh, Pashov, and Zennek. New pet parent to the dvisti colt Chompy.

ASHA (Ah-shuh)—A mated female sa-khui. She is mated to Hemalo but has not been seen in his furs for some time. Their kit died shortly after birth.

HEMALO (Hee-mah-lo)—A tanner and a quiet sort. He is mated (unhappily) to Asha.

TIFFANY—A "farm girl" back on Earth, she suffered greatly while waiting for Georgie to return. She has been traumatized by her alien abduction. She is a perfectionist and a hard worker, and the running joke amongst the human women is that Tiffany is great at everything. Resonates to Salukh.

SALUKH (Sah-luke)—The brawny son of Kemli and Borran; brother to Farli, Pashov, and Zennek. Strong and intense. Very patient and helps Tiffany work through her trauma.

JOSIE—One of the original kidnapped women, she broke her leg in the ship crash. Short and adorable, Josie is an excessive talker, a gossip, and a bit of a dreamer. Likes to sing. Family is everything to her, and she wants nothing more than one of her own. Resonates to Haeden.

HAEDEN (Hi-den)—A grim and unsmiling hunter with "dead" eyes, Haeden formerly resonated but his female died of khui-sickness before they could mate. His current khui is a replacement, and he resonates to Josie. He is very private and unthaws only around his new mate.

LILA—A shy, introverted deaf woman kidnapped from Earth with her sister, Maddie. On Earth, Lila had cochlear implants, which were removed by the aliens who took her. She resonates to Rokan after being kidnapped by Hassen.

ROKAN (Row-can)—The son of Sevvah and Oshen; brother to Aehako and young Sessah. A hunter known for his strange predictions that come true all too often. Resonates to Lila.

HASSEN (Hass-en)—An impulsive but kindhearted hunter who was exiled after kidnapping Lila. He finds a kindred spirit in

Maddie and they eventually resonate. Together they find the new home for the tribe.

MADDIE—Lila's older sister. She is tall, full-figured, blonde, and bossy. She feels out of sorts with her new world and pairs up with Hassen, who she eventually resonates to.

THE UNMATED

BEK (Behk)—A hunter generally thought of as short-tempered and unpleasant. Brother to Maylak.

HARREC (Hair-ek)—A hunter who has no family and finds his place in the tribe by constantly joking and teasing. A bit accident-prone.

TAUSHEN (Tow—rhymes with "cow"—shen)—A teenage hunter, newly into adulthood. Eager to prove himself.

WARREK (War-eck)—The son of Elder Eklan. He is a very quiet and mild hunter, with long, sleek black hair. Warrek teaches the young kits how to hunt.

ELDERS

ELDER DRAYAN (Dray-ann)—A smiling elder who uses a cane to help him walk.

ELDER DRENOL (Dree-noll)—A grumpy, antisocial elder.

ELDER VADREN (Vaw-dren)—An elder.

ELDER VAZA (Vaw-zhuh)—A lonely widower and hunter. He tries to be as helpful as possible. He is very interested in the new females.

THE DEAD

DOMINIQUE—A redheaded human female. Her mind was broken when she was abused by the aliens on the ship. When she arrived on Not-Hoth, she ran out into the snow and deliberately froze.

ELDER EKLAN (Eck-lann)—A calm, kind elder. Father to Warrek, he also helped raise Harrec. Dies in the cave-in.

KRISSY—A human female, dead in the crash.

PEG—A human female, dead in the crash.

ABOUT THE AUTHOR

RUBY DIXON is an author of all things science fiction romance. She is a Sagittarius and a Reylo shipper, and loves farming sims (but not actual housework). She lives in the South with her husband and a couple of goofy cats, and can't think of anything else to put in her biography. Truly, she is boring.

VISIT RUBY DIXON ONLINE

RubyDixon.com
 RubyDixonBooks
 Author.Ruby.Dixon

Ready to find
your next great read?

Let us help.

Visit prh.com/nextread

Penguin
Random
House